LETHBRIDGE-STEWART

WARRIORS OF MONTU

Gareth Madgwick

CANDY JAR BOOKS · CARDIFF
2021

Range Editor: Andy Frankham-Allen
Editor: Shaun Russell
Editorial: Keren Williams
Licensed by Hannah Haisman
Cover by Paul Cowan & Will Brooks

ISBN: 978-1-913637-74-3

Printed and bound in the UK by
Severn, Bristol Road, Gloucester, GL2 5EU

Published by
Candy Jar Books
Mackintosh House
136 Newport Road, Cardiff, CF24 1DJ
www.candyjarbooks.co.uk

For Gemma.

CHAPTER ONE
Can This Be Love?

'IT'S HIDEOUS, dear.' Alistair Gordon Lethbridge-Stewart peered over his fiancée's shoulder as she rolled the jar around in her hands. He risked a glance upwards. Through the clouds of incense and fluttering fabrics, the store holder was making his way towards them, his face a dour, affected grimace, impervious to the flies that settled around it.

Alistair cursed the man as he wafted away a few of the insects. The bazaar was a piece of pure theatre that he had wearied of through the late afternoon, going from amused, to irritated, to simply resigned in the hours' trip through the Khan El-Khalili Bazaar.

'Nonsense. Look at the pictures, Alistair. They're so detailed.'

He took the jar from Fiona's hands, running his fingers across the writing and little figures of birds, animals and men.

'They could mean anything. Like those youngsters at home that think they're communing with the infinite but end up meditating to a curry menu.'

Fiona stifled a laugh. He smiled himself. Somehow, she could always pierce his defences. That was why he had asked her to marry him.

'Let's ask Cosgrove this evening,' she said.

Alistair grunted. General Cosgrove might well give a very detailed account of what the markings on the jar meant. The trouble with their host was that it was hard to know when the act stopped, and reality began.

'What would you do with it anyway?' he asked Fiona.

She shrugged, taking it back from him. 'We could keep dry foods in it. In our kitchen.'

A pointed look, to remind him that this holiday was to mark their engagement.

'Oh, come on, we can't even get the lid off.' He struggled with it briefly. From the corner of his eye, he could see the stall keeper with a face still downturned like a dog staring at a closed biscuit barrel, but a glint of a sale in his eyes.

Fiona held the jar at arms' length, turning it and letting the reddish gold sunlight fall on the design.

'Well, I like it. So, we're getting it and that's final.'

That it was, she was haggling with the owner. The man's arms were flailing in a theatrical performance of horror at Fiona's supposed insulting starting point.

Alistair cast his eye over the rest of the goods, trying not to listen to the money being quoted. Not a single price tag featured anywhere in the stall. He didn't doubt for a second that a clipped British military accent would add a few pounds to any starting price. It was probably best to stay quiet and let his fiancée's City experience handle it.

His gaze must have lingered too long on the row of hats, because he found his own panama whipped away by the stall keeper and replaced with a garish fez.

Fiona clapped her hands with delight.

'Oh, darling, definitely. Fezzes are so cool! Come on, lighten up.'

Alistair caught sight of a tarnished mirror that hung crooked from a supporting post. Sweat stained the cream shirt and slacks of the man that looked back.

'Nothing here is cool in any way whatsoever,' Alistair said. 'I look like that comedian that keeps getting his magic tricks wrong.'

The stall holder grinned, a crack through his concrete face. 'Just like that, sir.' His cockney accent was flawless and, despite himself, Alistair laughed. He looked at Fiona, met her eyes in a moment of simple ease.

'Go on, buy the fez too. We'll need some plant pots. Just get my proper hat back too please, dear.'

General Charles Cosgrove's house was a short walk away from the bazaar, past the smells of cooking lamb and the stench of tanned leather, through foul smelling puddles that pooled in the dust next to men selling sugary treats and tea. They dodged athletic urchins and footless beggars that both wanted the same thing.

Then, away from the shopping streets to the residential areas, filled with cats that lurked on every corner, finally to arrive at the small door, set away from the street. The Bawab, an old gentleman in a traditional robe that minded the door, nodded with a sudden quick smile from his chair as he recognised them.

Inside, the steps led up and away from the noise of the streets, into coolness and darkened wood. Cosgrove was already sat out on his rooftop terrace, shaded from the blazing sun by a potted palm with a glass in hand and his pith helmet on a side table, next to a loose pile of untouched papers.

'Mr and Mrs!' he called to them. 'Try this brandy. It's absolutely exquisite.'

'Where do you get hold of the stuff?' Fiona folded herself on to a wicker settee across from Cosgrove, placing her purchases on a stained pine coffee table.

Cosgrove laughed. 'If the Egyptians can sell it to you, everything is easy to get hold of.' He waved at the city spread out in front of them, minarets decorating it like candles.

As if on cue, the muezzins began the evening call to prayer, the sound of hundreds of off-kilter voices bouncing around streets that sweltered in the late sunlight. Cosgrove listened as the wall of sound built then faded away.

'It's dreadful of me, but I've started to use that sound to decide when it's time to knock off work for the night. Join me, please.' He gathered his papers and deposited them in a nearby briefcase.

Fiona reached for the decanter and two glasses as Lethbridge-Stewart joined her on the settee. His every instinct forced him to sit up straight when in front of a general like Cosgrove. He accepted the glass but placed it in front of him. It seemed somehow rude to drink while so many in the city below rushed to pray.

'You've found yourself another fez!' Cosgrove tossed the object up into the air, catching it as it fell back. 'I knew that you were missing it. I can't think how you lost the last one.' He leaned forward, brandy sloshing over the rim of his glass and landing on the floor to soak into the stone tiles.

'No…' Alistair gave a half-grin. 'I think I must have mislaid it.'

Cosgrove leaned closer to Fiona.

'Do you know, that hat saved our lives last time Alistair came over here? Did he ever tell you?'

Lethbridge-Stewart waved the line of questioning away as Fiona leaned forwards, her head on one side and a sly smile on her face.

'I doubt Fiona would be interested in some old war stories. We're here for a holiday, pure and simple.' He felt the movement of Fiona against him. Enough for him to know that she wasn't happy about being kept out of yet another military matter. That part of his life being secret angered her.

'Now,' said Cosgrove. 'What else have you got?' He spotted the jar and lifted it up to his face, turning it this way and that, such that his handlebar moustache nearly brushed against it. 'Very good this is too. An extremely good account of the Contendings of Horus in the hieroglyphics.'

'The what?' asked Lethbridge-Stewart.

'Oh dear.' Cosgrove tutted. 'Horus was the son of Osiris and Isis, and nephew to Nephthys and Set. After Osiris' death, Horus became involved in a struggle for the Throne of the Gods with Set.' He settled back. 'You're going to have to brush up on all of this on the cruise you know, old boy. There's one of those professor chappies on the boat. An expert in this sort of thing. What did they teach you at your school?'

'I dread to think what school you went to, but the closest mine got to this was the Greek classics. You said that the jar's very good. What sort of money?' Lethbridge-Stewart could see the double bonus of getting rid of the hideous jar at the same time as making back some of what he had shelled out.

'A good copy, old man. Completely worthless in itself. Perhaps for the best. The ancients used them to store hearts and other organs ready for the journey after death.' Cosgrove laughed as he replaced the jar. 'Speaking of which, how were Saqqara and the pyramids this morning? A happy reunion?'

Lethbridge-Stewart thought of his previous visit to Khufu's pyramid, a good two years ago now, and the danger that he and Cosgrove had found themselves in. He had been glad to experience nothing worse on his trip with Fiona than a pushy local trying to sell him a plaster scarab.

'Wonderful!' said Fiona. 'But so busy. I almost expected them to be deserted. Instead, there were tourists and diggers everywhere.'

Cosgrove nodded. 'The necropolis is vast. It's what's left of Memphis after all. They uncover new finds all the time.' He took a deep breath, letting it out slowly. 'Sometimes, things are best left where they are.'

'How so?'

'Hmm?' Cosgrove paused, his lips moving before speaking. 'They're not the most careful with what they find. Go in there, break half of what they look for, trying to find whatever sells for most.'

'I thought that you were going to talk about curses.' Fiona giggled as she took a long sip of the brandy.

'I wouldn't write them off.' Cosgrove leaned back in his chair and turned his head, looking out across the city and beyond. 'We brought some dark things back in the Victorian days. I've heard stories.' He looked down into the brandy glass, swirling it around and watching the dark liquid settle. 'Running footsteps that followed a young man home after he bought a mummy. Strangled men in the woods next to artefacts they stole. No footprints leading away. And in, I believe, 1911 a Priory rammed with Egyptian artefacts was burned to the ground with no explanation.' He sighed, shaking his head like a dog leaving the water. 'We started it all. We can't really complain that a cemetery is like Borough Market now…'

'I daresay we'll get something more isolated further up the river.' Lethbridge-Stewart looked out of the window, past the minarets and tower blocks, where the Nile drifted through the city. 'Thank you for making the arrangements. We could do with the peace and quiet.' He meant every word.

'I hope you find it, old man. I was thrilled to be able to help when you contacted me. You deserve it after your last trip here.' Cosgrove raised a glass. 'To both of you. Happy travels from tomorrow.'

It was later that Venessa Cosgrove joined them on the terrace;

she had given instructions for dinner and was now concerned, more than anything, whether it was to everyone's liking and which was the correct wine.

'It's dreadful out here,' she said, sipping at the dry white she had eventually settled on. 'You simply can't get the better French vineyards, and as for the new world wines...' She laughed hollowly. 'Absolutely no chance.'

She was, Fiona noticed, entirely concerned with practicalities. When hearing of the trip up the Nile, her first reaction was to ask about the return journey.

'A train seemed the best option, dear,' said Charles. 'I think by that point they will have taken the slow route for long enough.'

'Well, yes, it would certainly be the fastest route. But they are very unreliable. I think you should have considered that at least. I've checked Ahmed's diary now that he's our driver.' Venessa took a deep breath like a schoolteacher dealing with a difficult child. 'I believe that he is free for the day in question if he is needed. Would that be preferable, Alistair...? Fiona...?'

Fiona would have genuinely preferred the train. Somehow being out of the umbrella of the Cosgroves, even in a train carriage, seemed much more private than sitting in their car for the long journey back to Cairo. She turned to Alistair, who did one of his characteristic eyebrow-raises back at her.

'It's very kind of you, Mrs Cosgrove...' he began.

'Excellent, that's settled then. I'll keep Ahmed's diary free for those days so that he can head up and drive you back. Much safer and more comfortable for you.' Venessa leaned closer to Fiona and said, her voice low enough that it at least appeared that she was trying to keep it from the two men, 'You're going to marry an officer, dear. It's like joining the aristocracy. Because his job is everything, you see. You've got to hold the fort at home, look after his officers and their wives.' She glanced over at Alistair. 'Whether they like it or not. You've got to be the lady to his lordship. That means organising him.'

'What happened here, the last time you came?'

They both lay in bed under the slowly rotating fan, wishing the heat of the room would escape through the now open window.

Alistair turned away, then back to Fiona.

'You know I can't talk about it. Official Secrets.'

'That's what you always say. Cosgrove seemed happy enough to witter on about it.' She sighed. 'Until you stopped him.'

He breathed out slowly. Cosgrove was happy to discuss it. To be fair, the fact that a bunch of bandits had tried to kill off a pair of British officers probably wasn't an official secret. The dead alien, on the other hand…

He smiled, to present a mask. 'I think poor old Cosgrove has gone native. Forgotten his job a bit.'

'I worry.'

'What about?' Alistair needed to get out of this disingenuous habit. He knew exactly what she worried about. It worried him too and that's why he didn't want to discuss it.

'If a fez, of all things, saved your life. Who was trying to kill you? And why?'

'They're not a problem anymore.' He levered himself up in bed and placed a warm hand on her shoulder. 'Don't worry. We're perfectly safe now.'

She turned to face him.

'Well, I should hope so too. *That* wasn't what I was worried about.' A pause. 'Until now.' Fiona sighed. 'I was worried about whatever it is about your work that means that people would try to kill you. And what happens if they get lucky next time?'

Alistair couldn't answer. He just held her and listened to the fan's whirr and the drone of the city outside as life surged through its veins.

Much later, Fiona opened her eyes to another call from the muezzins. She lay in bed, listening to Alistair's deep breathing next to her. For a man of action, he was a surprisingly deep sleeper. She glanced around as the echoing rise and fall of the call to prayer faded. There was no clock in the room and no daylight outside. Early morning then.

She slipped from under the thin cotton sheets, leaving Alistair under the whirring fan. Pulling on a borrowed dressing gown from Venessa, she went to the window. From there, she looked over streets that were quieter now, but far from asleep. It was mostly men that wandered, moving quickly from house to mosque. It seemed the most natural, normal thing in the world.

Why Egypt? It had been Alistair's idea, of course. A getaway to celebrate their engagement. Somewhere completely different. He'd spent some time posted to Libya a couple of years ago, which had been cut short. And he had wanted to get away from Britain. She had no idea what had happened recently at his work, but she could tell that something was bothering him every time she brought it up.

How could a posting in Scotland cause him such difficulty? He didn't have to deal with the problems in Ireland, or any conflicts abroad. The quietest decade in centuries for the British military and he managed to be in danger. She only hoped that he would open up and let her in.

He had wanted to come to this place. He hadn't had a chance to enjoy it last time, he said. Again, she had been unable to drag the details out of him. Charles Cosgrove, an old friend of Alistair, had arranged a cruise for them. Up the river to Thebes, to explore the ruins of ancient Egypt.

It was the whiff of adventure that had made her jump at the chance. Hers wasn't a military family, with the exception of her cousin Frank. Finance was the Campbells game. They liked stress and long hours but only coupled with the certainty that they could stay in one place to do it and not get shot.

There was movement on the rooftops spread out in front of her, sliding smoothly over one apex was a cat. Tabby with a flash of white that danced in the dark. It settled there, like a queen watching her kingdom.

Fiona thought back to what Venessa had said to her. *Be the lady.* That was the phrase that stuck with her. A jump from being the secretary.

Except that Alistair didn't tell her much about his job, or his colleagues. She knew of Sally who'd had that accident a few months back, but the rest of them were shrouded in secrecy. She occasionally heard talk of a Sam, someone that she understood to be merely an NCO, or Bill Bishop, Alistair's golden boy. She had yet to meet any of them. Bishop had a fiancée of his own. Anne. Fiona heard a lot about her because she was a civilian that worked with Alistair. Anne sounded like someone that she should get to know, probably over a nice polite cup of tea.

Fiona preferred wine.

Then she saw another cat, similar, sat on a different roof. Both of them stared at her through eyes that glittered silver in the lights. These animals had freedom, adventures. Things she might lose.

It hadn't sunk in until Venessa had said it. The marriage wasn't just about her and Alistair. She had taken a new role. One in which, no matter what name Venessa dressed it as, she would be the little woman. The little woman who didn't know the half of what her husband actually did once he kissed her and walked out of the door.

A third pair of eyes shone outside, fixed on her. There must have been a feral colony outside. Used to meeting up on the rooftops, suddenly met with a British woman, awake and adrift.

She didn't want to invite them in, so she reached for the shutters, closing them on her curious night-time colleagues.

'What do you think?' Cosgrove beamed as he pointed across the Nile's docks to the paddle steamer, its white hull low in the water supported the scaffold-like framework that surrounded the wooden upper decks. '*PS Keberia.*'

'Like an Agatha Christie novel,' said Fiona. 'It's delightful.'

'I 'opezere is nothing 'ere to exercise zebeetle grey cells.' Cosgrove tweaked the hairs on his handlebar moustache as if it were Poirot's own.

Lethbridge-Stewart groaned inwardly and clapped Cosgrove on the shoulder.

'You've done us proud, old chap. It's certainly got, erm, history.' He couldn't help but think that the thing looked like a relic from the last century. Even from the dockside, he could see paint that flaked from the windowpanes and rust flecks on the railings.

'The golden age of tourism is gone, I'm afraid,' Cosgrove said. 'The war saw to that. Then Nasser put the final nail in its coffin. Hopefully, it will pick up again soon. A bit of investment, a bit of touting. Get the Americans back over here and they'll soon be filling every berth again.' He walked ahead of them as Lethbridge-Stewart gathered up the suitcases to follow. 'But for now, stretch your legs a bit on board and enjoy the space. Enjoy the freedom. Tell your friends when you get back.'

Cosgrove gestured about him as he walked, pointing up the river.

'Up there, you see. Once you're out of this city, it will be like a breath of fresh air to your lungs. That river is the life blood of the country. The only reason it exists.' He stopped, throwing his arms in a theatrical gesture. 'The trouble is, a city like Cairo is like a living being. You take food and water in.' He pointed up the river where Lethbridge-Stewart could see barges laden with fruit and wood making their way down the waterway. 'But then it's all got to come out again afterwards.' Cosgrove pointed downstream, towards the smog of the city.

'You should come with us,' said Fiona. 'You should be a tour guide. Not a diplomat.'

'Alas.' Cosgrove sighed. 'Maybe when I've finally finished all the work Her Majesty has for me, I can be released from my bond. Goodbye, my dear.'

He kissed her on both cheeks. The sort of public display that only a British man with a pith helmet and safari suit could get away with. That, Lethbridge-Stewart knew, was why Cosgrove made sure to look as he did. The locals paid him attention, acted as if different rules applied and, most importantly, missed him if he disappeared.

'Old man.' Cosgrove held his hand out. 'I hope you find enough to occupy yourself.'

Lethbridge-Stewart scooped up the two suitcases into one hand. With the other, he reached out for Fiona. His fingers found hers, intertwined like children's. Then, as one, they scampered through the docks, past dockworkers, fishermen and tourists, towards the gangplank.

'Your room, sir, ma'am.' The porter, who had introduced himself as Azmy, dropped the cases onto the deck and pushed the key into the lock with a flourish and made to push it open.

It didn't budge. Azmy's smile froze as Alistair and Fiona

looked at each other on the deck that ran outside the rooms. Azmy tried turning the key further. Alistair could see the young man's muscles tense, before giving the door a nudge with his shoulder. The impression of poise and efficiency given by the pure white linen uniform finally collapsed as Azmy flew through the door.

Alistair raised an eyebrow and barely suppressed a laugh to Fiona as he picked up the luggage and stepped across the threshold. He could hear Fiona following, giggling. Azmy, to his credit, was back on his feet in as close an approximation to attention as one could get with a fez hurriedly reapplied to the head at an angle.

Alistair was impressed at the young man and fumbled in his pocket for a collar as a tip.

'Have you served in the Forces, young man?'

'No, sir.' A pause, as if searching for the right words. 'I hope to one day. Like my father and uncle.' The boy's English was exceptional. He backed out of the room, ignoring the proffered tip. 'Tea will be on the upper deck, sir, madam. Captain Ibrahim would love all of the passengers to join him. You know our itinerary?'

'I know that we will arrive in Luxor in six days' time,' said Alistair. 'The rest I'm leaving to you.'

'A quiet first couple of days,' said Azmy. 'Then we arrive at Minya tomorrow night. Then Assyut, Qena, we explore the ruins of Thebes and finally to Luxor.' He smiled again. 'I hope you enjoy our wonderful country.'

The freshly laundered sheets of the cabin matched the cotton curtains that fluttered in the breeze from the river. Fiona stood at the edge of the bed, her back to it, and let herself fall and sink into its welcome, soft embrace.

Smiling, Alistair could not help but join her.

CHAPTER TWO
The Nile

FIONA TRIED to keep her eyes on the green that outlined the Nile, separating it from the rocks and sand. The steamer was well underway, and the smell of coal and water vapour drifted across to where she and Alistair sat in wicker chairs on the deck. A smattering of other passengers lounged, watching the view. A view that was, so far, unremarkable.

It made a welcome change from the braying gargoyle that had sat at their table, without asking, and then proceeded to engage them in conversation. His name was Frederick Mortimer.

Conversation was the wrong word. It was really a monologue, punctuated by occasional assumptions that acted like replies. He had clocked poor Alistair as a military man the second they had sat down. And that meant he knew her fiancé's life story.

'You'll have started out on a commission, I expect. The easy life, that's what we chaps in the National Service called it!' A wink, and then a guffaw loud enough to drown out any attempt by Alistair to tell his own military history. One that Fiona knew involved a National Service with markedly more hostile action than the other man had seen.

She could see the effort that Alistair was taking to remain calm and polite. She put her chin in one hand and stirred some more sugar into her tea with the other. It was a mint blend, warming and relaxing. She hoped it was helping Alistair.

'Lunch, sirs, ma'am?'

Fiona knew the voice and turned to see Azmy approaching their table, his white uniform matching the curtains that fluttered out of the windows in the breeze. She opened her mouth to reply, when Mortimer cut across.

'Lunch, boy? It's barely past breakfast. Whatever times you people keep here are no good for us.' He waved one arm airily behind his head, as if dispatching a bothersome fly.

Azmy's smile froze, his eyes hardening.

'It is nearly noon, sir. A light lunch now before a full dinner later. Our chef can produce some fine—'

'A ham sandwich then!' Mortimer snapped.

Fiona winced. A request calculated to be both naïve and cause awkwardness to the other man.

'I will enquire, sir, but sadly, it may be difficult.' Azmy held his pose and smile, hands folded behind his back.

Mortimer was now leaning back in his chair to the two elderly ladies behind him, bringing them into the discussion, clearly hoping he'd found kindred spirits.

'Azmy is keeping his cool well,' Fiona muttered under her breath as she leaned away from the railing and towards her fiancé. 'You too, dear.'

'It's my "funding face",' Alistair said, barely moving a muscle. His eyes twinkled with amusement.

'Your what?' She giggled and lifted a hand to stifle it.

'You know, the face I have to put on whenever I'm forced to spend time with an odious civilian responsible for the purse strings. Usually a politician, or an industrialist. Troublesome beggars.'

'God help us all if he is…' Fiona nodded at Mortimer, just as he turned back from the two ladies.

'What would you recommend?' Alistair said to Azmy before Mortimer started again.

'We have some *Ful* today, sir. Fava beans cooked with oil, cumin and parsley.' Azmy beamed as he leaned back on to his heels.

'Sounds delicious,' said Fiona. 'That will do us both perfectly.'

Azmy moved on down the deck, greeting the other passengers strung out on the chairs and tables, checking each had enough tea, taking orders.

Fiona gazed past the lattice work of the railings as the suburbs of Cairo gave way to the landscape of Egypt. The noise of the city of barges, white sailed feluccas and poor families living in boats muffled by the steady, sedate pace of the old steamer as it breezed past.

Mortimer leaned in. His voice, however, continued as loud as ever. 'You don't have to be so polite to them you know. I wouldn't trust their recommendations. Grease and rotten food is mostly what they serve, to my mind.'

'I don't know where your National Service took you, *Mr* Mortimer.' Alistair let the slight emphasis lie on the man's citizen honorific. 'But my career has covered a lot of this globe. I tend to find that one man can eat much the same as another, if he approaches his meal with an open mind.'

Fiona's eyes searched across the deck, looking for escape. She was rewarded. At that moment, one of the ladies behind them sprang to her feet.

'There, there!' She pointed at the grey blue water, halfway between the boat's hull and the shore. 'I'm sure…'

Her companion leaped to her feet as well, gripping her friend's arm through her thin dress. 'What was it, May?'

'I'm sure it was a Nile—'

'Of course it's the Nile!' snapped Mortimer. 'Where do you think we are, woman?'

The first lady turned to him, a withering look extending over her spectacles.

'*Crocodylusniloticus*. A Nile crocodile, young man.' She turned back to the river with a sniff. Her friend simply let out a loud tut.

Fiona wished she had brought her camera on deck with her as her eyes cast themselves over the waters; little wavelets that could hide anything were all she could see.

'Not this far south, ma'am.' Azmy was leaning over May's shoulder. 'They tend to stay up by Lake Nasser. Are you sure it was a crocodile?'

'What would you know about it, boy?' snapped Mortimer, standing. There was a slight shake to his posture. 'In any event, I should check on the little lady.' He stalked off toward the cabins.

Fiona and Alistair watched him leave. He dropped to the next deck down, hugging the wall furthest from the river.

Alistair nodded with satisfaction and turned to Azmy.

'Well, what would you know about it?'

Azmy looked sheepish, as if caught out.

'I have a degree in Zoology, sir, from Cairo University. My thesis was on invasive species. A particular interest of mine.'

Alistair smiled, raising his cup to his mouth. 'You and I may have a lot in common, Azmy.'

Azmy smiled again. 'I'm glad to hear that, sir. I hope to progress my career soon.'

As he moved on again, the quiet settled across the deck. Alistair winked at Fiona and leaned backwards, stretching his legs out in front of him into the sunlight which shone off the linen suit he wore. With his moustache, sitting on the old wooden deck of the tattered, but proud, old steamer, he looked like a man out of time, a remnant of the colonial era. Given what she knew of his family, that probably wasn't far from the truth. She thought of Frank's congratulations when he heard the news of the engagement.

'With the Lethbridge-Stewarts, you're marrying into class,' he'd said. 'But not money!' After his own experience of marriage into the moneyed classes, Fiona could only assume this was an advantage in his eyes.

May and her friend had sat down again, heads leaning into each other.

'No luck?' called Fiona brightly.

May shook her head. 'These old eyes I think.' She moved her chair closer 'I used to have such a good eye for natural history in my day.' She sighed deeply. 'Sometimes, maybe you lose the skills you had when you were young. Or maybe I just wanted something too badly.'

'Well, it's not impossible. Maybe an escapee from somewhere? A zoo perhaps?'

May smiled. 'I hope so, dear. I always like to think of animals escaping those places. Especially the zoos you find abroad. My late husband was an entomologist.' She nodded with satisfaction. 'He always said that it was better to pin them to a page than keep them alive.' Her eyes flicked across Fiona. 'Have you set a date yet?'

Fiona started, her momentary surprise settling as she followed May's eye down to her left hand. Fiona flexed it, the sun catching the diamond within the ring, still unfamiliar to her.

'Not yet.' She smirked. Alistair opened one eye and gave a half-smile. 'But soon.'

'Did he go down on one knee?' May's face was that of a schoolgirl as she whispered the question, shining through the wrinkles and wisps of white hair. It was as if her age was something done to her, rather than what she was.

Fiona giggled briefly, caught by the question. 'Of course! Alistair is nothing if not traditional.'

'Children next then?'

Such a personal question, but there was something so naïve about the old lady. 'Not just yet, I think. But I rather suspect Alistair would like an heir. What about you, any children of your own?'

May sighed and shook her head, her happy expression dropping. 'No. No children for me or Tabby here.' She nodded over to her quiet friend, who slightly inclined her head.

'Tabitha,' she said before taking a long sip of her tea. 'Miss Tabitha Gordon.'

'Pleased to meet you,' Fiona said.

'Did you know that Mortimer fellow?'

Fiona shook her head.

'Try not to attract him in future.' Tabitha sniffed. 'I prefer to take tea in better company.'

Fiona looked about her, at the other passengers, searching for a way out of the conversation. Alistair was characteristically leaving women's talk to women.

Fiona's eyes moved further around the deck, where a middle-aged couple, blond and unsmiling, both sat up stiffly in their chairs, heads pressed together. Beyond, a man in a cream shirt lounged with a broad brimmed hat over his face. He could have been asleep for all Fiona knew.

At that moment, Azmy came to her rescue, depositing a plate on Tabitha's and May's table; a pair of still sizzling kebabs. Alistair brought himself from the depths of his own reverie as the bowl of fava beans, steam still rising from it, was placed between Fiona and him.

'Excellent!'

Much later, Alistair breathed a sigh of relief as he reached his and Fiona's table in the steamer's restaurant. Mortimer did not appear to have arrived yet. He pulled out a chair for his fiancée. The other passengers filed in, the heat of the day seeming to fall off their shoulders. May and Tabitha took a small table by the bar. They were joined by the blond couple that had been sitting nearby earlier; the two walked in, each taking their own chairs, a good couple of feet apart. He listened for their conversation and caught a few words. Russian. Very curious but not unexpected with old Nasser's policies.

'Do you mind if I join you?'

Alistair looked up. The newcomer had clearly dressed for dinner, his light shirt completed by a tie. Alistair envied the man's ability to stay cool in such weather. His hat had been left elsewhere, but he recognised the clothing from the man that had been dozing on the upper deck.

'Of course not,' Fiona said and introduced the two of them. 'Are you travelling alone?'

The man's smile flickered slightly on his face, like a bulb fighting to illuminate a room. 'Yes. I'm a bachelor.' His eyes jerked to the upper decks, where the cabins were. 'Maybe I enjoy my academic work too much. It's not very compatible with fair company.'

Alistair sighed inwardly. As much as he complained about the military lifestyle and its difficulties, he sometimes wondered if his original career path of quietly educating young minds would have left him any better off.

'What work is that?' he asked.

The other man gave an embarrassed shrug, as if being caught. 'Actually, I'm an Egyptologist. Professor Alexander Greaves.' He extended an arm, first to Fiona, who offered her hand for a gentlemanly kiss. Greaves took it as if unsure what to do before shaking it between two fingers. He then turned to Alistair and gave a similarly weak greeting. 'It sort of runs in the family. My own grandfather came here in the last century.'

'Was he a tomb robber?' said Fiona. 'Sorry.' She laughed self-consciously. 'I meant, explorer.'

Greaves shifted in his chair. If the temperature could have dropped, Alistair was sure it would have.

'Back then, the two things were much the same. And, of

course, even earlier, most tombs were stripped before the Europeans found them. You've seen Saqqara, I expect. I prefer to avoid the place.'

'So,' said Fiona. 'Was your grandfather lucky enough to get all the gold and curses that go with it?'

Alistair placed a hand on her leg, squeezing slightly. Greaves stared down at the table. The waiter deposited a basket of flatbread and hummus before them.

'He got ill,' said Greaves eventually. 'That's all I know. He recovered, eventually.' He took a bite of the flatbread. 'That's what the curse of the mummy usually turned out to be. Ordinary human viruses and bacteria, sealed away with the bodies and organs and released onto whoever found the tomb.' He sighed. 'Everyone is always so concerned with what was buried in the tomb. That's not the interesting part. The interesting part is the walls. What is written there.' His eyes had glazed now. 'Because mummies are dead. But the people they used to be and their lives, they are all in the writing.'

A white suited waiter deposited glasses before them along with a bottle of white wine that Alistair knew would be bitter to his tastes. The waiter had clearly overheard the conversation and gave Fiona and Alistair a weak smile, humouring the professor.

'Such as…?' Alistair prompted.

'Their gods. And the stories. Absolutely fascinating. Take the creation myth, for instance, found on the walls of the oldest temples. The oldest of the Ancient Egyptian creation myths, is all about Atum.' Greaves shrugged and poured himself a large glass of wine.

Alistair coughed with the empty glass in his hand, and, with a mortified look, Greaves hurriedly poured the two of them further glasses. Alistair took a drink, letting the cool wine slip down his throat and wash away the dust of the morning.

Greaves continued. 'He creates his own children by swallowing his own sperm, thus becoming both mother and father to the gods. Are you okay there, Alistair?'

'Fine, thank you.' Alistair finished his spluttering and wiped his eyes from where they had watered.

'But it is strange to go back,' Greaves said. 'Such detailed mythology is almost fully formed in intricate detail in the oldest temples and tombs.' His eyes drifted towards the window. 'Almost as if their gods really did drop out of the sky one day.'

'Atum? We've already heard of Set, Horus and Osiris. How many leaders did the Egyptian gods have?' Fiona took over while Alistair tried to recover his composure.

'Ah, that depends.' Greaves grinned. 'Their mythology is somewhat changeable. There are several different creation myths beyond Atum's self-fertilisation.'

'I'm glad to hear it.' Alistair took another sip of wine. 'So, which one is the real one? A world can't have more than one beginning.'

'All of them!' The expression on Greaves' face was of a man who was almost oblivious to his surroundings as his brain fired on all cylinders. 'They contradict, but the ancient Egyptians saw no problem with that. Each was true in a different context. And the places where things don't quite fit, where the brush strokes of history have left blank patches, well they are the most interesting parts of all.' The look on his face was one of pleasure.

'And you're looking for the secret behind these myths on a steamboat?' asked Fiona.

'Ah, no.' He looked embarrassed again. 'I'm afraid this is how I'm paying my way to get here and up the river. I'm to be your tour guide. Hopefully, at the end of it all, I can get out into the Western Desert.'

'The Western Desert?' said Fiona.

'Oh yes, I think that there's a lot out there that hasn't yet been uncovered.' Greaves coughed. Alistair noticed the man's eyes drifting away from eye contact again, like they had when he talked of his grandfather. 'At least, that's what my research has indicated. It's been difficult. My grandfather left many notes, but much of his work in Egypt from the late Victorian era is frustratingly incomplete.' He drummed his fingers on the table. 'It's as if someone has gone through his records and taken out pages, whenever he seemed about to make a major discovery.' He mimed ripping a sheet of paper. 'But that is where he was going, out into that desert, miles from anywhere. What he was looking for, and whether he found it…' Greaves sighed as he looked past them, towards the window. 'I might never know.'

Alistair looked at the remnants of the white wine in his glass that he hadn't managed to spit across the tablecloth.

'Wonderful,' he said. 'Tell me. Will you be delivering lectures at every mealtime, or will we be able to eat for some of them?' It was then that he felt Fiona's high heel scrape down the front of his leg, not hard enough to hurt, but enough that he knew that his future wife would definitely try to keep him out of trouble.

'I'm sorry, I think I've been placed here as well.' It was a new voice, somewhat sheepish as if apologising for even presuming that the owner should be fed that day.

Alistair looked up to see a small, bearded man with round glasses, his skin with a local complexion but his clothes very western, being a simple black suit and unbuttoned shirt.

'Sit down, please.' Alistair gestured. 'We were just listening to the professor here tell us far more of the ancient Egyptians than I think can be squeezed into one mealtime.'

The man bowed slightly and sat. 'That sounds enlightening.' He kept his hands folded on his lap. 'I am Mr Dawoud. I was hoping to learn much about my country's history on this trip. I would love to spend time with you, Professor…?'

'Greaves.' The man beamed. 'I must say, it's so rare that I have such interest from one of the locals in what I have to talk about. So many of you just seem to treat your past as a bit of a backdrop and a commercial opportunity.'

'Ah.' Dawoud kept his eyes staring down at the table, but gave a half-smile.

Alistair's heart sank as, behind the man's back, he saw Mortimer enter the room.

'But not all. You need people to do the digging, do you not?' Dawoud asked. 'My father was one. And my family are Coptic. Growing up, I felt a connection to those ancient times, both in language and culture. I am fascinated, Professor, with hearing all that you have to show us.'

Alistair felt himself frown. It was such a strong generalisation to make that Copts were somehow closer to the past than other Egyptians. Somehow it didn't ring quite true.

'Great to hear it.' Mortimer was already standing next to the table. Hanging off his arm was a dark-haired woman, her eyes as empty as hollow shells. 'It's fantastic to hear that good Christian values are triumphing amidst the savagery here.' He gestured to his partner. 'This is Viola.' The look on his face was that of a man expecting friends to admire his new car. 'You'll have to excuse her small talk, she's from Italy.'

The girl smiled, a cold expression that didn't reach her eyes.

'Hello,' she said.

'Charmed.' Alistair raised an eyebrow. 'I'm sorry that we missed you this morning.'

The woman's expression didn't change. She remained disinterested, as if all around her was a collection of someone else's holiday photographs.

'The air in Cairo makes Viola ill. She's such a delicate flower.' Mortimer pulled her close to him, squeezing her shoulders against his chest. 'I'm sure she only married me for my passport, but I can't complain.'

There was almost sufficient space for the couple at the table. Alistair leaned back in his seat, letting one arm dangle on the empty chair next to him. He hoped that Mortimer's sheer obliviousness wouldn't power through anyway. He was saved by Azmy's gentle intervention.

'A space on this table over here, sir. A lovely view of the river as it flows by.' With his towel looped over one arm, he guided the Mortimers towards the table where the Russian couple still appeared intent on refusing to speak to each other.

Mr Dawoud winced as the man left. 'I do not know how being closer to a culture that kept slaves and desiccated its cats ready for the after-life makes me less savage,' he said with the first smile that Alistair had seen from him.

Alistair glanced over to Mortimer's new table. Only to find that the Russian man was staring straight back at him.

'So, what do you make of the rest of the passengers?'

The question caught Fiona off guard as she and Alistair walked through the Beni Suef marina, watching the more expensive boats bobbing across the water as the sun played across them and onto the farmland and date palms across the river. The ever-present feluccas drifted across the water, their sails now orange in the reflected light. The *Keberia* had moored late on, but there was enough time for an evening stroll.

'I'm trying not to. I'm here with you.' She squeezed Alistair's hand and brought him to a halt under a lamp that shone down to the black water below.

'There's something about some of them. I mean, they just look…' He sighed, at a loss for words 'Out of place.'

'Out of place?' She laughed, nudging Alistair in the ribs. 'What do passengers on a Nile cruise usually look like? In your experience, I mean.'

His smile, she could see, was for her benefit. It faded as soon as he thought she wasn't looking.

'We'll avoid Mortimer,' she said. 'Please…'

He squeezed her hand back and gave her a sudden, genuine smile. They kept walking, dodging an occasional cat that dashed across their path.

'I can't put my finger on it,' Alistair said. 'I certainly couldn't narrow it down to somebody in particular. Well, the Russian couple barely seem to speak to each other.'

'That's just Russians, isn't it? Very taciturn. If you're going to suspect everyone for acting like a national stereotype, you're best off staying in Scotland and eating haggis.'

He laughed and shook his head.

'There's something a bit funny going on. There always is with Cosgrove.'

Fiona released Alistair's hand. 'Your old friend.' She tried to keep her voice as flat as she could. 'Who saved your life the last time you were here.'

'Yes…'

She should be proud of herself. There couldn't be many women that could make a brigadier look as uncomfortable as Alistair did right now. There was a hollowness inside her, however. Something that had first opened up when she had heard Cosgrove talking about that fez.

'What happened?' She released his hand, stood back and waited. As his face turned to her it looked pained, but she knew that expression. It was embarrassment. The face of a man that had forgotten to book a restaurant for a date. 'You can't even remember, can you?' Her nails dug into the palms of her hands.

'You can't even remember why you nearly died the last time you came here.' She folded her arms, kicked a pebble that bounced across the quay and disappeared into the water with a hollow splash that was quickly sucked up into the night air around them. 'So why can't you trust Cosgrove? He seems amiable enough.'

'That's his act. He plays the fool to make sure that he is noticed, so that if any foreign powers tried to get rid of him…' Alistair shrugged. '…he'd be immediately missed. He's as good a friend as any that I know. But the reality is that he has one friend above all that keeps him here. That's the Crown. He is more loyal to that than any friend.'

Fiona gave a grim smile. 'And you let him arrange our trip.'

Alistair arched an eyebrow. 'It seemed like a good idea at the time.'

Fiona took his arm and rotated him back the way they had come, past the cafés of old men smoking shisha and the children playing on the little park, watched by the women, some veiled, some bare faced.

'Well, until Thomas Cook is operating here again, I suppose that Cosgrove will have to do,' Fiona said.

As the sun set across the desert, they walked back to the steamer, arm in arm.

CHAPTER THREE
Just in Time

WARRIOR.

Lethbridge-Stewart felt the place rather than saw or heard it. Around him were others, a multitude of beings, ready for action. A flickering red light on the horizon and, under his booted feet, red dust. Dust that stretched for miles in every direction.

Lead them. Prove yourself.

He had a sudden sense of something other than himself. Clad in black robes, they had a vaguely uniform look, a series of silhouettes topped by animal heads of all types, from birds to crocodiles, cats and other animals.

Over there was something else. Someone else. Numerous enemies, clad in white, like an opposing side of chessmen.

He was at war.

The opponent was moving. The troops spread out, as if ready to try and encircle him and his *men*.

It starts.

As he thought it, they moved, spreading out as well, drawing themselves in a classic defensive position, staying deep and presenting a face to the enemy. But that was not enough. He had thought too slowly, directed them too late. They were surrounded, sheep penned in by dogs. And yet, the enemy did not move.

He waited. Finally, he picked two units. He wanted to test the line.

The enemy mobbed them. Those two black figures crumpled under an onslaught of limbs and axes. He caught a sudden wrenching feeling, one of loss and bitter iron, as if a part of himself was torn away.

It worked. He gritted his teeth as the troops he chose fell under the onrush of the enemy. Again, he felt that wrench, as if he had been punched in the gut. But the feint worked, and the enemy line thinned on the flank.

He was in the sortie that broke for that line, felt the rush of the wind and the red dust that seared his cheeks as they closed on the enemy. It was the purest combat imaginable.

Then he felt those around him falling. Pawns sacrificed and, as always, he had thought to lead the way. Here, there was no reliance on quick wits, good shooting. The outcome was inevitable, as the axes fell on them again and again. The red dust grew darker and darker; the black blood of his troops leaked from rends in the dark robes. He could feel the wrenching and bitterness rising like bile as around him bodies went down.

He stepped over the bodies before him, his mind whirring. The number of black robed bodies on the landscape was vastly outnumbered by the white robed ones. In his hand was a sword.

The last troops surrounding him were gone and, within a split second, he was next. As they reached him the sensation was unbearable, every nerve was screaming in agony at once, he felt his heart beat for the first time since the battle had begun, felt his very essence pulled from the shell that it inhabited as all knowledge of the battle faded from him.

Warrior…

Lethbridge-Stewart's eyes flicked awake. He felt the sweat on his pillow. He listened. Total silence. He remembered *Keberia* mooring a little way outside of Beni Suef. It should have been quiet out here. No muezzins to wake him. Just the dream.

He swung his legs out of bed and sat, his hands braced against his knees, feeling the sweat dripping down his body.

He was not going to touch that wine again.

Lethbridge-Stewart felt on the bedside table, sliding his hand across the sanded surface to pick up his watch. In the pale moonlight from the window, he could see the position of the hands. It was half past two. He could still feel a thudding in his chest, easing now as he sat there. There would be no sleep for some time now.

On the other side of the bed, Fiona stirred and mumbled.

'Just going for a walk, dear,' he whispered. He didn't know if she was awake.

Standing, he pulled on his slacks and shirt and slipped on a pair of deck shoes. At the door, he carefully pulled the handle down to avoid the latch springing and waking her.

The night outside was almost silent as Lethbridge-Stewart walked around the deck. They were a short distance outside the city, surrounded by date palms that clad the river's shore in a dark cloud. Past them was the black curve of rocks and sand dunes before the stars began.

It was rare to see them like that. He gripped the railings; his eyes followed them. A million tiny pin pricks of light, gathering at one point into a silvery river that flowed across the sky. He had always thought of the Milky Way as a slightly inadequate name for something so striking. If Anne were there, she could probably give them each a name and a distance, turning the spectacle to a mere set of signposts. She could also tell him where each of the races they had faced came from. Somewhere out there was the Grandfathers' home planet, the home world of the Dominators', whatever planet the Galdani came from… And somewhere, likely not in this sky, but another elsewhere, his father carried on his good fight.

That was the real reason Lethbridge-Stewart didn't want to be involved in the wedding planning. The Campbells were a big, old, close family. He had family, of course. His mother and grandfather, Great Uncle Archibald and his family, Uncle Matthew and his. But nothing like what Fiona had.

He also knew that his cousins, those not following the military traditions of course, all had the scent of profit in their noses with his grandfather's declining health and his uncle's rather less than military approach to land management. Lethbridge-Stewart couldn't see either the estate at Glen Cladach or the family harmony lasting long. Uncle Matthew's letter of congratulations on the engagement had been loaded with innuendo about his true feelings. Ever the civil servant.

Lethbridge-Stewart couldn't blame his uncle. Frank Campbell had tried to marry into money and things had turned out terribly. An outsider like Uncle Matthew would be right to be suspicious.

Maybe Uncle Matthew would have been assuaged if he knew about the unicorn breeding programme that had really put paid to Frank's marriage. He had, at least, offered Greyhound Lodge, the family's hidden little cottage on the other side of Scotland, as a honeymoon destination.

Lethbridge-Stewart smiled to himself and began to walk down the deck. One day, he hoped to be able to come clean about his career.

But there was no one in his family to come clean to. Not now. It was the gaps that hurt him the most. His brother he had only remembered a couple of years ago. His memory was a flickering image, like looking at the back of someone's head and never being able to see the front. His father was a stronger memory, and at least he knew that, somewhere, Gordon was still alive. He would not be returning for his son's wedding. Lethbridge-Stewart's nephew, Dylan, would be there, of course, how could he not be? Alas, his other nephew, Owain… Well, the Galdani-induced coma had put paid to him attending events of any kind.

The empty chairs that should have held his father and brother would hit Lethbridge-Stewart the most. It should be a time of his life when those men were there, to share a pint with, take advice from.

He shook his head to clear the thoughts. Melancholia was not one of his traits.

He'd been a warrior in his dream. A strange dream.

He leaned over the railings again, peering down at the water, tiny black wavelets that washed against the side of the boat.

His eyes caught something. A series of wavelets smaller than the rest, but rising on a larger mound of water, almost regular in shape. He was sure that something was moving down there, when a sudden change, like a small splash, obscured them. It was almost like a patch of scaled skin, rising out of the river.

No, he thought, it was exactly that. The old lady must have been right. There were crocodiles in the river. Large ones judging by that movement. If any crew members were awake, he felt that he should inform them. The bottom deck, mostly the bar, restaurant and engine rooms, was only a metre or so from the water level.

Lethbridge-Stewart rushed down the internal stairs to the small open deck next to the saloon. From there, the narrow corridor ran the length of the boat. The water slapped against the hull, an irregular sound as if the vessel were a punching bag for the river itself. Amid that hollow echoing, came something more rhythmic, at the edge of his hearing, a clanging against metal.

'Hello?' he called. No response.

The bar and restaurant were both in darkness. As he pressed his ear to the glass, he could hear nothing but the clanging of metal grow fainter. Clearly nothing in there. Possibly the engine room would be open.

The small metal door was further down the corridor from where he now stood. He approached, glancing about as he did so. He had no idea what was making that sound. He also had no idea how high the average Nile crocodile could jump out of the water. Could it clear the deck? It was an unconscious movement that brought his right hand down to the empty space by his belt.

What wouldn't he give for his revolver now.

The engine room door was closed. He gave it a slight push and it opened with the screech of hinges long since unlubricated and left to rot in dry sandy air. The scent of oil and the sensation of coal dust in his nose told him he had found the place. Muscles tensed as he crept in.

'Hello?' he called again.

In the light that was drawn from the bright night sky outside, he began to make out the shapes: piles of coal, ready for feeding into the furnace, the huge hulking boiler, pipework that covered every inch of the walls and the enormous cylinders that powered the drive wheels. All around was the smell of oil and soot. In the silence, he paused.

There was something about a steam-powered machine like this; it wasn't simply an engine that was turned on or off, it had to be warmed, fed, coaxed. This felt like a sleeping beast more than an inert vehicle. He almost expected it to answer.

Then, it did. The clang echoed around the room.

He rushed in its direction as it came again and again from the foot of the boiler, next to the coal scuttle. There, the huge iron door that opened to the firebox was closed and the bar was across it.

He needed some sort of weapon; whatever was in there could be angry. A shovel. What could be better?

He grabbed at the object, half-buried in the pile of coal.

Then, he tensed again, and kicked the bar with the heel of his foot, once, twice until it scraped clear of the rings that held the door closed. He used the shovel's blade to tap the door open as it too creaked in complaint. Then he stood back, the weapon raised.

'You'd better come out now.' He kept his voice as calm as possible.

It would have stayed that way if the soot and ash covered face of Mr Dawoud hadn't appeared, coughing and spluttering through a handkerchief. The shovel dropped out of Lethbridge-Stewart's hands in surprise, clanging to the metal floor as he rushed to pull the man out of the firebox.

'What the devil are you doing there?'

The man wheezed, appearing to draw something within himself as he rocked onto his hands and knees, before spitting out a wet black lump onto the floor. Lethbridge-Stewart nudged it with his toe. Saliva and soot.

'Come on.' He bent and gripped the man under his arms. 'Let's get you out of here and into the fresh air.'

Walking together, they staggered across the engine room. It was when they were halfway to the door that Lethbridge-Stewart saw the figure in the doorway.

A stream of Arabic erupted before a torch snapped on, directed straight into their eyes.

'Mr Lethbridge-Stewart! Mr Dawoud!'

'What…?' He recognised the man immediately. Azmy. The young man must have been on a night shift. 'I heard banging from the boiler. He was shut in there.'

Azmy came to take Dawoud's other arm and, together, they pulled him out of the engine room.

They lowered Dawoud onto a nearby chair and Azmy pulled a canteen from his jacket.

'Drink this,' he said.

Dawoud, his hands shaking, took the bottle and tipped it

into his mouth, but the first gulp must have been too large. He spluttered and gasped. The next left water trickling down his chin, before he was able to take a deep, clear breath.

'I don't know what happened. I was walking. I couldn't sleep and went for a walk.' He took another breath, before his throat erupted in coughing. 'When someone caught me from behind. I couldn't see him. He must have bundled me in there.' He nodded at the door to the engine room, swinging freely now in the light breeze.

'Get your breath back,' said Lethbridge-Stewart, straightening up. 'You'll need to get the authorities involved in this,' he said to Azmy.

The young man nodded. 'I will speak to Captain Ibrahim. We will have to deal with it in the morning.' He put a hand to Lethbridge-Stewart's elbow. 'Thank you, sir. You can go back to bed now. Please try to get some rest yourself.'

Lethbridge-Stewart went to leave, heading back to the stairs that would take him to the top deck.

'Wait, sir.' Azmy's voice sounded stronger, clipped. As if the 'sir' was merely an afterthought. 'Why were you down here?'

Lethbridge-Stewart turned slowly. 'I couldn't sleep. A bad dream.' He knew it was a poor excuse. If he had been investigating the matter, then anyone trying that one would have been a prime suspect. But even now, after dragging a man out of the firebox of the engine, he still couldn't quite forget the feeling that dream had given him, as if everything was happening behind his own eyeballs. But with someone else dogging his every step and marking his actions.

Azmy nodded.

'I see. Why come down here?' His voice was level. He wasn't the happy young lad of that morning, lugging bags and bowing to his passengers. There was a hard core beneath the boy's exterior.

In any other situation, Lethbridge-Stewart would have approved of it. But now, with what he was about to say, he felt even more under suspicion.

'I was looking for someone. I wanted to let them know that there was some kind of animal in the water.'

'Another crocodile?'

As Azmy said this Dawoud started to give a barking noise. Lethbridge-Stewart went to crouch down next to him before he realised what the noise was. The meek little Egyptian was laughing at him.

'What is it with you English people and your crocodiles? A man could live for a lifetime in Cairo and never see one. But you see them around every corner.'

The little grin was back on Azmy's face. 'Please, help me take him back to his cabin if you can, sir.'

Lethbridge-Stewart looped one of Dawoud's arms around his neck and nodded to Azmy to do likewise. Together they hauled the man to his feet and out on to the upper deck.

'He was in the firebox.'

Fiona watched Alistair pace from side to side in the cabin. She'd woken to find him already dressed in a white linen suit. She knew something was up from the way he stood. No longer the awkward man out of place and out of time, he was now holding himself straighter, his chin jutting out. He was like a man that had finally recovered from a bout of flu. He bolted his breakfast of sweetbreads and fruit and hadn't sat down since.

'If you don't sit down soon, I'll throw you in the firebox. You're making me dizzy!' snapped Fiona.

'Sorry, dear.' He dropped onto the bed and looked over to where she sat with her book in one hand. 'I suggested to that chap, Azmy, that he should keep everyone in their cabins. It seemed fair to set an example. I always do.'

'The pressures of command? Azmy isn't one of your NCO's, you know. He's a steward.'

'True. What I wouldn't give for Bill right now.'

Fiona coughed. 'Well, you've got me. And some would say that for a romantic holiday, that should be all you need. If you'd still prefer Bill…'

Finally, he grinned. 'I think I'll leave him to Anne.'

'If you're like this when you're in uniform, she's welcome to the pair of you.' Fiona leaned over and touched his arm. 'Please, Alistair. Leave this to the police. It's got nothing to do with you. Tell them what you saw, then let them handle it. We're on holiday.'

Alistair squeezed her hand. She looked into his eyes, at once so proper but so alive as well. Then he sighed, stepping over to the window and looking out over the tops of date palms outside, like a rippling green tablecloth.

'I know. I need to learn to leave well alone.' He leaned out and Fiona watched the light cotton curtains flutter around his shoulders.

It was at that moment that the steamer's whistle made them both jump as it barked out into the stillness of the morning breeze. As he turned, Fiona could see that Alistair's face had changed, hardened.

'We're moving.' He pointed out of the window at the blue waters of the Nile as they slipped past.

'Good,' said Fiona. 'I was wanting to see the tombs later today and I was worried that we would miss them with all of this fuss.'

'It is not good.' Alistair grabbed his jacket and headed for the door. 'Because there haven't been any police officers coming to speak to anyone and now there is a fire burning in the crime scene.' He rolled his eyes and sighed. 'Clearly, if I want a job done properly in this country, I need to do it myself.'

With that, he left.

Fiona drummed her fingers on the dresser. What had really happened down there last night? Clearly the strange little Egyptian man had been in the boiler, but how had he got there?

She pulled herself up and crossed to the window to look at the landscape as it slipped past. As she looked, she saw two oxen, in a yoke and ready to go, look up as the boat cruised past and sounded its whistle.

This didn't feel like the kind of place in which someone would try to murder another person.

She pulled the window and curtains closed. Even if someone had tried to kill Dawoud, it didn't follow that anyone else was in danger. The man was, after all, a Christian in a strict Muslim country. Maybe he had upset people.

Really, she didn't think she should interfere. She picked up her book and headed for the deck to enjoy the journey from a sun lounger.

CHAPTER FOUR
Hours After

LETHBRIDGE-STEWART KNEW his first port of call. He wasn't going to clear it with Captain Ibrahim or any crew members. As far as he was concerned, he needed to find out who had attacked Dawoud for one reason and one reason only. That was to make sure that Fiona was safe. He didn't believe that Dawoud knew as little about what had happened as he claimed.

'Mr Dawoud.' He rapped sharply on the door with his knuckles. In response, all he could hear was the swirl of the water as it foamed along the hull. The man had to be inside; where else would he have gone to recover? Lethbridge-Stewart tried again with the flat of his hand, hearing the slight judder as the door rattled within its own frame. Still nothing.

He glanced both ways along the deck. No one could see. Carefully, still looking around him, he pushed at the door handle. It clicked as it moved down, and the door cracked open. He took a deep breath, his eyes flicking from side to side.

'Mr Dawoud…' he called again. With no answer, he pushed open the door and stepped into the room.

Inside, his eyes adjusted to the slight gloom. It was empty, the curtains floated in the air, ghosts of an abandoned space.

Lethbridge-Stewart padded across the floor, his eyes casting about. Across the dark wood dressing table was the familiar detritus of a single man travelling: loose change, a shaving kit, cut-throat razor dried and stored and a bottle of aftershave. He recognised the logo but not the curled and dotted script. Behind it all was a tattered, leather bound book. He picked it up and flicked through the pages. Of course. No Gideons in Egypt. The man had to bring his own Bible.

There was another book beneath it. A tattered paperback.

It was in an Arabic script with scattered black and white photographic plates. The plates showed ancient Egyptian hieroglyphs. The man had an interest, but this looked less of an introductory text and more like a translation guide.

Lethbridge-Stewart flicked to the front page, which contained some English, in blue ink, and a stamp from the University of Cairo library. He checked the slip. Overdue.

He allowed himself a small smile. Librarians could be formidable. But they usually stopped short of attempted murder to collect a late fine.

The rest of the room was barely lived in, the bed made in such a way that it looked untouched. He ran his eyes and then his fingers down the gap of the wardrobe door. A single hair across the bottom of the two doors. Of course. He'd read enough Fleming that he'd have spotted that even without the espionage training he'd had at the Fifth.

Gently, he took it between finger and thumb and then placed it on the bedside table. Then he opened the wardrobe door, letting it swing inch by inch out into the room.

Inside was nothing but black suit on top of black suit. Lethbridge-Stewart pulled each aside in turn, rifling through like a shopper at a dreary department store in the last few minutes of trading. Nothing there except for a sense of the sheer futility and emptiness of Dawoud's life. He stood back and tutted.

Something there had to give an idea of why Dawoud was attacked. Somebody wanted him dead, or scared, for a very good reason.

No suitcase, Lethbridge-Stewart noticed. It had to be in the same place as Dawoud himself. Along with whatever was in it.

There was a chest of drawers in the wardrobe. He began to open them, and was unsurprised to see folded underwear. Nothing hidden underneath the garments. He tested the bottom. It was thin and real. No hidden compartments here. He sighed, tutting. He would have to leave the room soon.

Reaching into his pocket, he took the pencil and paper that he knew was there.

Pockets. Where is a better place to put something than pockets? He returned to the suits, running his hands down the sides. There, he felt it, a heavy weight, stuffed into one side of the jacket at the back of the row. There was another, on the other side of the jacket. He reached in, closing his fingers around a chunk of something flat and smooth. Pulling it out, into the sunlight, he could see it was some sort of stone tablet. He pulled out the other.

They fitted together, he could see that. Almost like a jigsaw, albeit with some scuffing at the join. Marching across it was an army of hieroglyphs. One figure appeared more often than the others. A man, dressed in the usual short skirt and ankh combination that ancient Egyptians prized so much. His head, however, was that of a bull with enormous horns rising. He looked like some sort of minotaur.

It was times like this when Lethbridge-Stewart wished his espionage training had extended to having some sort of camera on his person. But this was a holiday and the only camera that they had was securely attached to Fiona's wrist. Some use it was to him there.

He withdrew his pencil and paper, and placed it over one of the stone tablets. One etching later, he used a second piece of paper to repeat the action with the second tablet, all the while glancing towards the door. The click of the lock that he feared did not come. He folded the papers into his pocket and replaced the two tablets in the pockets of the jacket. He closed the door and, licking it slightly, replaced the strand of hair.

Lethbridge-Stewart had something to go on then. Likely more than he would have got from Dawoud if the man had been in to receive him.

He stepped up to the door and listened. Upstairs, he could hear the chatter of passengers and there was, of course, the gentle rumble of the pistons downstairs as the engine drove the steamer down the Nile.

There were no footsteps. He waited, holding his breath, until he was sure. The deck outside sounded, as far as he could tell, deserted. Excellent. He pushed the handle down before freezing.

Given all the effort to hide the tablets, why was the door unlocked? Now was not the time to ask. He simply had to get out of there as soon as possible.

He pushed open the door and stepped out onto the deck.

Evidently, he was not the only one that was avoiding any heavy footsteps.

Rounding the corner of the deck and walking straight towards him were Tabitha and May. He wasn't sure which was worse, the expression on Tabitha's face as if vinegar had gone up her nose or the knowing half-smile from May as she saw him leave the room. Who did they take him for?

'*Mesdames.*' He nodded to them. 'I found Mr Dawoud last night and wanted to ensure that he had recovered. Unfortunately, he appears to be absent at present. Have you seen him?'

'You found him once, Mr Lethbridge-Stewart.' Tabitha sniffed. 'Surely you can have another look. Have you tried another dirty engine?'

Lethbridge-Stewart tried to keep his face as impassive as possible as he closed the door behind him with a quiet click.

'Thank you for your suggestion, Ms…?' Her name escaped him.

'Miss Gordon!' Hooking her arm through her friend's elbow, Tabitha's heels clicked on the deck as she swept down it, impossibly dry and cool in her thick black dress.

Lethbridge-Stewart permitted himself a quick smile as he walked in the opposite direction, back towards the staircase to the lower saloon. *The two are pretty harmless,* he thought.

It was as he rounded the brass stair rail that he saw Azmy advancing up towards him, carrying a tray of drinks.

'Just the man I wanted to see.' Lethbridge-Stewart stopped dead in the middle of the stairway. 'Where's Mr Dawoud? His cabin is empty.'

Azmy's smile was a constant element but, at that moment, it faltered, just slightly.

'Sir?' He appeared to gather himself, as if shrugging off a heavy coat and letting it drop to the floor. 'He's in a spare cabin. For safety. He's resting at present, sir.' He looked at Lethbridge-Stewart in a strange way, his head cocked to one side.

'I see,' said Lethbridge-Stewart. 'Please could I ask why Captain Ibrahim thought that sailing to the next destination was more important than actually getting the authorities on board?'

Azmy looked down at his tray, still holding his head to one side.

'I believe that authorities were told, sir. They have decided that this is not a matter for them at present.'

'Not a matter…' Lethbridge-Stewart took a deep breath. 'A man was locked in a boiler for God's sake.'

'They think that he more than likely tripped.' Azmy shrugged.

Lethbridge-Stewart stood and stared at the boy. It was a dreadful excuse.

'And locked a door behind him from the outside? Come on, Azmy, you're brighter than that.'

'I'm sorry, sir. The police have a lot to deal with in Egypt at present. It is hard to get them to deal with something like this. Attempted murder is sometimes not an urgent matter.'

Lethbridge-Stewart clicked his tongue against his teeth.

'Do you know what he is doing on this cruise? The man's an Egyptian himself.'

'I understand he wanted to be guided through the history of Egypt.'

'Indeed.' Lethbridge-Stewart thought of the stone tablets. 'Do you know if he has a lot of prior experience of this sort of thing? It just strikes me that an Egyptian gentleman with an interest in such things could easily learn a lot himself, without having to resort to an expensive trip with a bunch of foreigners.'

Azmy smiled back, a frozen smile that didn't quite reach his eyes.

'I'm afraid that I couldn't possibly comment, sir.' He lifted the drinks tray, the condensation from the glasses now pooling on it. 'I must be getting these to their grateful recipients. It's getting a bit warm for you chaps.'

Lethbridge-Stewart stood aside to let Azmy squeeze past and head up to the upper deck. He was going to get to the bottom of this if it killed him.

He suspected that help may lie in the saloon bar. That certainly seemed like a good place to locate his second quarry.

Inside, the air was close, not helped by the dark wood panelling of the room. Sitting close to the bar was Greaves. Lethbridge-Stewart was relieved to see that the man had a cup of something hot and presumably caffeinated in front of him, rather than anything alcoholic. It was, after all, mid-morning. Not everyone had May and Tabitha's stamina.

Lethbridge-Stewart pulled up a chair. 'Professor. Looking forward to tonight's expedition?'

The man took a long sip of his coffee and smiled. 'Who wouldn't? The Beni Hasan tombs are some of the most spectacular examples of Middle Kingdom funerary practices that we know of.'

'I'm sure I'll tire of pyramids eventually.' Lethbridge-Stewart smiled.

'Oh no.' Greaves gave a little chuckle, as a teacher would do with a dull student that had failed to grasp a simple point. 'We've left the pyramids behind up the river. That's Old Kingdom stuff. These are shaft tombs for the lower classes. One shaft going down, then a chamber for the burial. Or built into the cliff side for the upper classes. Those are much more elaborate.'

'I look forward to you showing us around.'

Greaves shifted in his chair. 'I'm sure. I am doing a talk that will take in the majority of the tombs that are accessible.' He coughed. 'However, I do have to remain behind afterwards. I have been asked to do a private piece of work in a nearby temple not open to the public.'

Lethbridge-Stewart pulled the etching from his pocket. 'I was hoping to play on your knowledge somewhat. Can you help me at all with what this means?' He smoothed it out on the table.

Greaves peered at it, a small smile on his face. 'Mostly, it's a bit rough, as etchings go.'

Lethbridge-Stewart smiled in what he hoped was a convincing fashion. 'Do they make any sort of sense?'

Greaves smoothed the paper out, drumming his fingers on the table next to it.

'It's somewhat hard to say.' He reached into his pocket for a packet of cigarettes. Camel, Lethbridge-Stewart noticed as he shook his head at the proffered packet. 'There's a few missing lines that could fundamentally change the meaning, but I think I can piece it together.'

Greaves flicked a zippo from his pocket open and lit the

cigarette. As he dropped the lighter onto the table, Lethbridge-Stewart noticed the crest engraved. He picked it up between two fingers as Greaves continued to pore over the paper. Two lions, holding an off-set shield showing a plumed helmet. Not so different to the Lethbridge-Stewart crest.

'Family crest.' Greaves didn't even look up. 'I'm not such a fan, but my elder brother got to deal with that sort of thing.'

Lethbridge-Stewart thought of his uncle, Matthew and his own father, Gordon. Two men in very similar positions. The heir and the soldier's son. He said as much to Greaves.

'Could I be the archaeologist's son?' The man winked. 'I'd have been an appalling soldier.'

'Not even in the last war?' Lethbridge-Stewart looked at Greaves. He was what, mid-fifties now? He must have been of fighting age in '39.

'No,' was the short reply. Then Greaves stabbed at the paper. 'This figure…' His full attention was now on it. 'It is clearly a deity, but which one? Associated with Osiris, but how so?' He tapped a specific figure, the man with a bull's head. 'Mont…' He caught himself, looking up at Lethbridge-Stewart. His hand left the paper, reaching for the fine chain that dangled around his neck. 'Where did you find this?' Greaves fingers shook as they closed around it.

'I'm not sure that I am at any liberty to say.' Lethbridge-Stewart straightened his back in response, as if bracing it.

'Well, that makes two of us.' Greaves reply was cold now and precise, a man that had picked up the pieces of his scattered thoughts into a bucket that he now threw at Lethbridge-Stewart. He stubbed his almost new cigarette out in the ashtray. 'It's gibberish, sir. Good day.'

Lethbridge-Stewart hoped that his mouth did not drop open for too long. 'What did you just say?' he eventually managed.

'This etching, it makes no sense. There is no internal logic to what it says at all. If it… I suggest it has been rather a waste of time for you.'

'No, you were about to talk about it, some name?'

Greaves sniffed. 'I think that you are mistaken.' He pulled himself up and headed for the door.

Lethbridge-Stewart banged one fist on the table as he

stood up to follow. Greaves was already out of the door and away up the panelled corridor by the time that Lethbridge-Stewart reached the saloon door.

That was as far as he managed to get before Mortimer barrelled through it like a bulldog, knocking him back into the room. Lethbridge-Stewart caught Mortimer's glance just long enough to see the sneer on the other man's face before he drove onwards into the room.

'Watch where you're going!' Mortimer snapped.

Lethbridge-Stewart was about to continue out of the door when he heard Mortimer snap at the barman.

'You, boy! What is the meaning of me being cleared out of my room?'

Lethbridge-Stewart paused at the door. Greaves could wait. Slowly, he turned and began to creep slowly back to the bar where he could see the barman had quietly put the glasses down that he'd been drying.

'I have no idea, sir,' the man said. 'I serve drinks. I don't allocate rooms.'

'Then you can damn well find someone that knows what they're talking about. And you can tell them that I am not moving until I get my room back.'

The barman shrugged. 'I know what I'm talking about.' He smiled. 'I can make the best drinks on the river without tasting a drop myself.' He shrugged. 'I don't see what that has to do with your room.'

Mortimer sighed. 'Look, you obnoxious little man. We built this country for you. If it wasn't for us, then backwards little drinks servers like you wouldn't have anything to pour anyway. Now, you will give me the keys back to my room and you will move my bags back out of my wife's room and into mine. Now hop to it.'

Lethbridge-Stewart stifled a surprised laugh as the barman paused and leaned over the beer tap towards Mortimer.

'Your wife's room.' He simply repeated Mortimer's words. There was no need for a question.

'Yes. I can't stand her perfumes and all those clothes. A waste of space. She claims I snore. We always book separate rooms. And if I am not reinstated in mine, then I will not be leaving this bar.'

The barman picked up another glass and began polishing it. 'Since I am still a barman, sir, you may have a long wait. Would you like a drink?'

'Wait now, boy…'

Lethbridge-Stewart coughed, at which point both men whirled around to face him.

'I have to butt in, sirs.' He emphasised that last word, as he glanced between the two men. 'I can see if I can help you, Mr Mortimer.'

'Are you lowering yourself to running around after these people? Somewhat of a comedown for an officer, isn't it?' Mortimer turned his back fully to the barman, who simply beamed behind him.

'I'm on holiday,' Lethbridge-Stewart said simply. 'I'll revert to parade ground etiquette when I have to. I'll give my voice a rest for now.' He coughed. 'Which room is yours?'

'Seven. Next to my wife in number six.'

Well. At least they hadn't booked rooms on the opposite ends of the boat. Still, he supposed, it seemed to work for them. Given how things had gone with Sally, perhaps he shouldn't mock.

'Excellent. I'll see what I can do for you. I'm sure it's just a silly mistake. You know how these foreign types are…' *Smarter than you ever give them credit for* he wanted to add.

Mortimer relented. 'I hope you have more luck than me. I came back after my round of the decks to find that it had been bolted from the inside. That boy, Azmy, was outside having a fag and told me that all of my things were in room six. Then he just stalked off.' He tutted. 'That boy needs to be put in his place.'

'I'm sure, Mr Mortimer.'

'Please, Freddie.' The man put his hand out. 'Thank you, Alistair. I'm sure a military manner will get more out of these people than I have managed.' He turned back to the barman. 'I'll have a G&T, man. And I hope it doesn't appear on my tab.'

'I also hope for many things, sir.' Lethbridge-Stewart saw the barman rummage for a bottle of Greenalls. 'I suspect we will both be disappointed.'

Lethbridge-Stewart left quickly, before he became embroiled in a further conflict.

Outside the saloon, he turned to climb the stairs. There, sat on them, just a few steps up, was one of the Russian passengers. Lethbridge-Stewart nodded to the man.

'A strange place to sit,' he said.

'Just thinking if it is time to have another vodka.' The man didn't smile, barely looked at Lethbridge-Stewart.

'Did you hear anything last night?'

The man looked up now. 'No,' he said.

The conversation was clearly not going to get him anywhere, so Lethbridge-Stewart went to continue up the stairs.

'You found the Egyptian last night.' It was a statement.

Lethbridge-Stewart stopped. 'Yes. What do you know?'

'Nothing. Strange man. I don't think he worships the god he claims.'

Lethbridge-Stewart nodded. 'Thank you.' He kept walking.

He knew exactly who was in room seven. It was possibly fortunate for Azmy that Mortimer and his wife had such a bizarre sleeping arrangement. If they hadn't then there was perhaps no other room on the boat.

Lethbridge-Stewart rounded the deck. He was now at the opposite end to his and Fiona's suite, in a quieter part of the boat. He paused, letting the breeze from the Nile blow through his hair. They were a long way from Cairo now. Out there was still nothing but farmland, the narrow strip of green on both sides of the river that soon gave way to rock and sand. It was like the country itself was simply a line of oxen, date palms and fields that stretched from north to south, like a frontier between civilisation and barbarism that covered the entire nation.

At door number seven, he struck sharply with his fist. No answer. He swallowed. In for a penny, in for a pound.

'Mr Dawoud?' he called. Still no answer. He tried the door itself. Locked, just as he expected really.

He sighed, stepping back and drumming his fingers on the door frame.

'Mr Dawoud?' He tried again. 'It's Alistair Lethbridge-Stewart. The man who pulled you out of the boiler.' Somehow, that came out worse than it had sounded. 'I need to talk to you.' He sighed at the silence that greeted his remarks. What else could he actually offer this man, in fear of his life? He thought. 'Or rather, I need to listen to you. I'm an officer in the British Army. I might be able to help.'

This time he heard a shuffle behind the door, a clunk as a bolt was pulled back and the door opened a crack. Dawoud's round glasses peered through.

'Are you alone?' he hissed.

'Yes.'

'I don't know if that is good. Come in.' He pulled open the door further and Lethbridge-Stewart stepped through.

Inside was like a deathbed room, the curtains pulled tight and the smell of human sweat clung to the air inside, suffocating.

'You need to open a window,' mused Lethbridge-Stewart.

'I hope that is a joke, because if it isn't, I am worried that you are the best England can send.'

'Ah.' Lethbridge-Stewart swallowed. 'Now that I am in here, I should be clear. Firstly, my grandfather would be very angry if I didn't point out that I am Royal Scots Guards. So, I can be clear that England certainly did not send me. Secondly…' He sized up the room as he spoke. The wardrobe was closed. 'Secondly, no one has sent me. I'm actually on holiday. But that makes me even more determined to find out who tried to kill you.'

'Why, Mr Lethbridge-Stewart?' Dawoud's eyes were flicking from Lethbridge-Stewart to the door, like a rodent cornered. 'What do you care?'

'Because my wife and I are on this boat as well. I want to make sure that we are safe.'

Dawoud's lip curled 'You are safe.' He fixed Lethbridge-Stewart with a glare. 'This is an Egyptian matter.'

'Ah, but is it, Mr Dawoud?' Lethbridge-Stewart picked a chair, wicker like so much furniture on board. He sat down, his eyes not leaving Dawoud. 'Because when I walked in here, you thought that someone had sent me. Someone from my government by the sounds of it. I don't believe they have, but that makes me certain that you have asked Britain for help.' The niggling doubt at the back of his mind wore Cosgrove's pith helmet. He tried to block it out. 'So, what did you ask them?'

'I don't know what you're talking about.'

Lethbridge-Stewart tapped his knee, staring at the little man in front of him. 'Okay.' He took a deep breath. 'Let's try something else. What do you know that others might want to find out?'

'Nothing.'

'You seem very sure.' He took in the man's face, the slight shake. Mr Dawoud was scared, but was he scared that Lethbridge-Stewart was on to him? 'You were very interested in Ancient Egypt.'

'It's a hobby. An interest.' The man was stoic. His face not moving a muscle.

Lethbridge-Stewart thought of the university library book. 'I'm sure. But you're still on this boat after someone tried to kill you.'

'Why would I be safer on the shore?' Dawoud snapped back. 'At least on here there's only a small number of people that could be trying to kill me.'

'And if you can't tell me why, then they will carry on doing just that.'

Dawoud sighed. 'This is nothing to do with you.'

'Fine.' Lethbridge-Stewart leaned backwards and folded his arms. 'Let's stop beating around the bush. I've already been to your cabin. I found the tablets. Very old, stone tablets left over from who knows when. Now, I know Greaves didn't want to tell me what was on them, so that makes me even more suspicious that there's a lot here that I don't know about. And more where those tablets came from.'

Dawoud shook his head. 'I've never spoken to Greaves before in my life.'

'I never said you had,' snapped Lethbridge-Stewart. 'What does the tablet say?'

Dawoud shrugged. 'It's a curio. Of very limited interest, nothing more. I think I picked it up in a souq in Cairo.'

Lethbridge-Stewart snorted to stifle the laugh. 'Oh please, Mr Dawoud. I may be British but I'm not a complete idiot. That tablet isn't a cheap knock off. It's old. Very old. Now, I'm fairly hopeless at French, let alone Ancient Egyptian, so I'm going to need someone to tell me what it says. Greaves claims that it is simply gibberish, but it rattled him. Now.' He paused for effect. 'I don't really care for this sort of thing. Someone is going to tell me what is going on.'

'I wish I knew. Please. I would like to be alone now. I can assure you, there is no danger to you. Please.'

Lethbridge-Stewart sighed and stood up. 'Very well, Mr Dawoud. But if I find that there is any risk to me or my fiancée, then I will be back to speak to you.'

CHAPTER FIVE
Of Heavenly Things

'**SO, IT** went well then?'

The alcohol seemed to flow more freely that day. Perhaps it was a form of bribery for the events of the previous night. Fiona was already on a gin and tonic by the time Lethbridge-Stewart caught up with her and kissed her.

'Dawoud won't tell me why someone went for him, but I'm convinced it had something to do with that tablet. Greaves knows what's in the tablet and he won't tell me. And without his input, well, I'm a little short on experts in ancient Egyptian hieroglyphs.' Lethbridge-Stewart grimaced. If one of his troops had come back from a morning's work with that sort of result, he'd have been unimpressed.

Fiona sighed and took another sip of her drink, tapping the side of her glass with her stirrer and pulling her sunglasses back down over her eyes.

'So, in other words, it's got nothing to do with us and we're quite safe.'

'I don't know how you can be so sure.'

Fiona patted the sun lounger next to her and picked up her book. It looked like a rather trashy romance. Not his sort of thing at all. He settled next to her, propping himself forward so that he could still see the rest of the deck. Mortimer was there, still barred from his own room and being forced to spend time with his wife. Tabitha and May were also present. Both still shooting occasional glances in his direction. There was a stillness here. Not oppressive, but a sense of contentment as the steamer trundled down the river, its steam drifting and falling on to the nearby fields in the windless air.

'Listen,' Fiona said.

'To what?'

'Exactly. Everything is exactly as it was before. It's just a boat steaming down the river to visit some ruins. That's all it needs to be to us. If Dawoud has upset some people, just let him upset them. You don't need to go trying to solve it.' He smiled at her. 'I mean, I know you're a brigadier and everything, but you're pretty much desk bound, aren't you? Leave it to the police, Alistair, that's what they're there for.'

Lethbridge-Stewart leaned back on the lounger. That was the sensible position. He knew that, but there was a lot more to this than he knew about so far.

'Which ruins are going to today?' he finally asked.

Fiona lifted her sunglasses again. 'Alistair?'

'Which ruins are we headed for?'

'The Beni Hasan tombs.'

'Ah yes.' He recalled his conversation with Greaves. 'Shaft tombs for the lower classes. One shaft going down to a burial chamber. Some are built into the cliffside. They tend to be for the upper classes.'

Fiona looked at him, a strange expression on her face, somewhere between incredulity and amusement.

'See,' said Lethbridge-Stewart. 'I haven't completely wasted the morning.'

Much later, *Keberia* pulled into the river docks next to the tombs. Off the river and away from the constant breeze of the boat's motion, the sweat sprung to Lethbridge-Stewart's brow. He mopped it with his sleeve and shielded his eyes with his hand to gaze up at the cliffs, looming ahead of them. Already he could see the dark spots that marked the entrances to the tombs. He watched as the rest of the passengers disembarked, one by one, to be met by souvenir sellers and hawkers of dubious food.

A hand caught his arm and he turned quickly, his left hand ready with a defensive jab, to see the earnest face of a local, his teeth gleaming white beneath his moustache. The man held up his other hand to show the rope that he held. Lethbridge-Stewart's eyes followed it to its, somewhat inevitable, terminus.

It's always going to be a camel, he thought. The beast

grunted and fluttered its eyelashes in a way that put him in mind of a woman long past her prime trying to entice a young man.

'Ten dollar, sir. You and your pretty wife. Ride to the tombs. I can guide. Yes?'

Fiona hugged Lethbridge-Stewart's free arm. 'A camel, in Egypt, what could be better, Alistair?'

'We, ah….' He saw Greaves finally making his way down the gangplank, calling for the rest of the passengers. 'We already have a guide, thank you,' he told the local.

He knew that he said this with more relief than he should have done. The animal's stench was already beginning to overpower him. He had bad memories of the last time he had ridden one of the beasts. That had been essential. This wasn't.

'Ladies and gentlemen,' called Greaves. 'Please feel free to make your own way to the tombs. I will join you there in fifteen minutes.'

Lethbridge-Stewart's heart sank as he turned back to the local, all arguments crumbling to the sand.

'Five dollars, sir. Camel ride only. No need for guide.' The man's expression hadn't changed one bit.

Lethbridge-Stewart had no idea why he was forced to ride the younger camel while Fiona sat astride its easygoing mother. As the creature grunted and swayed up the long looping path to the tombs, there was something unreal about the animal's dry, short fur. As if it was something already dead and tanned but reanimated just for his journey. Lethbridge-Stewart looked longingly at those who had taken the quick route up the face of the hillside. It wasn't the trip he minded; it was the heat. The chance to be inside the cool caves was one that he yearned for.

At last, they reached the point where the rest of the group had gathered. Lethbridge-Stewart braced himself as the beast dropped to its elbows first, pitching his seat forward, before finally dropping its hind quarters so that he could climb off.

Then the blasted local was holding his hand out for a tip. Lethbridge-Stewart pushed another dollar into it with a muttered thanks. He was about to ask how much the man wanted to not turn up to take them back, when Fiona rounded the bulk of her camel and enveloped Lethbridge-Stewart in a hug.

'Thank you!' she cried. 'Horses are one thing, but these are so exotic.'

He couldn't help but smile as he hugged her back and pecked her cheek. 'How else can we travel in Egypt?'

That was what was important. He would ride a thousand animals that smelled worse than a camel if it meant something to Fiona.

He looked around. They stood on a flat plateau. To one side the ground fell away to the irrigated green of the river valley below, to the other the cliffs rose, stark white against the blue sky. Dotted at intervals were the tomb entrances, some covered in rusted iron bars, others open as a few tourists drifted in and out.

Even up there and so far from Cairo, he could see that the entrepreneurial street theatre wasn't far away. Already May had a monkey dancing on her head as Tabitha glared in disapproval at its handler. Lethbridge-Stewart didn't blame her, removing the dratted thing would almost certainly cost money. He nudged Fiona with one arm and pointed, sufficient for both to share a quick giggle.

'Ladies! Gentlemen!' called Greaves. He stood at the centre of the plateau, as his passengers gathered around him. Lethbridge-Stewart and Fiona went to join them, Fiona nudged Lethbridge-Stewart as they did so.

'Dawoud,' she hissed. 'He's out and about.'

He was indeed. Behind dark glasses and with his hat pulled down hard onto his head, he lurked at the back of the crowd, as if he wanted to avoid being seen at all costs. He had probably only made himself more conspicuous.

'It's a load of old holes in the rock!'

Nowhere near as conspicuous as Fred Mortimer could be with no effort at all. His wife, at least, had the decency to look embarrassed as Tabitha shot an angry glance at the pair.

'These tombs date from the Middle Kingdom,' Greaves began. 'That's four thousand years ago to those of you that haven't read my books.' He paused. 'If you want a copy, let me know. I have them available at a very good rate.' He spread his hands out, indicating the tombs behind him. 'Up here are thirty-nine tombs. These are the most important and highest status tombs. The people buried up here include local dignitaries, governors and chiefs.' He grinned. 'Of course. Had we died back then, such tombs wouldn't have been for the likes of us.' He pointed back down the cliffs. 'We'd have been buried down there with the rest of the plebs. Over there,' he pointed south, 'a couple of klicks away, is the temple of Pakhet. She's a minor goddess of war. Often depicted as a cat. It is usually known as the Grotto of Artemis, because the Greeks, like the British, assumed that everyone thought the same as they did and renamed the place.'

The crowd tittered at the self-deprecation.

'Now, that temple is a bit far to go in this heat, so we're going to start over here at Amenemhat's tomb. He was a chief priest and overlord of this area back in the twelfth dynasty, during the reign of Pharaoh Senusret.'

Greaves trudged off towards the tomb, detailing the various scandals and points of interest that had been gleaned by archaeologists over the years.

As they were led inside, Lethbridge-Stewart's military mind kicked into gear as he realised that he was surrounded on all sides by solid rock with one narrow entrance. Nearly twenty people crammed into space designed for just one. And that one wasn't expected to move around much. As Greaves gave his lecture about the history of the tomb and the meaning of the various images to the life of the occupants, Lethbridge-Stewart found his attention was on the entrance, the sounds outside, listening for any change as the life of the place slowly ebbed away as the day faded.

Of the fellow passengers, he expected little and they delivered it. May giggled like a schoolgirl at every naked picture within, Tabitha asked numerous questions of the politics of the long dead officials, Mortimer tutted at the slightest indication that any culture outside of England could have a value, and the two Russians continued to pretend that their other half didn't exist while each wearing identical expressions of disinterest at each tomb or fresco.

'Do you think we'll be like that one day?' said Fiona in a low voice as she squeezed Lethbridge-Stewart around the waist.

'If I end up like Mortimer, you know where my revolver is.'

Lethbridge-Stewart wondered if it was perhaps the third set of pictures of wrestlers in the fourth tomb that was when the agitation vanished, and the weariness set in, or if it was when Greaves began describing the specifics of the moves that the small characters were using. What utterly defeated Lethbridge-Stewart was that such a detailed account of, to be honest, naked men grappling with each other, was somehow a fit subject to decorate a grave with.

An opinion not shared by May.

'Seeing them enjoying themselves really brightens the place up, don't you think?' she chirped.

'Shall we take some fresh air?' Lethbridge-Stewart asked Fiona.

She nodded in relief, and they emerged from the coolness of the tomb back into the late afternoon.

He was glad that they decided to leave at that moment. The two of them found that they were alone on the plateau and faced with the image of Egypt, dropping away in front of them from the edge of the terrace and stretching out to a horizon that blazed a brilliant orange as the spring sun started to sink towards it. Lethbridge-Stewart reached for Fiona's hand just as she did the same to him, then spun her around in an embrace that lifted her off her feet, finding her lips easily. They fell into each other both laughing and smiling as she lay her head against his chest and they both looked out across the landscape.

'Alistair?'

'Mmm?'

'How on earth will we top this when we take a honeymoon?'

He smiled. 'I like a challenge.'

Their joy was short-lived as they heard the crunching footsteps and babble behind them of the rest of the passengers leaving the tomb to join them on the rocky terrace. Lethbridge-Stewart heard their gasps and whistles as they emerged to the once white landscape now bathed in the rich orange.

It was then that he heard another sound, one that was far too familiar to him. A miniature sonic boom that was invariably produced by a bullet. The crack of a rifle.

He grabbed Fiona around the shoulders and yanked her down and to the floor behind a boulder.

'Head down!' he shouted as he looked around.

The rest of the group looked at him in confusion until the first bullet was followed by further shots that ricocheted off boulders and shattered stones into gravel. Then the gasps and shrieks started as they rushed in different directions.

Lying across Fiona, Lethbridge-Stewart could feel her breathing as he scanned the landscape, trying to see past the milling crowd. Fortunately, none of them seemed to have been hit. A further volley of shots came. This time he could tell that the gun fire came from the north, where the path from the river emerged. The sounds of the bullets striking rock came from the south, behind him.

'Get behind those rocks!' he yelled at the rest of the passengers as they continued to call uncontrollably to each other.

There. The figure was coming towards them. He could now see why they were only getting a few shots at a time. The man was carrying some sort of antique semi-automatic from the war. The thing looked like it had been looted from American supplies and then resold at least ten times. The man carrying it had clearly never fired it before, the thing kept jamming and he struggled to get it going again each time.

Lethbridge-Stewart wasn't fooled. Incompetent gunman or not, the weapon could still kill if he were unfortunate enough to get in its way. He glanced at the other passengers, just long enough to see that most were under cover. Two faces caught his eye. Dawoud, he was surprised to see, was in a classic military prone position where he could see the maximum distance while lying as flat as possible behind cover. Perhaps that was just random chance, but Lethbridge-Stewart was starting to doubt that such a thing existed. Greaves, meanwhile, was in the entrance to the last tomb they had emerged from, his back flat against the supporting column. He caught Lethbridge-Stewart's eye and gave him a questioning look. Lethbridge-Stewart raised one finger to indicate the number of gunmen.

This was a fine time to spot hidden depths in his most

suspicious fellow passengers. Lethbridge-Stewart kept his eye on the assailant as he approached the group. It was then that he realised that the man was familiar. The face was one he knew. One that, so recently, had annoyed him so much.

It was the local who had brought them here. The camel hawker.

The man was still approaching, quicker now, his breath coming in ragged gasps as he staggered from side to side across the terrace. Lethbridge-Stewart watched the man. His head occasionally lolled backwards so that he was staring up at the sky, then threw itself forward to hang like a rag doll towards the ground. He was like a puppet, yanked along on strings. Every so often, he would squeeze another shot away, letting it fly off the cliff face or cannon harmlessly into the rock.

Lethbridge-Stewart braced himself.

'I love you,' he whispered in Fiona's ear.

'No…' was her only response.

He ran, jumping straight from behind the rock, he zig-zagged along the terrace, kicking up dust as he went.

The gunman barely seemed to notice him, still staggering towards him as if drunk. Lethbridge-Stewart kept to a running crouch. If he got close enough, he could maybe rugby tackle the hawker, prepare to pull the weapon away, and find out what he was doing.

It was then that the man locked eyes with him. This time, he didn't change course, his head stopped it's wobbling, uncontrolled dance and the gun remained at his side.

'Montu,' he said.

Lethbridge-Stewart froze. That word, he had heard it before, the half name that Greaves had said when looking at the etched hieroglyphs.

'What did you…?' Lethbridge-Stewart started to say before the other man turned and lurched away from him, towards the cliff edge. 'Wait, stop right there, man, you're going to fall!'

Lethbridge-Stewart wanted to talk to the man more than ever now. It was no good. As he raced after the man, trying to catch hold of his clothing, the other picked up pace towards the edge. His right foot went over first. There was no leap, no sudden stop, and then a tumble as he realised where he was. The man simply kept running at the cliff until there was no ground left to support him. No cry came as he fell, but the sound of gravel and pebbles skittering down the hillside came shortly after he vanished from view.

Lethbridge-Stewart slowed as he reached the edge, steeling himself for what he would see.

It must have been quick. The man lay many feet down, his head twisted to an unnatural angle and limbs splayed randomly. Lethbridge-Stewart could already see the growing red stain across the grey dust coming from the man's head.

He turned as the rest of the passengers started to emerge. He shook his head. 'Nothing to see here. He didn't make it. Please don't gawp at him. I don't think he was in his right mind.'

The lingering thought remained: *Whose mind was he in?*

Fiona was the first to reach Lethbridge-Stewart. He opened his arms to her before seeing her expression. She was furious.

'Never do that again!' Her fists flew into his chest, hammering against him. 'How was that your job?'

Who else was there? he wanted to say, but he knew that deep down, she knew this. She was angry because she was scared.

Although an Egyptian with an old gun that barely knew what he was doing was far from the worst that Lethbridge-Stewart had faced in recent years, it was still a far bigger deal than anything Fiona had been prepared for. He held her as the others milled around, chattering to each other like hens.

Mortimer was shouting at anyone that listened, and many more that didn't, about whose fault it was: Greaves, the steamer company, the Egyptian police, the UK government… His list of blameworthy persons knew no limits. The Russian man stood next to him, enthusiastically nodding at every word that left Mortimer's mouth. With no smile on his face, his eyes had lit up.

Lethbridge-Stewart could see that, standing slightly further back, his eyes still buried behind his dark glasses, was Dawoud. His face was almost inscrutable, but the panic that had been apparent earlier in the day was gone.

Lethbridge-Stewart followed his gaze to the other man

that wasn't reacting like the rest of the passengers. He was unsurprised to see that it was Greaves. The archaeologist simply stood by the edge of the cliff, looking down at what was left of the trader. Finally, he turned to Lethbridge-Stewart.

'We need to get everyone back to the *Keberia*.'

Fiona released her hold on Lethbridge-Stewart and looked up. He knew that she wanted to get back to safety as soon as possible.

'Let's go.'

Lethbridge-Stewart knew that a parade ground shout was required and gave it.

'Ladies, gentlemen,' he bellowed. 'We need to get back to the boat as soon as we can. Please, let's take the quickest path. No more camels or mules. I will let the authorities know what has happened.'

The authorities turned out to be one policeman on a motorbike who visited the boat that evening. He wrote down everything that Lethbridge-Stewart told him while Azmy acted as an interpreter.

When Lethbridge-Stewart finished, the policeman nodded.

'He was a very sick man,' Azmy translated back into English. 'The officer doesn't think that there's anything more to it than that.'

'So that's it,' Fiona muttered as they lay in bed later. 'A man nearly killed us, and lies in a heap at the bottom of a cliff and it just gets shrugged off.'

Lethbridge-Stewart drew her into the crook of his arm and let her head rest in his shoulder. 'It can't possibly happen again.'

He listened to the sounds outside, the water lapping quietly and the occasional roar of a car engine on the road that ran up and down the Nile valley.

'I looked into that man's eyes, you know. There was no intent there. He was a sick man.' *There was almost nothing human there* was that familiar niggling feeling. One he hoped was wrong.

'Still, that really got to me up there,' Fiona said. 'We were shot at, nearly died, and then it's just a shrug and "carry on".'

She stopped. Lethbridge-Stewart knew there was something more she wanted to say. 'And you just seem to accept that.'

He paused again, thought hard.

He was dismissing it. Apart from the fact that Fiona had been there, it was the sort of thing that would have merited very little thought at the end of many of the operations that he worked on. That was how he saw it, and he knew that Fiona knew it too.

It was a gap that, no matter how close they were to each other, he could not bridge. Nevertheless, he held her as they both lay in the darkness, lost in their own thoughts.

Lethbridge-Stewart must have drifted off eventually. Dreams came once more. It felt again that he was on trial, performing tasks that he felt rather than heard or saw. Tasks in which he simply knew where things were and was expected to change things, to find a solution to some amorphous problem that was just beyond his understanding.

As before, he woke eventually, when he was sure that he had failed, and found himself lying in a pool of sweat under the bedsheets. He peeled them off and stepped away. At the very least, he would need to cool off before he clambered back into bed. He should be used to the temperature by now and no longer suffering these strange fever dreams. He pulled on some clothes and deck shoes.

He looked back at the bed. Fiona slept, peacefully. Lethbridge-Stewart was glad. It had been such a shock of a day for her. Something that he had hoped she would never have to see, and never would again.

Outside, the air was cooler and he shivered as he leaned on the railing and looked out across the valley and up to the tombs. There was no light there now, simply a dark shape of the cliffs that partly occluded the stars. Across on the other shore glinted the lights of towns and farms. There was nowhere along the Nile that was truly wilderness, he reflected. The water was far too valuable to waste on land where no one lived.

He paced around the deck, listening to the water lapping against the boat's hull, as always with the occasional hollow slap. Beyond that, all was silent. He took a deep breath of the air. There was a pureness to it out here, far from the cities.

There was something else, at the edge of hearing. A rhythmic sound from behind him, like footsteps. He turned, looking back down the deck towards the stern. There was nothing there, an empty deck.

'Hello?' he said. Not loud enough to wake anyone, but enough to be heard.

Nothing answered but the night. He turned back to the view of the hillside.

The sound came again, a soft tread but steady and sure and getting louder and closer, nearly behind him. Lethbridge-Stewart turned around again, his heart beating, unsure what he would find.

Again, there was nothing, simply the deck curling away into the dark and silence. He took a deep breath and held it. He then let it out, hearing his own breath shaking as it did so. He was never one to back down, so he took a step back towards where the sound had come from. That was when he heard more steps, quicker and from further away, the other side of the boat.

Lethbridge-Stewart put a slight sprint on to reach the centre of the boat where the stairwell down to the lower decks was. He was just in time to hear the sound of footsteps retreating down it.

'Hello?' Lethbridge-Stewart called again to no answer.

He crossed to the railing that hung above the gang plank and looked down on it. Just as he thought, a figure was crossing to the shore, the gait hurried, and a cylindrical object under the arm. Lethbridge-Stewart almost knew who it was before the man below turned around to look back at the boat.

He nodded to himself in satisfaction. It was Greaves.

Lethbridge-Stewart counted himself happy to be fitter than the man that he was pursuing as he followed across the moonlit, rocky landscape, cutting behind boulders and trying to keep himself far enough away that Greaves didn't hear his movement. The man was heading south of the place where they had climbed up to the tombs, crossing diagonally up to the terrace rather than heading straight up.

When Lethbridge-Stewart crested the lip of the plateau,

he could see what Greaves had been aiming for. Pillars surrounded a rectangular opening in the hillside, just visible in the darkness. Greaves was nearly at the entrance and disappeared inside as Lethbridge-Stewart watched. He remembered the man talking about a temple, south of the tombs themselves. That had to be it, a spartan building. Secreted away from the world in the shadow of a big tourist attraction. Lost and forgotten.

Lethbridge-Stewart reached the portico that was framed by the pillars, and saw the faded and defaced hieroglyphs that covered the interior, like graffiti covering a church's notice board. However, he could see that this writing had been hacked at many millennia ago. He gave himself a wry smile. Younger generations never really respected what came before.

He gathered himself. Inside, he could see a flickering light, as if from a candle. He peered around the edge of the entrance to see a short stone corridor, ending in a small chamber. An inner sanctum. He slid along the side of the passageway, until he reached the end and looked into the sanctum.

There were a few small candles, set into small alcoves and sufficient to cast a brief, flickering light to the chamber. Of Greaves, there was no sign.

'Greaves!' Lethbridge-Stewart snapped. 'Professor Greaves!'

Outside the night wind whistled around the pillars of the portico.

He ran his hands across the walls, thousands of years of history lay in them, buried beneath the scrapings and impressions of successive generations. He hoped for some sort of response, something to show that he was on the right lines, some light or noise, like the tourist's technology with its eggs slotting into place. He sighed and slumped to the floor. The room appeared to be exactly what it was, a bare room cut into rock.

A sound from outside, the same regular plod of steps that he'd heard creeping behind him on the boat. Steps that he now realised sounded very different to the hurried scampering of Greaves.

His arm went to his hip. Of course, no gun here. He had a hunch that it would do him no good even if he had it. The damn thing that came after him now couldn't be seen, and he doubted very much that his luck would allow bullets to stop it. Still, he pushed himself back to a standing position, casting around for some sort of weapon, finally grabbing a candle from near his feet.

The steps were coming down the passageway now, heading for the inner sanctum. He gripped the candle holder, keeping it at an angle so that wax fell away, his eyes fixed on that entrance. The steps grew closer.

Lethbridge-Stewart couldn't be sure what he saw, just a flash, a shadow, something like a tree branch that briefly obscures a light to cast a brief shade across the landscape. He couldn't even make out the shape before, with an air of weary inevitability, every candle in the room flickered out, leaving him in total darkness.

In total darkness with whatever had just walked in.

He backed against the wall, feeling the wind whip up where before all had been still. He cast the candle around him in an arc, trying to keep whatever had entered at bay.

His wrist hit something. Whatever it was, was hard, rock rather than flesh or cloth. He yelped in pain, before feeling a crushing sensation on his chest, something squeezing his lungs, forcing him to gasp for air like a fish plucked out of the water. The candle dropped and rolled away. He fell first to his knees.

Purple explosions danced before his eyes, and Lethbridge-Stewart slumped across the floor.

CHAPTER SIX
What's That?

IT WAS the light that brought him back round. Moving across his face as if scanning him, caressing. Blearily, he opened one eye.

'Alistair?' the voice said. He knew the dry tones instantly. It was Greaves.

'What the devil's going on?' Lethbridge-Stewart croaked.

'You tell me, old chap.'

Lethbridge-Stewart felt the other man's hand on his back. He must have been lying prone across the floor of the temple. There were bruises across one side of his body where he had landed.

'I've just found you,' Greaves continued. 'I've been doing a bit of night-time research. What on earth brought you here?'

'I followed you. You disappeared.' Lethbridge-Stewart brought himself to his knees to see the sanctum lit by the beam of Greaves' torch. 'Why did you go in here? What have you been up to?'

Greaves laughed, almost convincingly.

'I'm afraid that you are mistaken. I just told you, I've been doing a bit of research.' He cocked his head to one side, looking around, as if seeing the inside for the first time. 'Didn't I mention it earlier? It doesn't matter. Look around you.' He cast the torchlight across the hieroglyphs on the walls. 'The writing in here is absolutely fascinating. Several local governors have managed to put their own stamp on it, altering or deleting as they went along. As a social record of the society, it's unique.' He shone the light directly at Lethbridge-Stewart. 'It must have been a bad bump you got. Perhaps you stumbled against one of the pillars?' He indicated the roof supports.

Lethbridge-Stewart stood, stumbling as more purple spots scattered in front of his eyes. He leaned against the wall, before bringing himself to fix his eyes on Greaves.

'I might be a bit unsteady, but I can assure you that my faculties are fully intact thank you, Professor Greaves.' He shook the dust off his shirt. 'Now, perhaps you can tell me, honestly, what that is under your arm?' He pointed, and Greaves looked at the thing as if he had never seen it before. A cylindrical object, wrapped in the sort of fine cotton that Egypt produced in such quantities.

'It's a canopic jar. A rather valuable one.' Greaves shone the torch down as he unwrapped the cotton, revealing a design of orange, ochre and blue. It was an old carved jar. The sort of thing that wouldn't have looked out of place in a tomb. 'It's been in my family for a while, you see, and I brought it with me in case it helped my interpretation of some of this stuff.' He waved at the writing on the wall.

'And has it?'

Greaves shook his head, quickly. Lethbridge-Stewart noticed the golden chain around his neck. He'd seen it before, when Greaves had reached for it in the bar. It somehow looked out of place on the scholarly gentleman.

'Oh, no no no. Nothing of the sort. It's a shame, I fear that I may never find the place.' The man was clearly lying; he lacked the practice to make a convincing denial.

'What place?'

Greaves made a lopsided smile, as if embarrassed. 'Zerzura,' he said simply.

'I've never heard of it.' Lethbridge-Stewart was getting his strength back now and started to head for the door, ensuring that Greaves was also going to walk with him.

'No, you wouldn't have.' He breathed out slowly and motioned Lethbridge-Stewart down the stone passageway out into the night.

The air felt cooler now and Lethbridge-Stewart wondered if he could see the tell-tale flicker in the east that showed that the sun was heading for the horizon.

'Zerzura is a mythical city. Like Eldorado or Atlantis. Supposedly, it is mentioned in the *Kitab al Kanuz*, a missing manuscript. A city of pale people, threatened by black giants and home to a sleeping king and queen.'

Lethbridge-Stewart tread across the scattered stones and pebbles towards the path that led back to *Keberia.*

'Sounds like a hodgepodge of a load of toot to me. What do you want with it?'

'Ah, well, that's the thing, my grandfather found the place.' Greaves eyes flicked across Lethbridge-Stewart's face, searching for some sort of reaction. 'I don't mention it often. Prattling about lost cities gets one thrown out of even the worst archaeology departments.' He held the jar up.

With the steady growing pale light of dawn, Lethbridge-Stewart could see the pattern now, and the carved head of the bull that sat at the top of the jar.

'And this is what he brought back. This amulet as well.' Greaves reached beneath his shirt and pulled at the chain, revealing a sort of beetle. It looked like something cast in gold, adorned with green stone.

'It makes you look like a barfly in a Mediterranean nightclub.'

Greaves laughed. 'It's a scarab. An amulet. It protects me. Something that I feel I sorely need after yesterday. There aren't many places that he could have found such a thing. And the thought of a lost city is one that is not to be missed. It's a sad dream, but I hoped to go and find it myself.' He tucked the scarab back into his shirt.

'I imagine those missing pages in your grandfather's notebooks were the route to Zerzura then?' Lethbridge-Stewart knew that he had seen that bull shape before, and there was something about the curve of the horns that was familiar.

Greaves grunted. 'The pages leading him there are all gone. Along with his notes of other places. He located a notorious tomb in Saqqara for instance, seemingly from his explorations further afield. Professor Scarman excavated that afterwards, about sixty years ago. He came to a bad end when his ancestral seat burned down. Misfortune tends to follow the objects we bring back.' Lethbridge-Stewart's eyes went to the jar as Greaves continued. 'I know my grandfather went to those places. But I don't know how or what he found. Except for what he brought back.'

'And you hoped to find clues here?'

'This is the last place I can pinpoint him at. After this, he disappeared into the desert. And brought back this.' Greaves held up the jar. The head seemed somehow larger in the gloom, the eyes watching in the darkness.

'What's the name of the horned chap on top of that jar?' Lethbridge-Stewart thought he already knew the answer, he just wanted to try and see just how much Greaves wanted to hide. The man was silent. 'Let me have a stab,' said Lethbridge-Stewart. 'Montu.'

He saw Greaves start at the name and shrugged.

'You need to hide your surprise better, Professor. So, what's in the jar?'

Greaves rolled it around in his hands and gave a sudden grim smile. 'His heart, if you believe the inscription.'

Lethbridge-Stewart thought of the description of the Egyptian creation myth from the meal the other day. He supposed he should be grateful that of all the organs the ancient Egyptians imbued with power, this jar only contained a heart.

'And does it?'

'No idea, old chap. Never been able to get the lid off. Montu is a god, mind you. Why on earth would a god be buried in the style of a pharaoh. With his heart in a jar?' Greaves snorted. 'Gods don't exist. There's no heart to extract.'

Lethbridge-Stewart pointed at the bull head. 'It's the same chap that was on the paper I showed you, isn't it? What did that paper say? No directions there I imagine.'

'No, the paper wasn't directions,' said Greaves quietly. 'And according to it, the place that my grandfather found this…' He held up the jar. '…was just as cursed as anything from Tutankhamen's tomb. Every appearance of Montu in that sequence of hieroglyphs showed him taking revenge on those that stole from him. As well as their families and descendants. It was a hard thing to read for me.'

'You're worried about an Egyptian curse?' Lethbridge-Stewart thought back to his experience inside the temple, already a receding memory as they negotiated the path down. What was the thing that had attacked him? 'Gods don't exist. As you just said.'

Greaves paused on the path. Lethbridge-Stewart saw him take a deep breath as he gazed out onto the river, now quiet with just *Keberia* bobbing on the water.

'My brother died. A matter of months ago.' Greaves let the words hang in the air. 'We were close.'

'I'm sorry to hear that.' Lethbridge-Stewart stopped, thoughts running through his head of how he had lost his own brother, his father and, back just after the war, his little cousin. 'How old…?' he eventually ventured.

'Old enough that I don't feel guilt, only sorrow. He was a grown man. He always talked of following in our grandfather's footsteps and finding Zerzura. It seemed right to come here.' Greaves looked down at the jar in his hand again. 'And bring old Montu for a bit of help.' He seemed almost wistful as he gazed out again. The sun was definitely starting its rise now, the orange light filtering down onto the white rocks around them.

'I hope you find what you're looking for,' was all Lethbridge-Stewart could think to say.

Deep down, he knew that Greaves knew more about where Zerzura was than he was letting on. The man had found something in that tomb. Lethbridge-Stewart knew that the jar had something to do with it.

And it would be on the boat with them. Watching. Waiting.

'Where have you been?' Fiona could barely contain her anger as Alistair arrived back in their cabin.

He dropped onto the bed. She could see that he had dust covering his clothes and new bruises to one side of his face. 'And what on earth have you been doing?'

He was silent for a moment. She could tell that he was turning over in his head how much to explain to her, how much he trusted her.

'I've not been sleeping well,' Alistair finally said. 'Very strange dreams that keep waking me up in the middle of the night.'

'I'm sure that mountain climbing is a good solution.' She couldn't help it. Even though she knew that she should let him finish, it was such a trite excuse that he gave, she couldn't help but cut him off. She could see his jaw set. He really was a man used to command rather than compromise. He was going to have to learn.

'I saw Greaves heading off towards the hills, I followed him. He's looking for clues to some lost city or other. There's some connection to a god there. Montu the chap's name is. He's the same one as the bull-faced chappy on the tablet in Dawoud's room.' Alistair looked very pleased with himself.

Fiona took a deep breath, letting it out slowly. 'So?'

'So, what…?' Alistair looked confused.

'Exactly. So, what has any of this to do with our holiday? With us taking time off to really get to know each other? It's like you're running around like some '30s matinee hero while I sit here, alone, drinking dreadful wine.' Fiona bit her lip to stop herself from carrying on. 'What happened to your face?'

He looked past her, straight at the wall. Now she knew he was lying.

'I must have tripped inside the temple. I fell a bit awkwardly.'

She stood. 'Well, that doesn't bode well for the British Army. Come on. You might have been up for hours, I haven't, and I need some breakfast.'

It was mid-morning as Fiona sat on the upper deck, watching the never changing Nile slip past at a speed steady enough to breeze away the heat but still nowhere near fast enough for the steamer to be in a hurry to get anywhere. The watching water buffalo occasionally lifted a head to watch the boat pass, but the voyage was otherwise unremarkable.

She looked up at the tall funnel and the clouds that drifted from it across the blue sky, dropping back down behind the boat in the still air. This was safe, this was secure. So why was her heart still thudding and fluttering in her chest?

The answer she knew from every time she closed her eyes, and her mind was drawn inexorably back to the events of the previous evening. She could hear the crack of the rifle, the thud of the bullets. She could feel the thump of the ground after Alistair had pulled her down, see the grit, just inches from her face as they crouched there, the bullets still scattering around them.

Yet, here she was, sitting alone while Alistair slept off the night's adventure. As if it was nothing more than a late night.

The server appeared next to her with the silver teacup and small glass that she knew heralded the arrival of mint tea. She took it gratefully and sat back.

As the server moved on, she saw the bustle in the background as May approached, leaving Tabitha behind her. Fiona was unsurprised to see that the woman had somehow secured something in a long glass with ice.

'I needed something to settle me after yesterday, dear.' She plonked herself down in the chair opposite Fiona. 'I don't know about you, but it really put me about.'

Fiona laughed; she couldn't help herself. 'More excitement than I needed.'

May leaned forward, placing a hand on her knee. 'You coped admirably, dear. Like a woman under fire.' She smiled. 'And your chap, Alistair. He was like an action hero when he raced towards that man.'

Fiona simply nodded quickly. She wanted to steer the conversation away, but this woman was like a surgeon, probing a wound and not caring about the discomfort.

'What's his job?' May asked. 'Police? I've done a bit of work with them myself.'

'Army. A brigadier in the Scots Guards,' said Fiona. 'His whole family is from that background. My cousin Frank served with him on National Service.'

'I knew it.' May clapped her hands together. 'You have that look, my dear.'

'What look?'

'The slight dread of a woman marrying a military man. It won't be a normal relationship. There's always another woman you see.'

'I doubt that very much.' Fiona jerked away. Alistair was such a direct and moral man; she simply could not see him ever playing away.

May placed another hand on her knee. 'A figure of speech, dear. The other woman wears a crown. The job always comes first.'

Fiona gave a weak smile. 'Frankly, I would prefer it if his job stayed at arm's length from me if it is anything like yesterday.' She took a deep breath. Her heart was still thumping away. Almost without any action on her part. It was simply exhausting. 'Alistair has a desk job. In Edinburgh. He doesn't see much, if any, active service.'

May stared at her, her face looking like a doctor on the verge of breaking bad news. 'He reacted very well for a man that doesn't see any action.' She leaned in, conspiratorial. 'But I can see that it's a strong relationship. Look at them.'

She nodded over to where the Mortimers sat on their wicker chairs, opposite sides of the table, both looking out of the Nile, Frederick to the stern, Viola to the bows. Fiona giggled, despite herself.

'Go on, dear,' said May.

Fiona leaned in, whispering. 'They weren't even in the same room. To start with. Dawoud was moved into Frederick's room after the attempt on his life. Imagine. Being on holiday and sleeping in separate rooms.'

'I couldn't possibly. Fancy that. What do you think goes on behind that door?'

'I don't think I want to know.'

'Really?' May looked genuinely shocked. 'I can't get enough of finding out things like that. You really get to see how people tick.'

Fiona looked at her a moment, running the conversation back in her mind.

'The police,' she said. 'What work do you do with them?'

May's face clouded. Just for an instant before her mischievous smile returned. 'I'm a consultant. About a lot of things.' She stood up. 'Thank you so much, dear. That has given me a great deal to think about. I'm sure that I will see you later.'

Fiona sat alone after May moved on. The river flowed past, a darker blue here upstream than the dark greys and browns of the lower reaches.

What had the woman meant? Fiona felt like she had just walked away from a smiling man in a market, unsure if she'd said or done the right thing.

Winding his way along the deck was one of the servers. As he drew level, Fiona caught his eye.

'Azmy not working today?'

The boy shook his head. 'Working with the captain. Can I help you, miss?'

She nodded, settling herself back. 'A G&T, please.'

The boy looked up at the sky, as if making a point about the early hour.

'I got shot at yesterday,' said Fiona. 'I need a damn drink.'

The lad smiled, humouring her.

The drink was, as usual, warm by the time it arrived. She sipped it and gazed around. Her eye was caught by the Mortimers as Frederick stood, walking away from Viola without a backwards glance. Fiona wanted to know what was going on there. She stood, and headed for the empty chair that Frederick had just vacated.

'Hi,' she said, sitting down.

'Good morning.'

She could see that Viola had only a glass of water in front of her.

'So. How are things after yesterday?' said Fiona.

The other woman shrugged. 'We hung back. Inside the tomb with the Russian couple.'

'Oh yes? What did those two do?'

Viola shrugged. 'They didn't do much. When they heard the shooting start, they told us not to move. We didn't see much of it. It was all over when we got out.' Short staccato speech. Uninterested or simply Italian?

'Being trapped would be more frightening I think,' said Fiona.

Viola took a deep drink of her water. 'I didn't think of that.' She shrugged. 'Probably for the best. We didn't have much choice.'

'You seem very calm.' Fiona sipped at her gin, mirroring Viola. The other women simply nodded. 'Is Frederick okay?'

Viola avoided her eyes, looking down at first and then out of the boat. Like everyone, she seemed to be searching for an answer that would come from elsewhere, rather than in front of her.

'He sleeps badly,' she said, finally turning back to Fiona.

'Really?' Fiona instantly thought of Alistair and his own midnight jaunts. 'How so?'

The woman shrugged. 'He doesn't tell me. He simply wakes, thrashing around in a pool of sweat.' She sighed. 'He shouts too. Nothing comprehensible, just random yells from the back of his throat. I don't ask why, but all that talk of crocs in the river disturbed him a lot.'

'Do you wish you were back in separate cabins?' Fiona wasn't sure if this was prying too far. It probably was, but there was something unreal about this pair.

Viola looked back to her, her eyes staring straight into Fiona's. 'Oh yes.'

CHAPTER SEVEN
Transition

LETHBRIDGE-STEWART STEPPED out onto the deck, knowing that Fiona's scowl would be there to greet him. He was lucky to find her sipping a gin and tonic in one hand. With her other, she reached for him and pulled him close.

'You're an old fool and I love you,' she whispered.

He relaxed, kissed her, and dropped onto the chair next to her.

'Thank you,' was all he could think of to say.

She looked over her sunglasses and nodded towards where Greaves sat, hunched over a textbook.

'Perhaps you should say thank you to the professor. For picking you up from the dust that you fell in. And apologise for stalking him out there.'

It was certainly a gentlemanly thing to do. He hauled himself off the seat and went to join Greaves.

'Really, don't mention it,' the man said. An actor reading a script that he knew he should recite.

It was then that Lethbridge-Stewart caught sight of the pictures in the book. Tall, powerfully built and bull-headed with a sword and spear.

'Montu,' he said.

Greaves looked down at the page, as if seeing it for the first time. 'Some research in depictions. You see, he is usually shown as a hawk-faced god of war.'

'War?'

'Indeed. One of the main such-gods in the pantheon. Yet in later periods he started to be shown with a bull's head instead. I've always wondered why.' Greaves coughed. 'And now I'm starting to find references to a bull-headed war god at the very start of Ancient Egypt history.'

'I see,' said Lethbridge-Stewart. He had little appetite for a history lecture.

'But I don't think you do,' continued Greaves. 'Because this means that the depiction of Montu as bull-headed in the later kingdom reflected an earlier practice that predated his hawk-headed visage. It was a revival. But what was it reviving, I wonder?'

Lethbridge-Stewart was saved the rest of Greaves' musings by the unmistakable and painful sound of a metal spoon being rapidly hit against a glass.

He turned to see Tabitha Gordon, now the centre of attention, standing at the centre of the sun deck.

'Ladies and gentlemen. Miss Day has been watching everything on this boat with great interest.' The passengers began muttering to each other before Tabitha coughed loudly. 'She has put her skills to work on our situation and would like you all to join her in the saloon.'

As the passengers stood glancing at each other, Fiona approached Lethbridge-Stewart, still with her glass in one hand.

'See, no one appreciates it when people go poking their noses in.'

He nodded. 'Still, let's see what she can offer us.'

Beneath them, the rumble of the paddles stopped, while from the front came the sound of the anchor chain spooling out.

In the dining room, Mortimer slouched in his seat, clearly unhappy at being dragged away from whatever had been occupying him before Tabitha had done her rounds. Viola was bolt upright next to him. His hand rested absently on her knee, maintaining some contact, even if it didn't extend to their eyes meeting. Dawoud was alone at the opposite end of the room. Tabitha and May were perched on the edge of a small sofa that had been dragged into the middle. The rest of the passengers and crew filed in, including the now ubiquitous and taciturn Russian pair. They both leaned against the wall, their faces identical masks.

The last two in were Captain Ibrahim and Azmy, who

closed the door carefully behind him with a click.

'What's this all about?' Lethbridge-Stewart said.

May smiled. 'Please sit down, Brigadier Lethbridge-Stewart.' She folded her hands and gazed around. 'I thought it best to bring you all here after everything that has happened.' She was studiously calm. 'The fact is that someone attempted to kill poor Mr Dawoud just two nights ago. I think we are all worried about the danger this presents.' Her face froze. 'Except for the man that did it.'

'The police weren't interested, woman.' Mortimer's hold lolled back on his chair. The man's sunken eyes and full water glass made it clear that he was either hungover or suffering from a lack of sleep.

'They weren't, Mr Mortimer. But I've not been entirely honest with you all. You see, I've been keeping my eyes open a lot since then. I am actually something of an investigative consultant to our own constabulary and I am very interested.'

Fiona turned to Lethbridge-Stewart, and he caught her eye; her expression was one of amusement.

'Beaten to it by Miss Marple,' she said softly, stifling a giggle.

He nodded. 'What have we walked into?' he whispered back.

A cough behind them came from Azmy. Lethbridge-Stewart saw for the first time that the man was carrying a rifle, currently held down by his hip with the butt resting on the floor. It looked to be a military model. Likely army surplus. Azmy nodded towards May, who began talking again.

'The man that attacked Mr Dawoud was a man we know was awake that night. A man that has military training that he has demonstrated before our eyes outside the tombs. He is a man of good standing which is why he was so eager to remove any trace of himself from Mr Dawoud's cabin after he failed to do away with him.' She sniffed. 'Because you see, ladies and gentlemen, the man that tried to kill Mr Dawoud wanted to cover up his intimate relationship with him.' She paused, looking around the now silent room. 'Didn't you, Mr Lethbridge-Stewart?'

Her eyes, and that of everyone in the room, turned to rest on where Lethbridge-Stewart and Fiona sat. Beyond a few hastily drawn breaths there was no sound at all from those assembled. Lethbridge-Stewart heard the sound of Azmy lifting his rifle. Not cocking it, just clearly keeping it ready in case he needed it.

Dawoud was having a coughing fit in the corner, shaking his head vigorously. He lunged forward, shouting in Arabic, his perfect English forgotten until he broke into simply shouting 'No!' repeatedly.

Lethbridge-Stewart felt his own jaw dropping, but before he could say anything, the silence was broken by Fiona as she burst into uncontrollable laughter.

'Him?' she said pointing towards Lethbridge-Stewart. 'He wouldn't have tried to off a man in a million years. Much less lie about it.' She held her head in both hands, and lifted it up to look around the room before her eyes rested on Lethbridge-Stewart.

The Russian man stepped forward, grabbing Dawoud's shirt and pulled him backwards.

'They must be hiding something. Something important. Between them.'

Dawoud shook his head, pushing the Russian away with force. The man stumbled backwards over a low stool, his blond head bounced against Mortimer's table, knocking his glass. It hit the wood with a thump, spraying water across the Englishman's shorts and shirt.

The Russian leapt to his feet, his hands fists. His partner stepped forward, a hand to his shoulder, restraining him. The room fell silent.

'Well, I've heard enough and had enough.' Mortimer pulled himself upright, standing unsteadily as he brushed water off his clothes. 'I need to go back to my cabin.' Gingerly, he stepped over the tables and chairs scattered around the saloon.

'Right.' Lethbridge-Stewart stood up. 'Enough of this messing around. I'm sorry to tell you, madam…' He nodded to May, still sat imperious on the sofa. '…That you are very much mistaken. I have been looking into the same matters that you have.'

'Miss Day seems to have managed without sneaking around in people's cabins.' Tabitha sniffed, as if catching a whiff of some acrid odour.

'Madam!' snapped Lethbridge-Stewart. 'I happen to be a brigadier in the Scots Guards, and I decided that there were clearly matters of interest in that cabin.'

'Mr Lethbridge-Stewart.' Azmy stepped forward behind him. 'I fear that you may be somewhat outside of any jurisdiction that will allow you to enter someone's cabin. After what we have heard, perhaps we should refer this matter to the police?'

Lethbridge-Stewart rolled his eyes. 'They weren't concerned about an attempted murder. It seems scarcely likely that they would want to get involved in a trespass of all things.'

Azmy and Ibrahim quickly conferred before Azmy continued. 'Nevertheless, sir, the captain's wish is that the authorities be involved in this instance.'

'Oh?' Lethbridge-Stewart raised an eyebrow. 'You seemed to be only too happy to sail *Keberia* away from them after I found Mr Dawoud in the firebox.'

As Azmy translated, Ibrahim's face clouded over. He snapped back a reply to Azmy, one that ended in a very short and harsh word.

Before Azmy could translate back, a single piercing voice stabbed into the assembled gathering from the deck outside.

'No! No! Keep back!' There was then a shriek followed by a hollow splash. More splashes and screams followed.

'Mortimer!' shouted Lethbridge-Stewart rushing to the window.

Outside, he caught glimpses of the man's arms thrashing in the river.

There was something else thrashing around him, scales and teeth that rose from the water.

'Crocs!' Lethbridge-Stewart shouted, running for the door to the saloon and the small portion of the lower deck that bordered the water. Azmy blocked his way, holding his rifle at shoulder height. 'Really? A man is drowning out there. In fact.' Lethbridge-Stewart grabbed at the rifle. 'Give that here, I'm going to need it.'

'Sir, I can't let you—'

'You can stop me after I've saved that man's life. You haven't had the training to hit the animal.'

Azmy paused, his hands tensing over the weapon. Then he sighed and handed it over.

Lethbridge-Stewart pushed him aside, stepping out of the saloon and rushing down the corridor to the lower deck. He could hear the others following him.

He reached the wooden parapet, a part of the hull really, past which he could see the continuing thrashing of water. Mortimer was still in the centre of it all, occasional glimpses of his head or arms showing through the foaming water alongside the head and body of the crocodile.

'It shouldn't be here!' shouted Azmy.

'Try telling it that!' snapped back Lethbridge-Stewart, raising the rifle to his eye level and sighting down the barrel to try and hit the croc.

It was a pig to draw a bead on the thing, as it thrashed. Eventually, he saw its back arc out of the water, at least a couple of feet from Mortimer. He squeezed the trigger and felt the rifle kick into his right shoulder as a fountain of blood erupted from the beast.

The bulk sank out of sight. The bubbles and foam that had filled the water faded, leaving only the dark red stain of blood surrounded by water tinted with the silt that had been churned up from the river's bottom. There was no sign of Mortimer.

Next to Lethbridge-Stewart, Azmy kicked off his shoes.

'No body,' he said. 'Bodies should float. I'm going to try and find him.'

Lethbridge-Stewart placed a hand on the boy's shoulder. 'Unconscious men also float. But neither man nor corpse floats if every major organ is punctured.' He pulled the rifle back and handed it to Azmy. 'And the same will go for you if there's any more in there. You once told me that there's no chance of any crocodiles this far north. Would you bank your life on that being the only one?'

Azmy sighed deeply. 'Someone must tell the man's wife.'

Lethbridge-Stewart closed his eyes. Now, the man was being deferential to him at the worst possible time. He turned back to where he knew the crowd would be gathered and opened his eyes again.

In front of him was Viola Mortimer, her lips pursed. Behind her was a gaggle of the passengers; May, Tabitha,

Fiona, Greaves, Dawoud and the Russians among them. Captain Ibrahim appeared to be looking right past Lethbridge-Stewart at Azmy, his expression unreadable.

'You are sure he is gone?' Viola asked, her voice level, her eyes flickered, fire dancing behind a grate.

The two men turned to each other. Lethbridge-Stewart turned back to the widow.

'Certain. He couldn't have survived that.'

Her expression did not change. 'Thank you.' She turned and pushed her way back through the crowd, her shoulders shaking, heading for the steps up to her cabin.

Azmy risked a glance behind him, back towards the water that now stood calm again, apart from its spreading red stain. Lethbridge-Stewart saw him swallow.

'We should return to the saloon, ladies and gentlemen,' he said, opening his arms to usher them all back inside.

Inside was silence as the crowd tried to process what had happened. May and Tabitha returned to their sofa in the centre of the room. Gradually, the whisper of conversation built up around the room as the passengers each began to talk about Mortimer and how dangerous Egypt could be.

Fiona stood next to Lethbridge-Stewart, and he felt her hand squeeze his. He turned to her and smiled grimly, before quickly pecking her cheek.

'I think I've had enough of this now,' he whispered in her ear. Behind him he could hear Azmy and Captain Ibrahim deep in conversation in Arabic.

There came the same high-pitched rattle of metal on glass that had summoned them. All eyes turned to the source of the sound to see Tabitha now standing. May remained seated and coughed once. She looked around the room before speaking.

'Clearly, new information has come to light. Even the best of us can only work with what we have.'

Lethbridge-Stewart nodded. 'If we are all here, who pushed Mr Mortimer?'

'Exactly. All we can say, Mr Lethbridge-Stewart, is that another person on this vessel, as yet unknown, may have had the means, motive and opportunity to try to kill Mr Dawoud and to kill Mr Mortimer.'

'Another person *may* have had the opportunity to kill Mortimer?' Lethbridge-Stewart spluttered. 'Just how long do you think my arms are, madam? I was standing in front of you when he screamed and fell.'

'Please, ladies and gentlemen.' Azmy stepped forward. Lethbridge-Stewart was glad to see that he now had the rifle very much down at his side. 'What is abundantly clear is that we can go no further than Asyut tonight. We must wait there for the authorities. We will call ahead and then a full search will be undertaken of the vessel.' He shrugged. 'The man who did this may well have jumped ship in the confusion, but he would be a strange man that throws his enemy to a crocodile and then jumps in after him.'

'So, what do we do now?' asked one of the Russians. 'Should we not hand these two over just in case?' He pointed at Dawoud and Lethbridge-Stewart.

Dawoud snapped a short answer back in a guttural tongue. From the shock that suddenly hit the Russian's face, Lethbridge-Stewart guessed that Dawoud had calmed down enough to recover his skill with languages.

Azmy shrugged. 'We have had enough of supposition today, I think. I cannot confine any of you to your cabins. But if you do leave, please do so in groups of at least two people.' He looked directly at Lethbridge-Stewart as he said this.

'Great!' said Fiona softly to him. 'You need some salt on your tail after the last few nights.'

The atmosphere on the top deck for afternoon refreshments was remarkably relaxed for a vessel that hid a murderer. That may have been down to Azmy, who now sat at the entrance to the sun deck with his rifle while the other deck hands dealt with the passenger's needs.

'Or maybe everyone secretly knows that they could never antagonise anyone as much as Mortimer antagonised everyone before his killer finally snapped,' said Fiona over her spritzer.

Lethbridge-Stewart had opted to put a small ice cube into his whisky. It was completely justified by the weather, he told Fiona, and she was not to breathe a word of it to his uncle if she ever met him.

'Perhaps.' He smiled wryly. 'As much as his wife seemed

happy to see him go, she can't have been the one that pushed him.' He chuckled. 'A death on the Nile. Perhaps Cosgrove was right.'

'I'd rather have a holiday here,' said Fiona.

'Maybe I can help.' They turned to see that Greaves had arrived and sat down next to them. His expression was an eager one.

'I think that the idea of a relaxing holiday is almost ruined by now. Egyptian police don't work fast,' said Lethbridge-Stewart. 'We may be in Asyut for a long time while they deal with us. And then the best we can hope for is train tickets back to Cairo.' He thought for a moment. 'This time, I think we'll get a hotel.'

'I could possibly offer you something less…' Greaves smiled. '…shall we say *tedious*.'

'Go on,' said Fiona. 'Less tedious is what I'm looking for at the moment.' She stirred her drink. 'Safe would be nice as well, for both of us.' She made a sidelong glance in Lethbridge-Stewart's direction.

'Well, the two of you would be with me, and no one else. So hopefully you would be safe from any further murders.' Greaves shrugged. 'You would have to cope with my driving, however. Has Alistair filled you in on my plan to head into the Western desert and try to find the lost city of Zerzura?'

Fiona laughed. 'He mentioned that you were thinking along those lines, yes.'

Lethbridge-Stewart bit his tongue. The words he'd actually used probably shouldn't be repeated to Greaves.

'I could do with some company. I'm planning on leaving from Asyut. As soon as the police let us. I'll arrange a vehicle and supplies.' Greaves sipped on his wine and winced. 'This is from the King of Morocco's own vineyard? I think he should convert it to an olive grove.'

'Why not stay with the steamer?' asked Lethbridge-Stewart.

Greaves shrugged. 'It won't be going anywhere for a while. At least not with any passengers. What place for an overqualified tour guide like me? They'll pay me or they won't. Either way, I'm due back to teaching in two weeks. I won't get much of a chance at this for a long time, so this could be it.'

Lethbridge-Stewart blew air out between his teeth. 'I'm not sure about this.'

He knew what he wanted first. A squad of troops in case of bandit activity, and an airlift.

'Well, feel free to spend the rest of your holiday in Asyut,' Greaves said. 'But I think my plan would be a trip to remember. Even if we don't find the city, you will at least see some of the real Egypt. The desert sands, the oases, far from the queues of locals lining up with flea bitten camels.'

Lethbridge-Stewart thought further. For all its political issues, hopefully now far behind them, this remained a safe country. Not quite an ally to Britain, but not somewhere he would expect anything too dangerous to happen. Certainly, he expected much less danger to the three of them on a drive out to the desert than in the confines of the boat. A boat where someone had clearly already made attempts, one successful, on people's lives.

He looked to Fiona. She nodded once at him. He turned back to Greaves.

'Agreed,' said Lethbridge-Stewart. 'But only once the authorities have finished with us. And then I will come with you to pick some provisions.'

'Excellent.' Greaves smiled, holding his hand out. 'I do hope we find something worth searching for.'

As he left, Fiona leaned into Lethbridge-Stewart.

'I thought you said he didn't know where to start looking for this lost city?'

Lethbridge-Stewart watched the man's retreating back.

'That's what he told me. But I didn't believe him then, and I believe him even less now.' He took a sip of the whisky. 'But it convinced me that he is such a bad liar, that must be all he is keeping from us.'

'Glad to hear it.' Fiona gripped his hand and looked out at the desert, off on the right, as they cruised down the river. 'At last, an adventure rather than a cruise.' Her voice broke as she said it.

Lethbridge-Stewart squeezed her hand back. He could see that her eyes alone told him that it wasn't the boredom that she despised.

'I'll be glad to leave this boat too,' he said.

'You're more used to this than I thought.' Fiona released his hand. 'Being shot at, grabbing a gun, seeing a man die. You take it all in your stride.'

'I've had a varied career.' He picked up her drink and held it out to her, a peace offering, a pleading to drop the subject before he was forced to lie to her.

'And this shouldn't be a part of it. But you just seem to slide all too easily into your role. You're not a desk bound officer at all, are you?' Fiona asked. 'You still see a lot of action, firefights and death.'

He put the glass back down. 'I can't talk about it...'

'But.' It was a statement.

'But, yes, you're right, I do a lot of this. I can't tell you why, but I can only hope that there's a lot less of it out there.' Lethbridge-Stewart waved over at the western bank of the Nile, past the green fields.

Fiona nodded. 'I hope so too. We'll find out.'

Lethbridge-Stewart reached for her, wrapping his arms around her. 'We will, after we get to Asyut.'

He couldn't wait. Even in the sunshine of the afternoon, his mind flashed back to the previous night. The footsteps behind him in the dark, the presence in the tomb.

There was something inhuman on the boat.

'Please sit, sir.'

The khaki clad police lieutenant gestured at the single wooden chair behind a nondescript desk. It was the only furniture in the concrete room that Lethbridge-Stewart had been led to in the police station at Asyut. It was, he had been assured, a formality. Simply a way to remove him from the police enquiries.

Lethbridge-Stewart gathered this lieutenant was called Nasir. He sized him up as the other man sat down opposite, pulling out a notepad and pen and scribbled silently in it, not looking up. Lethbridge-Stewart was familiar with the technique and reacted as nonchalantly as possible, crossing his legs at the knee and resting the back of his neck in his hands.

Nasir coughed.

'Mr Stewart.'

'Lethbridge-Stewart. Brigadier, actually.' Lethbridge-Stewart dropped both feet to the floor and sat up in his seat.

'Mr Lethbridge-Stewart.' Nasir's English was accented but good. 'Why are you travelling on the boat?'

'A holiday. With my fiancée.'

'How long have you known each other?' Nasir didn't look up from his writing.

'A little over four months.' That didn't sound long. 'We've only just got engaged.'

'Why not wait for your honeymoon for a trip?'

Lethbridge-Stewart looked around at the grey walls and bare light bulb. 'Why wait to visit your beautiful country?'

At this, Nasir looked up, putting his pen down. 'I'm not in the mood for mocking, Mr Stewart.'

'Neither am I. As I have already pointed out, my name is *Brigadier Lethbridge*-Stewart, not *Mr Stewart*. Now, what has my relationship with my fiancée got to do with anything?'

Nasir sighed and resumed writing. 'Very well, then perhaps you can tell me…' He looked up again. '…why you locked your fellow passenger in a boiler.'

Lethbridge-Stewart sat there, aware that whatever cockiness he may have had, had now simply expired. The rug of certainty, or knowing that he was just here to clear up some loose ends, had been pulled from under him.

'I had nothing to do with that,' he said, feeling his own voice break as he became horribly aware that he was here, in a cell in Egypt, separated from everything he could rely on and suddenly being accused of murder.

'It will be easier if you just explain why.' Nasir produced a cigarette box and pulled out two, holding one out to Lethbridge-Stewart, who shook his head. The policeman shrugged and lit his own, taking a long drag and letting the smoke fill the air between them. 'We can make things easier from here. Our prisons are not as nice as yours, I understand.'

Lethbridge-Stewart thought back to his brief stint at Her Majesty's pleasure. He doubted that he would find anyone like Stanley to look after him inside an Egyptian cell. Still, it couldn't be any worse than his time at the prison camp in Korea. He also doubted, very much, that this man meant a single word of anything he had said.

'I still had nothing to do with it.' He tried to keep his voice level. Mysterious happenings, spaceships and alien invasions were one thing. The very real and very deadly conditions of a north African prison were something else.

'Very well. If that is what you want to say.' Nasir drew a line, doubled, under the text and tapped his pen before looking up. 'We will, of course, have to keep you here while we gather more evidence. Perhaps even move you to another prison.' He left the sentence hanging in the air, like a guillotine ready to fall.

'I won't admit something I haven't done.' Lethbridge-Stewart realised as his hand shook harder with a clenched fist that he was far more angry than scared.

The other man appeared to relent and turned a page, his head down again before he suddenly snapped it up to look directly at Lethbridge-Stewart.

'What had Mr Mortimer done to deserve his death?' he said.

'Nice try. I think I should be requesting some embassy assistance at this stage, don't you?'

Nasir sighed and closed his book, tucking his pen into his jacket. 'This really is just drawing everything out you know, Mr Stewart.' He stood and went for the door. 'We have not so many cells in this station. I don't think you want to wait here for too long, do you?' The expression on his face was encouraging. Perhaps if Lethbridge-Stewart was a weaker man, it may have worked.

'The answer's still no. I still want the embassy.' Lethbridge-Stewart kept his hands folded on the desk.

The corners of the lieutenant's mouth, turned up slightly. 'Then I will find you a room for the night.'

CHAPTER EIGHT
Thither and Yon

THE CELL was cramped with stained concrete walls and a slab of a bed with a moth-eaten piece of cloth to cover it. Lethbridge-Stewart remained standing, confining himself to the dry end and trying not to think what sort of liquid would seep into a room from a desert.

They brought him food. Pushed through the door was a plate of cold, congealed brown mush complete with flies already crawling across it. He stared at the spoon briefly, thinking of prison escape movies. This was reality and the walls were solid and so roughly made that the thin cotton of his shirt caught and scratched as he leaned against them.

He left the stuff lying on the floor. At least the flies could continue their lunch.

The police had taken his watch, leaving him with no idea of the time. As the light began to die, he hammered on the door. It was eventually opened by an officer.

'Yes?' the man grunted.

'I need to tell my partner where I am.' Lethbridge-Stewart held out a hand, expecting a phone handset. The man's face was confused, but quickly settled.

'You want to confess?' he eventually said, his English far more broken than that of the lieutenant.

'No.' Lethbridge-Stewart kept his voice level. 'I do not.'

The man shrugged. 'You tell me when you confess.'

The door slammed in his face.

'This isn't going to work on me,' Lethbridge-Stewart shouted after him.

Much later, there was a hammering on the door.

'Stand back!' snapped the voice behind. Lethbridge-Stewart did so. Nasir entered, one hand on his pistol in its holster. 'You have a visitor.'

'Fiona?' Lethbridge-Stewart was hopeful, for at least a familiar face.

'Doesn't look like it.' The man smirked at him, but then his face fell. 'Follow me.'

He was led back through the myriad corridors of the police station to the interview room that he had originally faced the lieutenant in. They stopped outside the door. Lethbridge-Stewart went to enter. As he did so, Nasir placed a hand on his arm.

'Please, sir.' It was such a change in tack that Lethbridge-Stewart stood frozen for a half a second before laying one hand over the lieutenant's.

'Yes?' Lethbridge-Stewart didn't want to give this corrupt individual any more indication that he was open for negotiation than he had to.

'I was doing my job. Please remember that.' At that, the man stood back, giving Lethbridge-Stewart plenty of room to walk into the room.

The reason for Nasir's nervousness was apparent the minute that Lethbridge-Stewart entered the interview room. Sat at the desk, with two steaming mugs in front of him and still wearing his safari suit, was Cosgrove.

'Alistair!' he called. 'Take a seat! I brought my own tea bags with me. None of this mint rubbish. I thought you could do with a taste of home after today.'

Lethbridge-Stewart sat down and gratefully took a sip of the black tea in front of him. He inhaled the aroma.

'Earl Grey?' he hazarded.

'Bang on, old boy. I never leave Cairo without some. Helps the crazy Englishman persona. And you don't need any milk. There's no lemon, I'm afraid.'

'Well, you've certainly got the chap outside spooked.'

Cosgrove at least had the decency to look embarrassed. 'Yes, I think I may have laid on the intelligence officer stuff a bit too heavy. They've probably got me down as being here to blow up a villain's secret base.'

'And are you? Why are you here anyway?' It was too large

a coincidence that the man would be in this exact city at this exact time.

'For you.' Cosgrove looked confused. 'To help you get out of this mess.'

'Oh, come on, I've only just got into this mess. Cairo is days away.'

Cosgrove grinned. 'Oh, good God boy! You've gone a bit cuckoo on that boat. You know how slow they move, don't you? Cairo is a few *hours* away by car. I left as soon as I got word that they were going to try and pot you.'

Lethbridge-Stewart sipped the tea further, feeling the warmth of it trickling down his throat.

'Then I am incredibly grateful and owe you far more than a cup of tea. So, what next?'

'Don't mention it, old boy. As for what next. The answer, if you want, is nothing.' Cosgrove shrugged. 'They've got nothing on you, but I heard about one of your fellow passengers' dotage driven stunt today.'

'I'm sorry?' said Alistair.

'The old biddy. May. She married a man called Day you know. May Day.'

Lethbridge-Stewart burst out laughing before Cosgrove continued.

'Fancies herself as a PI. The only inquiry she's helped the constabulary in Blighty with is wasting police time. But I think her accusation was all the Egyptian plod felt that they needed.' Cosgrove shook his head. 'I don't think they're quite up with Scotland Yard's finest. A few choice words and it's all dropped. You're free to go.'

'Excellent.' Lethbridge-Stewart drained his cup. 'Please don't take this amiss, but after today, I think that Fiona and I need to get out of this country as soon as we possibly can.'

'I'm sure that sounds attractive right now.' Cosgrove leaned forward. 'But I do have another option if you wanted to stay in Egypt. Consider it a way to make things up after this trip I arranged went so badly wrong.' He sighed. 'I don't think I'm going to go into travel agency when I retire from foreign intelligence, Alistair. It's simply too much stress for me.'

*

'What is that?' Lethbridge-Stewart stared at the vehicle in front of him, parked outside the police station in the now cool city streets.

Mostly sand-coloured, there were places where its previous green paint showed through, a white star on the bonnet made its origin obvious to anyone with a passing interest in military history.

'US Army Jeep,' said Cosgrove proudly. 'It was left here after the war.'

'Was that when it was last serviced?' asked Lethbridge-Stewart.

Cosgrove coughed. 'I will have you know, this vehicle is tried and tested in the deserts of Egypt. I thought it would make a fantastic way to see the country properly, rather than having to trudge around after a load of geriatric murder suspects.'

'As a matter of fact, we already have tentative plans to that very effect. Accompanying an archaeologist out into the desert.' Lethbridge-Stewart looked at Cosgrove as he told him, searching for any reaction.

After a slight pause, maybe even a twitch, the other man rubbed his hands together.

'That is absolutely splendid, old boy.' His eyes twinkled. 'Then you will be glad to know that I have already provided you with provisions.' He started pointing out the objects inside the rear of the jeep as he did so. 'Map of the western desert and oases. Very useful. Jerry cans. They've got enough gas in to get you two thousand miles in this. Water.' He pointed at several enormous bottles. 'Easily enough for a week.' He smiled with a broad grin. 'That's a bit boring, so I also threw in this.' From under the seat he produced a green glass bottle.

'Aha,' said Lethbridge-Stewart. 'That's an excellent malt. Where on earth did you get it?'

Cosgrove shrugged. 'I had to raid my own provisions. Don't worry, I have plenty left where that came from.' He turned back to the bags stacked in the jeep's rear seats. 'Right, trail rations, dull as dishwater I'm afraid. A small amount of firewood. It doesn't get too cold and there's no large animals in Egypt.' Lethbridge-Stewart kept his own counsel on crocodiles. 'A couple of tents…'

'A couple? We're engaged!' Lethbridge-Stewart was secretly happy to have somewhere to leave Greaves.

'Well, I didn't know what your approach to that sort of thing would be. I mean, you can be a bit old fashioned sometimes can't you, old boy?' Cosgrove saved the last item until the passing traffic had dissipated before he reached into the footwell again. 'I don't think anyone travelling in Egypt has needed one of these for decades, but just in case…' He produced what Lethbridge-Stewart immediately recognised as a British Lee-Enfield rifle. He could see from its shining surface that it had been well cared for. 'You never know, eh?'

Lethbridge-Stewart took it, checking it over. 'I imagine this was left here at the same time as the jeep?' He checked the breach and barrel. 'And in considerably better condition as well.'

Cosgrove laughed and slapped the bonnet. 'Look here, if that thing lets you down, I will buy you a whole crate of single malt.'

Lethbridge-Stewart looked around at the provisions piled high in the jeep's rear and the rifle that now sat in his hand.

'Deal. I don't suppose you packed us any Scrabble, did you?' He hoped the joke would be taken in the spirit it was intended.

'For an engagement holiday? I didn't think you were that old fashioned.'

Lethbridge-Stewart leaned over the tailgate of the jeep, taking it all in. 'I can't thank you enough for this.'

Cosgrove clapped him on the shoulder. 'Don't mention it at all. My treat. I promised you a holiday, didn't I?'

Cosgrove swung himself up into the driver's seat. On the left-hand side, Lethbridge-Stewart noticed. 'Come on. If you and your good lady are joining me in the hotel later, we will need to go and pick her up. Unless you want another night on *Keberia*?'

Lethbridge-Stewart smiled and jumped up next to Cosgrove. He went to check the glove box.

'I wouldn't bother, old chap,' said Cosgrove 'That thing might as well be welded shut. Can't seem to get it open for the life of me.'

'That really doesn't bode well,' Lethbridge-Stewart said

as the jeep juddered, its ignition turning over before it rattled away down the road.

The hotel in Asyut that Lethbridge-Stewart and Fiona eventually arrived at ranked above *Keberia* in terms of security. However, it was sorely lacking in terms of comfort.

'I don't think this bed is designed to be this soft. I think the springs have gone.'

They had dropped into the bed and both managed to sink and slide into the middle. Lethbridge-Stewart stared up at the ceiling and the bare wiring jutting out of the broken fan. As he watched, a bug crawled into the cavity that the fixture housing had left uncovered when it had slipped down the flex an unknown time ago.

'Do you think we'll miss this luxury on the road?' Fiona asked.

'We can but hope,' he replied.

'Did you invite Cosgrove to join us as well as Greaves?'

Lethbridge-Stewart rolled away, needing much of his upper body strength to pull himself up. 'I didn't think he was angling for an invitation. He would have made it more obvious.'

'I'm worried about what he's up to.'

Lethbridge-Stewart stopped dead as he was pulling himself up from the bed. 'He did drive up from Cairo to spring me from an Egyptian jail. I owe him a lot.'

'Yes, and he just happened to hand you exactly the type of vehicle needed for the journey that we already had planned. That makes me worried.'

Lethbridge-Stewart sat down on the edge of the bed, watching the lights of Asyut playing through the patchy and shredded curtains.

'Me too. But we'll never get anything out of Cosgrove as to why he wants us to head into the desert outside of what he's already told us.' He drummed his hands on his knees. 'That's the problem with the man. You only get the surface.'

'And yet, you trust him. And that's what got us on the murder boat.'

Lethbridge-Stewart could hear a clock ticking. It must have been his own watch, but now ticking loud enough that its sound entered the conversation to fill in the space that couldn't be filled by words.

'He can't have known what was going on. No one does. That's why we need to get away from it all.'

'He seems to know everything else. And it's about time he stopped knowing it,' Fiona said. 'I want my own holiday back. With you, not with Mortimer, or Greaves or Dawoud. And definitely without Cosgrove.'

Lethbridge-Stewart swung round to her. 'Wait, you wanted to go with Greaves into the desert.'

'Yes, anything to get away from that boat.' She threw her hands up. 'Fine, it's Greaves' expedition. That's not the point. You're still far too relaxed about this. We've been shot at, seen a man eaten by crocodiles, another man was locked in a boiler…'

'Relaxed?' Lethbridge-Stewart restrained himself from barking at Fiona. 'I was chasing around that boat, trying to find out what was going on, even chasing after Greaves through the mountains to find out where he was going.'

Fiona's eyes had grown cold and distant. 'You were revelling in it,' she said. 'I thought I knew you, but one little glimpse at things out of the ordinary and you start running around like an action hero. Who do you think you are, anyway? Come on, I need to know who I'm marrying. I was ready to give up my job because I thought I would be taking a new role. Supporting you. But how can I do that if I don't share any part of it?'

Lethbridge-Stewart could feel the blood rushing to his face. That strange mix of embarrassment and unfairness that always marked an argument like this.

'I'm a soldier,' was his only answer.

'Oh, is that all you can say? You're a soldier so you have to go rushing around like Bond when the reality is that you're on a bleedin' paddle steamer on the Nile. I've barely seen you in the last couple of days.'

'I was locked in a prison cell.' He knew he was being petty. 'Anyway, do you think Dawoud walked into that boiler himself? Or Mortimer decided that a swim with the crocs would be a bracing dip?'

'Don't be flippant, Alistair. You know that both of those men were likely mixed up in something dodgy. We…' She emphasised this by stabbing her finger into his chest '…were never in danger.'

'You can't know that.' It was a poor retort.

'I can't know it. But it seems pretty likely, don't you think? The only person who came even vaguely close to actually targeting me or you on this trip was a drunk camel guide.'

Lethbridge-Stewart thought of that man's last words. *Montu.* The name of the deity whose heart was in Greaves' jar, whose grave they were now heading for. He hoped that the man had been drunk. It was such a simple explanation for something that otherwise terrified him.

'That was enough!' he snapped.

The watch ticking again, filling up the room.

'You're scared as well,' Fiona finally said. 'You're trying to play the knight in shining armour and protect me.'

He slumped next to her. 'Of course.' He reached out for her hand. She grabbed it quickly and squeezed it.

'Well don't. You've clearly had adventures out there on your own, now it's my turn to join you.'

Sally's face. That's what rose up in his mind's eye. This was not the time, but when he heard that Fiona wanted to join him in his life, in his working life, and experience that for herself… How could he tell her that he was scared about what she would find? The likes of Dominic Vaar, James Gore, and the rest. It was a world that he wanted to keep a long way from Fiona.

'Just a small trip. We'll be back on the plane in a few days, won't we?' she said.

He squeezed her hand back. He hoped so, he really did. He checked that damn watch. 10 o'clock, yet his eyes were already heavy.

'What's wrong?' Fiona said, following his eyes.

'I've not been sleeping well,' Lethbridge-Stewart said. 'The last two nights, waking up in the early hours.'

'That's what led you to find Dawoud and follow Greaves up to the temple.'

'Exactly. I don't like a coincidence like that.' He realised as he said it that he had maybe said too much.

'Really?' Fiona laughed. 'You've got a secret spiritual side, Alistair. Maybe a higher power is looking out for you.'

'Experience, my dear.' He forced the indulgent smile onto

his face. Deep down, he was more worried. In his experience, higher powers were not something he wanted to draw the attention of.

'Anyway,' Fiona continued. 'It's probably the food on the steamer. Viola Mortimer said that Frederick was sleeping badly as well.'

He felt his heart beat faster as his skin grew cold.

'What did you say?' he asked. 'How was he sleeping badly?'

'Screaming in his sleep, then waking in a pool of sweat.' Fiona pulled him closer. 'Like I said, probably the food.'

Lethbridge-Stewart looked past her shoulder, through the gaps at the city lights, hearing the yowls of feral cats and occasional car horns as life went on.

They set off early, before the sun's heat started beating down on the car and the road. As they threw their bags into the back of the jeep, Lethbridge-Stewart realised there would be some careful packing needed to ensure that there was enough room for three of them and luggage in the back.

'Good luck out there.'

He turned to see Cosgrove standing by the jeep's wing. The man had finally removed his pith helmet and stood in darker clothing than he usually wore. He had even trimmed his moustache down, making it far less noticeable. He must have seen Lethbridge-Stewart staring at him.

'You've got the car I drove up in, old chap. I'll need to take the train back, it's always best to look a bit more inconspicuous than I normally strive for.'

'Sorry. You're very welcome to take it back.'

Cosgrove held his hand out, ruddy and strong, for Lethbridge-Stewart to shake.

'Wouldn't hear of it. The two of you deserve an adventure. And what is better than seeking a lost city with an expert in the field.' He shrugged. 'You'll need to get going. Goodbye.' He turned to Fiona and held both arms out to embrace her. 'My dear, you're in the safest of hands.'

He stood back as Lethbridge-Stewart took the wheel. Lethbridge-Stewart wrenched the gearstick back, using brute force to get the thing into the right gear. He could feel the clutch had very little bite left as the jeep moved off, the stick shaking as it kicked into motion down Asyut's narrow streets.

'I wonder if anyone else got offed during the night?' mused Fiona from the passenger seat as she waved to Cosgrove.

'Let's hope not. May Day and Tabitha will probably find a way to pin that on me as well.'

Fiona giggled. 'They're quite cute in a way, aren't they?'

Lethbridge-Stewart spun the wheel as the jeep reached the waterfront, ready to find *Keberia* among the other boats moored up and pick up Greaves.

'You weren't locked up in the cell,' he retorted. 'I've gone off the Miss Marple act now.'

Ahead was the familiar smokestack of *Keberia*. Still and silent in the morning air; the boat was unlikely to be steamed anytime soon. When they reached its mooring, he could see Azmy and a young police officer, both sat on folding chairs at the end of the gangplank. They shared a cigarette.

Lethbridge-Stewart jumped out of the jeep and strode towards the pair.

'Sir?' said Azmy brightly. 'You had a good night?'

Lethbridge-Stewart thought briefly. 'Yes. For once.' *Maybe it was the food.* 'Is Professor Greaves about?'

Azmy nodded. 'Yes. He's been released from the inquiries now.' He turned towards the boat. 'Professor!' he shouted up the gangplank.

The man's face, a panama hat perched above it, appeared from the cabin deck. He waved below. Unlike Lethbridge-Stewart and Fiona, the professor clearly travelled light, just a small canvas bag swung over one shoulder.

'She's a beauty!' he said when he saw the jeep. Lethbridge-Stewart turned to Fiona and smiled.

'That sounds like an offer to drive. I'll sit on shotgun in the back.' Lethbridge-Stewart took Greaves' bag and wedged it into the one remaining space in the back seat of the jeep. 'Literally,' he muttered to himself.

Azmy walked over to him. He appeared to now be holding his rifle at all times, despite the presence of the Egyptian police officer also standing guard.

'Going far, sir?' he said brightly.

Lethbridge-Stewart nodded. 'A bit of an expedition for the professor. And an adventure for us.' He slipped a pair of sunglasses on as the light brightened with the day. 'Searching for a lost tomb.'

'I didn't think any tombs were still left, sir.' Azmy crouched next to the jeep suddenly, looking underneath it.

'What's the matter, man?' Lethbridge-Stewart tapped his foot. He wanted to get moving.

Azmy rummaged under the car for a second, before jumping back upright. 'Sorry, sir. You get used to these old things when you live here. I thought there was something loose around the drive shaft, but it was just some vegetation.'

Lethbridge-Stewart smiled. 'You should try and join up again once you get off this boat. I think you'll go far.' He looked back over at *Keberia*. 'Much further than that thing is going anyway.' He stuck his hand out, aware that Fiona and Greaves were already in the jeep. 'Thank you for everything, Azmy. You've brightened our trip.'

'Glad to help, sir,' the boy said with a flash of teeth as he shook Lethbridge-Stewart's hand. '*Inshallah*, we will meet again?'

'I hope we do,' Lethbridge-Stewart said as he scrambled up to the jeep's rear seat.

The oases of Egypt marked a ring of human habitation that arced away from the Nile, starting at a point near to Cairo in the north and stretching all the way down to Aswan, far to the south. Asyut was roughly halfway between the two and so as far from the apex of the arc as it was possible to get.

'And, of course,' said Greaves, as he coaxed the jeep expertly along the roads leading out of Asyut, 'we've got to go far beyond the oases to find the place. With any luck.'

The road leading from Asyut to the oases was half dirt track, half tarmac. The half that was tarmac was the most dangerous. Cracks and potholes caused the jeep to buck and jump as it rattled across them. The lush irrigation of the Nile plain soon gave way to date palms, olive trees and finally to desiccated scrubs dotting a landscape of scree and boulders. As they continued, even the scrub disappeared, leaving them with no other life for miles. Every so often, they would pass a cattle truck, its passengers looking too haggard to provide much milk or beef, or a lorry carrying mineral water.

Finally, Greaves had to pull in for a break from the drive and for the three to stretch their legs. He had managed to find a small shop, merely a shack in many ways, situated next to the road such that they could see for miles the plumes of dust sprayed up by lorries and bikes that thundered up and down the road.

The three climbed unsteadily from the jeep in the sudden silence. Lethbridge-Stewart felt the gritty film that came from travelling on the road across his skin as he paced back and forth, unsure whether to chance an entrance to the shack itself. It seemed that out there, their footsteps were the only sound. Finally, Greaves made the decision for them, pulling some dollars from his shirt pocket and counting them before he entered.

As they entered the shop, the flies seemed to lift off the produce at the sight of new faces and then swarmed across the newcomers. Greaves picked up a snack that seemed more sugar than pastry and three bottles of warm local cola. At least, thought Lethbridge-Stewart, it wet the throat and the food gave him some energy. He ventured to the toilet at the back of the shack, but the stench and the sight of more black flies lifting from the seat in unison drove him back. On reflection, he would wait until they passed a convenient boulder.

'I'll take the wheel,' he offered as they regrouped at the front of the store.

'I'll try and catch some sleep,' said Fiona. 'Then I'll take the next driving shift. You two can try and give us some shade.'

Greaves nodded wearily and, between them, he and Lethbridge-Stewart erected the canvas roof of the jeep. It was unlikely to offer them much protection from the sun that was now pushing its way to the zenith, but anything would be of some relief.

'So…?' asked Lethbridge-Stewart further down the road.

Greaves was beside him for navigation and wrangling purposes, while Fiona slumped in the back seat, trying to chase the scant shade around the jeep as much as she could.

'You know where we're going now?'

Greaves looked up from his map. 'I can't get much past you, can I?'

'Would you mind telling me how you found out where this lost city is?'

Greaves sighed, looking away from the road and towards the horizon that lay in the haze so many miles distant. 'You'll laugh or get me locked up if I told you.'

'You'd be surprised, Mr Greaves.' Lethbridge-Stewart risked a quick glance back. Fiona was dozing. 'Fire away.'

'Right, you remember the Temple of Pakhet, near the tombs?'

'There's something about being knocked unconscious somewhere that sticks in the mind.' Lethbridge-Stewart, shifted in his seat, the leather sticking to his clothes in the heat.

'Well, yes.' As Greaves paused, Lethbridge-Stewart knocked the car down a gear for a sudden twisting rise up past a rocky outcrop. 'When I went into the temple, before you arrived, I discovered a door.'

Lethbridge-Stewart turned in his seat to face Greaves. 'There was no door. I checked every wall of that place.'

'I know. I've read a lot about that temple. The inner sanctum is a small room and is well documented. But here's the thing.' Greaves tapped the dash with one hand. 'Pakhet was a local goddess, but she is thought to be a god of war, amongst many other things.'

'Hence the connection to the Greek goddess, Artemis,' said Lethbridge-Stewart. Greaves looked sidelong at him. 'Well, I didn't fall asleep in all my classics lessons. Carry on.'

'So, Pakhet was a goddess of war. The same is very much true of Montu.'

'Your god in a jar.'

'My god in a jar as you put it, yes. Their depictions obviously differ. Montu is usually an ibis, but can be a bull. Pakhet is usually a cat.' Greaves jabbed at the dashboard. 'Now this is where you're going to think I've got hold of some hashish. I swear that when I approached the alcove at the rear of that temple, the jar with the heart inside grew warm. It was almost like electricity or pins and needles shooting through my hands.'

Lethbridge-Stewart nodded. He could well believe it, but wasn't going to be the one that tipped Greaves off about that.

'Then,' continued Greaves. 'And look now, I swear I wasn't drinking… That wall opened in front of me. One minute solid rock. And that temple is built into solid rock, no single brick walls to slide or swivel here. That wall was solid rock and then it simply dissolved.'

'Dissolved?'

'Like a mist. Obviously, I stepped through. Who wouldn't?'

'Who wouldn't? I should think an archaeologist that was worried about damaging the artefacts beyond,' said Lethbridge-Stewart.

'I challenge any archaeologist not to do exactly what I did. We all thirst for knowledge and it was there, in front of me.'

'What did you find?'

'Well, first of all, the rock closed back behind me. That was a shock, let me tell you.'

'I imagine that it was,' said Lethbridge-Stewart. 'You at least had your torch.' He remembered it being shone in his own eyes by Greaves when he woke up.

'I did. And let me tell you, that inner passageway was not like any Egyptian architecture I have ever seen. Polished stone, sheer, no adornments, nothing.'

'I see.'

'You don't believe me.'

'On the contrary, I believe every word. I just wish Anne were here.'

Greaves started and swung round to check that Fiona was still asleep.

'Instead of your fiancée?' He was incredulous.

'Instead of both of us. She's my science bod. Well, she is when she wants to be. Anyway… what was down the corridor?'

Greaves laughed. 'Another smaller chamber, but this one contained a map… Well, several in fact.'

'Maps to where? Zerzura?'

Greaves nodded. 'Amongst others. Some strange ones, circles and dots. If they weren't thousands of years old, I would have sworn that they were star maps. Others to tombs near Cairo, back in Saqqara.'

Lethbridge-Stewart kept his own counsel. He knew enough not to discount the idea that ancient Egypt may have had the sort of contact with alien races that Earth was not currently short of.

'And the map to the city?' he asked.

'Yes, I saw that, sketched it, took a couple of Polaroids, as well. Obviously, it's not a trusty Ordnance Survey, but using the maps that I've got of the area, I think I can guide us there.' Greaves' voice dropped. 'It's going to be a bumpy journey, I'm afraid. There's absolutely no guarantee that this thing will even make it there in one piece.'

Lethbridge-Stewart made up his mind to give the Fifth a call when they reached the next oasis and found a room for the night. If there was a chance of getting trapped in the desert, he was going to make damn sure that Colonel Douglas and the rest knew where to start looking. Egyptian Government or no Egyptian Government.

'Did this map say anything about the city itself?'

Greaves fanned himself with his hat, briefly. 'Actually, it did. What do you know about the Contendings of Horus?'

'It's one of my favourites.' Lethbridge-Stewart smiled sideways at Greaves. 'I lie. Fiona's got a knock off pot with the story on. I understand that Horus and Set came to blows over who ruled the gods?'

Greaves pursed his lips and turned his face out to the desert to avoid letting Lethbridge-Stewart see his expression.

'That's one interpretation, yes.' He sighed and scratched his face in an irritated way. 'This is going to need a full monograph when I get back to my studies but, you see, the glyphs around the map gave the impression that Pakhet and Montu fought alongside Horus in his battle with Set.'

'Well, you said they were gods of war. That seems likely, doesn't it?'

'But that's not the point.' Greaves wrung his hat in his hands. 'The gods of Egypt don't really follow a simple straightforward narrative from start to finish, you see them change role and even their entire natures depending on location and time and so on.'

'You've mentioned.' said Lethbridge-Stewart, staring ahead as the road rumbled on beneath their tyres.

'Well, that's the point. Montu and Pakhet have had no previous relationship with Horus and Set. In fact, they're separated from most accounts by over a thousand years. This will drive the Egyptologists crazy.'

'The myths aren't the truth though, are they?' Lethbridge-Stewart raised one eyebrow at Greaves.

'How do you mean?'

'Well, whatever caused the Egyptians to believe in gods and their mythology, it must have been there before them. Something real inspired them, and the priests just copied it and got things wrong. Perhaps the memory of Pakhet and Montu fighting alongside Horus, as they must have done, just wasn't as strong in most of Egypt as it was here.'

'Ancient astronauts, you mean?' Greaves' hand went to the chain on the amulet around his neck. 'Egyptian mythology is a corrupted version of real aliens. That's a theory that has been comprehensively debunked. I could give you a list of actual historians and archaeologists that know about the history and mythology of Egypt and all its contemporaneous civilisations in Mesopotamia, Central America, South America, wherever. None of them would have any truck with the idea of little green men coming down and helping the civilisations that built their cities and temples.'

'Has anyone asked the little green men?'

'I'm sorry, are you telling me that you actually believe this sort of rubbish? Alistair, come on now. You're a much better man than that.'

Lethbridge-Stewart grimaced and gripped the wheel. Official Secrets Act or not, making sure this man knew the possibilities caused by the existence of aliens could be crucial to ensuring that he got all the right information.

'I work somewhat on the edge of official matters.' He paused and checked over his shoulder again. Fiona was still asleep. 'And I have to say that I have received quite a lot of information in my time that indicates that there may well be other intelligences out there.' He was fairly sure that he was skirting the edge of what he could say. At least he hadn't told the other man that robotic Yeti had attacked both the London Underground and New York's subway.

'I see,' was Greaves' only reply.

'Well,' Lethbridge-Stewart said. 'Imagine that the people of Egypt witnessed these extra-terrestrials coming to blows. Seeing a race of men from the sky fighting a war between themselves. Surely that would have some influence on their culture, their art and, most importantly, their mythology.' He thought of the war that he had fought in his sleep, something that he was now convinced was a test, a simulation from this Montu chap sent to him and Mortimer at the very least.

'It could.' Greaves continued to idly twist the chain around his neck that held the scarab amulet. 'Take this, for example, you see the green gemstones?'

Lethbridge-Stewart glanced over and saw them embedded in the scarab's shell. He had seen the stones before in the darkness after the trip to the tomb. Somehow, they now looked duller in the bright sunlight that blazed around them. He nodded sharply and returned his eyes to the road.

'They're made of glass that resulted from a meteorite impact, possibly around the time that Egypt's civilization was just starting. That said, I've always thought that it will protect me. And, up until now, it always has.'

Lethbridge-Stewart shrugged. 'Exactly. Now, we say that it was from a meteorite, and my understanding of that is that they're just something from space that hit the earth hard. I wonder where those little gems came from before they landed in your amulet?'

CHAPTER NINE
New Horizons

IT WAS early in the year and the sun was not at its zenith for long. After lunch, consisting of the least stale flatbread in another roadside shack, Fiona took the driving for an hour or so before Lethbridge-Stewart offered to take back the wheel. The sun was heading for the horizon by the time the jeep was moving again.

'Right,' said Greaves. 'I've come clean about my matinee serial adventure. I think you can tell me where you really found that inscription you showed me.'

Lethbridge-Stewart shrugged. He had nothing further to hide.

'There was a pair of tablets hidden in Dawoud's room. I found them when I searched it.'

Greaves nodded. The reality was that they both knew that this was the answer. With one hand on the wheel, Lethbridge-Stewart reached up into his shirt pocket and handed the folded paper to the man next to him. As Greaves unwrapped it, Lethbridge-Stewart heard Fiona shift in the seat behind.

'You been tracing again, Alistair?' she said.

'You awake, dear?' he called back.

'Mmhmm,' she responded. 'I'm starting to miss the *Keberia*. Murderer and all. At least you could get a good drink. My mouth is dry from the dust.'

'Sorry. We've still got the whisky.'

'Can't wait,' she said, leaning forward. 'So, what does it really say?'

'As I said before,' said Greaves. 'It is mostly a series of promises of revenge on those that steal from Montu's tomb. All very straightforward.'

'There's more, isn't there?' said Lethbridge-Stewart.

Greaves nodded. 'There is.' He took a deep breath and let it out slowly. 'The final line is a warning and an instruction. Montu will follow whoever takes his *ab*, his heart, from him. He will follow that person forever, pursuing them until their heart is weighed against a feather.' He took another breath. 'Death, basically. And the only way to prevent it is to return his heart.' He folded the paper and handed it back to Lethbridge-Stewart. 'And yes, it is geared directly towards the heart. It's a very important thing in the religion of the Egyptians.'

Lethbridge-Stewart risked a glance backwards at Fiona before flicking back to watching the road ahead. She raised both eyebrows at him, sceptical of such a claim. Lethbridge-Stewart was less dismissive.

'You believe that then?' he finally said.

Greaves turned to face both of them. 'I think the key question is, what does Dawoud believe?'

'Damn,' said Lethbridge-Stewart. 'The man must have been on the boat to get that heart.' A thought occurred. 'Wait… Professor?' They were now nearly a day out from Asyut with this man. Had he been the one that had attacked Dawoud?

'I'd never heard of him before the morning after you found him. In any event, if he was after something I owned, don't you think the easiest option for me would be just to have Captain Ibrahim kick him off the vessel? I was the chief attraction for God's sake. You'd think that would give me some clout.'

Lethbridge-Stewart nodded. It made sense to say that. As much as anything did. 'That still doesn't explain what he was up to,' he said. 'Or indeed who wanted to take him out.'

'A secret sect of Montu worshippers?' said Fiona.

Greaves laughed sharply. 'Those only exist in 1930s pulp novels. Think about how many complete changes in Egyptian society they would have had to hide from.' He nodded, almost to himself. 'Dawoud is a Copt, nothing more than that. And it makes sense that, as such, he would perhaps know more about the history of this country. Perhaps legends passed down within the community, but secret sects? Definitely not.'

'Wait.' Lethbridge-Stewart thought back to the search he made of Dawoud's room. 'He had a book. A university textbook from Cairo. It looked like a translator from ancient Egyptian writing to modern Arabic.'

'Ah.' Greaves was silent for a moment.

'Well. Are secret sects more likely in universities?' asked Fiona.

'Only American ones. But one of the professors at Cairo is a little unorthodox.' Greaves clicked his tongue against the roof of his mouth. 'Mariam Salem. She has a tendency to head down some very strange directions in her studies.'

'Or send her students in those directions first, in disguise,' finished Lethbridge-Stewart. 'Any idea why someone would want to kill her students?'

Greaves grinned. 'No one outside of academia. And they'd only resort to that after peer review failed.'

Fiona thought that the Hotel Royale looked like it had never come within a thousand miles of real royalty. No wonder, out there on an oasis.

The Egyptian flag on the pole outside hung limply in the still air, but was clearly tattered and ripped so much that half of it had simply disappeared. Greaves now had the wheel and dragged the jeep across the car park, which was really a simple square of bare rock with gravel and pebbles filling in the larger cracks.

They all jumped out, grabbing for bags and water as they did so. Fiona, as always, took her luggage off Alistair as soon as possible. She was glad, all she wanted now was to wash away the interminable dust. It formed a film that felt like a second skin.

As Greaves led the way toward the hotel's lobby, Alistair suddenly shouted, 'Stop!'

He dropped the bags and walked back to the jeep; he knelt to the side, peering underneath it. Finally, he started rummaging around in the undercarriage, before pulling something free.

'What is that?' asked Fiona, leaning in to look.

It looked like a small grey tube with some sort of magnet on one side. Alistair brushed the dust away from it.

'Radio tracking device,' he said. 'Military issue. Looks like someone wants to know where we're going.'

Fiona and Greaves both stood in silence. There was one name that jumped into her mind.

'Cosgrove,' she said.

Alistair shook his head. 'I doubt it. It's a Russian design.'

'The Soviets? The pair on the boat? What do they want from us?'

Alistair raised one eyebrow. 'I would hazard a guess, nothing. It's an old model. It's been sold on since they last used it. I imagine it's the Egyptian Government that are after us rather than our friends. They tolerate Cosgrove, but they wouldn't work with him to track us.' He tapped the thing against his hand. 'There's enough crossing and double crossing in Cosgrove's world that I don't imagine for a minute that he doesn't know that they are following us.'

Fiona stared at the thing, her mind turning quickly. 'They'll know that we're here.'

Alistair's hand closed around the little metal object; she could see his knuckles whiten as he did so.

'We'll have to stay at another hotel,' he said.

They both turned to face Greaves. He slowly shook his head.

'There isn't one that I know about.' He looked around him, at the plain box-like buildings that made up this little frontier settlement, the dust roads that petered out into the rocks that surrounded.

'Even if there was, they will have tracked us to the town.' Alistair shrugged. 'They can easily find us here.'

'So now what? Wait for a lift back to Cairo and hope for another fix from Cosgrove?' asked Fiona.

Alistair drummed his fingers on the jeep's wing. 'They want us to go into the desert and find this city, or tomb or whatever it is. That's my hunch. If we hang around here too long, we'll be shanghaied before you know it and be heading out there with half the Egyptian security service.' He walked to the back of the jeep and rested his hands on the tents that were stowed there in their canvas bags. 'Sorry, dear. No bath tonight.'

Fiona rubbed at the dust that lined her face. Well, she had

wanted an adventure. She only had herself to blame really.

'Why do you think they want the tomb?' asked Greaves. 'It's probably just a ruin in the desert. My grandfather's diaries were rather sparse on the subject. It would be a miracle if it's still there.' He looked out to the desert, away from the couple. 'I'm only going out there to satisfy my curiosity.'

Alistair slapped the rolled tent one last time. 'I have no idea. I suspect that it's something I won't appreciate when we find out. My real concern is with who put this on the jeep.' He held up the tracker.

'That could have been anyone,' said Fiona. 'We were parked outside the last hotel all night.'

Alistair grimaced and looked at her. He looked both pained and embarrassed at the same time. 'I know,' he said. 'But we were only parked in Asyut for a few minutes after we told someone we trusted where we were going.' He gave a grim smile, without happiness or humour. 'I trusted him too.'

'Azmy.' She barely needed to repeat the name. The little smiling server had been so helpful. And so very competent. Perhaps a little too competent for a steamer whose glory days were behind her.

Alistair nodded. He turned to the hotel. 'Right, assuming that the barmen in there aren't also secret government agents, I need to make a phone call before we set off.'

'A phone call?' Fiona almost choked as she said it. 'Who on earth are you going to call out here?'

His face gave nothing away, except that it had a lot to give away.

'Work. I need a bit of insurance before we head out there…' He nodded at the desert that stretched away to the western horizon. '…in this thing.' He slapped a hand down on the jeep again. Fiona noticed that this time, a flake of paint dropped into the dust.

'You'll need these.' Greaves held up a small wad of notes.

Alistair looked confused. 'Payphones don't take notes,' he said.

Greaves smiled. 'There are no payphones. You'll find that the hotel's only phone won't work until the receptionist has a few of these.'

Alistair grinned, took the notes and strode off towards the

doorway. Fiona watched. He was already starting to act more like an officer.

Inside, the counter was simply a wooden table shielding a bored-looking youth. A wilted yellow plant drifted slightly in the breeze from the ceiling fan that clunked as it revolved.

'Phone?' Lethbridge-Stewart made the appropriate hand signals at the youth who simply smiled and rocked his head from side to side as if sizing the other man up.

Lethbridge-Stewart sighed and handed over a couple of dollar notes, repeating the question. In return, the youth nodded and, reaching below his desk, pulled out a battered Bakelite with a rotary dial.

Lethbridge-Stewart knew the number he needed. As the call connected, he began to breathe easier. He looked over his shoulder. The young man from the reception was still there.

'Scots Guards Special Support Group,' came the voice of Sergeant Jean Maddox.

He knew he had to keep this casual. The youngster didn't appear to understand a word he said, but Lethbridge-Stewart had already been fooled by someone only slightly older than the boy.

'Is Bill there? It's Alistair.'

That surprised the voice at the end of the phone. 'Sir? Is that you?'

'Slight change of plans on our trip. Just want to make sure that Bill knows where we're headed.' He heard the retreating footsteps as Maddox went to find Captain Bishop.

Lethbridge-Stewart's mind worked on overdrive. He had to ensure that Bishop knew what was going on, despite him knowing less than Lethbridge-Stewart did. He heard the phone being picked up.

'Sir…?'

'Bill, good to hear you, I just wanted to update you on our itinerary, my dear fellow.'

'Ah, I see.' Bishop understood immediately. 'Can I speak freely? Can they hear me?'

'Oh, I shouldn't think so.' The Egyptian Government would be doing well to have a wiretap on this phone of all phones. 'The important thing is that we've decided against doing that last thing I told you about this trip.' He crossed his fingers. He really hoped that Bishop would realise that he had never told him anything about this trip before.

'You mean, you're not doing what you're about to tell me. You're doing the complete opposite.'

Lethbridge-Stewart let his genuine smile replace his mask. Bishop was good. One of the best, in fact.

'Absolutely. Now, see here, we've reached the end of the road at the Hotel Royale in this oasis in Dakhla, so we've decided to head back north-east of here.' He gave the bearing. 'Now, you remember how to calculate our destination from that?'

'From what you've said so far, knock off top dart score.' He could imagine Bishop smiling as he said it. He was right, of course, take 180 degrees off that bearing and you would have the line that Greaves had found leading straight to the city.

'Wonderful, old chap. I'll see you soon, I hope. No need to worry if you've not heard anything after three days. I'd give it a week.' *In other words*, Lethbridge-Stewart thought, *come and find us if we haven't checked in after three days.*

'Duly noted, sir. Stay out of trouble.'

Lethbridge-Stewart replaced the receiver. He had no idea how much an international call was from this country. He dropped another couple of dollars down just to be sure that he'd covered it.

Off the road, the going was much worse. Greaves took the wheel, but his inexperience at handling desert driving was telling as they struggled to crest some of the smaller dunes or slipped sideways down the edges of the larger ones.

'Just think, this thing must have played a role in the North African campaign, eh?' he shouted over at Lethbridge-Stewart.

'The North African campaign was fought by tanks. Not by battered jeeps,' replied Lethbridge-Stewart. 'Try going around the dunes and—'

The jeep launched itself partially into the air. Lethbridge-Stewart left his seat for a split second and heard the luggage leap and resettle behind him. Fiona gave a grunt of discomfort.

'You could also aim to miss the rocks,' Lethbridge-Stewart

added.

Greaves eventually followed the advice and began following his bearings less slavishly. Conversation thus became easier.

'I can't stop thinking of Azmy,' said Fiona eventually. 'If he planted that tracker, what else was he up to?'

Lethbridge-Stewart frowned and turned back to her. He would have joined her in the rear, but it was no time to reorganise the luggage and make space.

'He was the man that turned up after I found Dawoud in the boiler. I wonder if he put him there. And, if he did, was it anything more than to put the frighteners on the poor fellow?'

'You mean, he was coming back to let him out when you appeared anyway?'

Lethbridge-Stewart nodded. 'That would make sense. Clearly, they both have some kind of interest in the city of Zerzura. So, one of them tries to scare the other one away.'

'Right,' said Fiona. 'What do both of them want with some lost city?'

Lethbridge-Stewart paused, looking out at the shifting landscape as the oasis shrank away far in the distance and the rocky desert opened out in front of them, inviting them further in.

'Who knows?' he said brightly. 'Do you know, I rather think that the Egyptian Government probably just want to make sure they know where it is. After all, it's their cultural heritage. As for Dawoud, well maybe Professor Salem wants to get there before the government?' Lethbridge-Stewart laughed, knowing he was forcing it, just to try and calm Fiona down. 'The most religious and the most nationalist tend to go crazy first I think.' He thought for a second. 'That's probably why Mortimer jumped in the river.'

'It's not all connected then?' Fiona sounded slightly more certain, more confident all of a sudden.

Lethbridge-Stewart raised one eyebrow, a gesture he knew that she loved. 'Of course not. Conspiracies tend to unravel much easier than they come together. Right now, we can leave the Egyptian police to sort it all out. I'm sure they will once May and Tabitha stop trying to pin a murder on everyone.'

'That sounds fantastic, Alistair,' said Fiona. 'Can I ask one thing for the rest of this trip?'

'Of course.'

'That you don't lie again to try and make me feel better.'

She turned away so that he faced only her blonde hair. Lethbridge-Stewart didn't want to let her into what he was really concerned about. If Fiona thought that he was mad, the wedding may never happen at all.

'Do you think this is far enough yet?' asked Greaves.

Lethbridge-Stewart stood up on the rocking, swaying jeep and looked back across the desert behind them. They had covered several miles of rocky landscape, leaving barely a trace of a tyre track as they went. The oasis was now completely out of sight. Tracking them was going to be very difficult and the sun was now starting to drift quickly towards the horizon, as the dune shadows lengthened around them.

'Let's stop,' he called, fearful of losing the light.

It was nearly dark by the time the tents were up.

Lethbridge-Stewart decided to risk a small fire as the temperature plummeted. It was too little too late for Fiona, who kissed him with a short stiff embrace before retreating into bed, leaving him and Greaves sitting on a pair of boulders, staring at the thin flames that licked around their meagre firewood. They poured the whisky into mugs. The warming glow of the whisky as it slid down gave Lethbridge-Stewart a slight twinge of regret that this wasn't a more pleasant holiday all round. He could really have enjoyed a malt like this.

He poked at the fire with a stick, waiting for Fiona's breathing from the tent to settle into a rhythmic rise and fall. He took a deep drink of the whisky and held it in his mouth before he pushed Greaves further.

'So, I'm assuming that we can agree that Azmy may have dropped Dawoud in the boiler. But that leaves a lot else that has happened. The man that attacked us all by the tombs, whatever knocked me unconscious in the temple, how Mortimer went into the river. I'm starting to wonder if these aren't all connected with each other. And, also, with the lynchpin to both Dawoud and Azmy.' He nodded towards the jar, sat with the rest of Greaves' gear, just within reach of the archaeologist. The god's heart.

Greaves sat hunched on his boulder, staring at the fire as the wood cracked and spat. Finally, he spoke. 'You're familiar with the works of Arthur Conan Doyle?'

Lethbridge-Stewart smiled, thinking back to his childhood in Bledoe.

'Somewhat. I read most of his Holmes stories when I was a child. How are some old detective stories relevant?'

Greaves blew air between his teeth. 'Doyle's published work, I understand, was not always entirely fictional. He changed the names, but a lot of what happened was based very much on fact.'

'Sherlock Holmes was real?'

'Oh no. Not quite. The original detective that Doyle wrote about had a very different name and several other aspects that were much less palatable to the Victorian audience than even copious amounts of opium.' Greaves tapped the jar that sat next to him. 'It was just an example. In any event, he wrote other stories. Including one about a mummy.'

Lethbridge-Stewart hadn't heard of it and indicated as much with a short shake of his head.

'It's the original mummy-comes-to-life story. Some Oxford bod keeps it in his room and, of course, strange things happen. The interesting thing is that in that story, unlike many that came after it, the mummy doesn't move. Instead, its spirit roams the rooms and corridors of Oxford, attacking those that its master wants out of his way. It follows people down deserted lanes.' Greaves tapped the jar again. 'The mummy isn't the corpse. It's the spirit of the corpse.'

Lethbridge-Stewart fixed his eyes on that little jar, the bull's head and horns sat atop it. Suddenly, they looked even more life-like, the representation of something within. He took another drink. It felt like he was going to need it.

'Also based on fact?'

Greaves nodded.

'How do you know if this has the same…?' Lethbridge-Stewart searched for the word. 'Manifestation?'

'This has been in our family for a long time. It is somewhat of a curse. There are a lot of stories, you see. A lot of staff went running from the house with no reason. It almost became a running joke. When dinner was late, people would ask if the curse had got the cook.' Greaves paused, stared out at nothing but emptiness in front of him, firelight reflecting in his eyes.

Lethbridge-Stewart breathed in. He knew there was more to this than a few stories.

'It's more than a joke now. Tell me more.'

Greaves swallowed. 'My brother. I told you he died recently. I found him in a forest near our house. He must have been up that tree for… I don't know how long. Hopefully only an hour or so.' He breathed in again and let the air flow back out slowly, as if trying to steady his breathing. 'I don't like to think of him hanging there in the cold.'

'You said he died, but you never said…'

Greaves turned away. 'We went through his belongings, of course, trying to find a reason, any reason, why he would have done such a thing. We found his diary.' He poked at the fire. 'I didn't want to read it, but forced myself. I needed to know what had happened.'

'And…?'

'And it told me a lot. He had been followed for months. Always the same. Footsteps behind him, like the stories. When he turned, there was nothing. But there was a voice. One that spoke to him. This figure would appear without warning in his room, waiting behind the dark corners on the way home. It had chased him home more than once.' Greaves looked pointedly at Lethbridge-Stewart. 'It wanted him to fight a war. To command troops. My brother was a pacifist. He wanted no part. So, he took the only way out he knew. Not a coward's way. A brave man's way. I'm proud of him.'

It wanted him to fight a war. Lethbridge-Stewart knew then that the power inside that jar, that had tortured Greaves' brother, was the same that had been visiting him in his own sleep. It had visited Mortimer too. More than that, it was the thing that had followed him, knocked him out in the tomb. He could feel the rage build up inside him. He felt like the thing was inside him.

'Why did you bring that thing onto the boat?' The chill settled on his spine despite the desert heat and the fire. 'And why did you not warn us before you brought us out here on this fool's errand? That thing is a danger to all of us. To Fiona and to me.' He realised, as Greaves shrank back from him, that his fists had clenched.

'I'm a poor scholar. My father wouldn't pay for an expedition like this, so I had to find someone else that would. I was just lucky to find that the consortium that owns that boat were planning an archaeological tour. A way to bring in the tourists.' Greaves shrugged. 'It seemed like a good idea. Work my way up the river, and then head out into the Western Desert.' He sighed. 'You see. I need to find Montu's tomb. I need to return his heart.'

'Because the tablet says that you need to return it,' Lethbridge-Stewart finished for him.

Greaves moved one of the logs closer to the centre, the better to make it burn quicker. 'Not that tablet. I knew it existed, of course, and I had read a transcription at my college. That's how I translated it so quickly. But Dawoud, or Professor Salem, must have another with the same text.' He drummed his fingers on his mug.

'Who is this professor? A woman. Teaching in the Arabic world. Not usual.'

'She's very unusual. She specialises in the very ancient history of Egypt. A very murky area that can give a careless archaeologist a free reign to make up what they like. Not my style at all. I much prefer the Middle Kingdom. The bureaucrats and middle classes of that era led fascinating lives.'

'Professor,' said Lethbridge-Stewart. 'What about Salem.'

'Sorry.' The man grimaced, like a schoolboy that has been caught out. 'She has some strange ideas. About civilisations that existed before the Old Kingdom. That rivalled it. Not many take her seriously but her students are notorious. They believe every word. And they can get very fanatical. I've come across them at conferences.' Greaves grinned. 'They are very irritating. I wonder if Dawoud is one of them and that's why he's chasing this city.'

'And what about me? Why am I here?'

Greaves looked at Lethbridge-Stewart curiously. 'You're the only man on that boat that I trust. I'm afraid that I'm going to need your skills to get to that tomb. You see, I'm just a simple scholar. I couldn't make it all the way across the desert to that city.' He looked up at Lethbridge-Stewart. 'I'm very glad you came by the way, it's a massive load off my mind.'

'Why didn't you just smash and burn the damn thing?' Lethbridge-Stewart snapped.

'Do you know what would happen to the spirit inside if I did that?'

'No.' Lethbridge-Stewart gave a curt response.

'No,' agreed Greaves. 'Neither do I. But I can't imagine it would be a pleasant experience for anyone concerned.'

Lethbridge-Stewart sat, staring at the pot, his mind turning.

Greaves' brother was dead; hung himself in terror of a stalker. Mortimer had screamed and jumped into the river when no one else was looking, as if the man had lost all control of his mind.

Like the camel handler that had, suddenly, started taking shots at the group.

Lethbridge-Stewart remembered the man's last words. *Montu.*

It had got to him too. Lethbridge-Stewart dropped his mug as he jumped to his feet, anger coursing through him again. He marched at the jar, getting close before Greaves put his hand out, getting to his own feet.

'What are you doing?'

'It needs to go in the fire. It manipulates and tests people. And when they are found wanting…' Lethbridge-Stewart realised that his fists were whitening. '…When it finds them wanting, it twists their minds to destroy themselves.'

'Then I've got two questions for you.'

'I've got a lot more for you,' snarled Lethbridge-Stewart.

'How strong is your mind, and why would it find you wanting?'

Lethbridge-Stewart took a step back. 'Strong enough,' he said. 'But for how long?' He dropped his voice, turning back to the tent where Fiona lay sleeping. He thought of her, excited to be joining him on her own adventure. Every time he tried to summon Fiona's face in front of him, Sally's would appear instead. The look he remembered as they broke off their engagement, sad but almost accusing as she walked away. He could still remember the scratches on the table in that Edinburgh pub, the lights in the window.

This trip was too dangerous. He couldn't possibly lose Fiona as well.

Yet, by sending her away, he could well end up losing her anyway.

'Why aren't you affected?' He tried not to snarl the words.

Greaves held up the amulet, pulled it from his shirt. 'Remember when I told you about this?'

Lethbridge-Stewart nodded in recognition. 'An amulet that seems to protect the wearer, made out of rocks that fell from space. What I wouldn't give for a detailed report from Anne on that thing. After she's chopped it up of course.'

'You'll be waiting a long time. I'm going to keep it with me until we've dealt with this thing once and for all.'

In the silence that followed, Lethbridge-Stewart drained his mug. He forced his thoughts to more practical matters.

'Someone needs to watch this camp. Look out for the government.' He gritted his teeth. 'Or ancient vengeful spirits.'

Greaves sighed and stretched. 'Well, I'm old, so I need less sleep. I'll take the first watch. You need the rest, my friend.'

Lethbridge-Stewart knew the older man was right. He checked his watch. 'Agreed. Six hours each should be sufficient.' He turned towards the tent.

CHAPTER TEN
Dreams Come True

IT FELT like an age before Lethbridge-Stewart finally dropped off and nearly an instant later before Greaves woke him for his watch by reaching through the tent flap to shake a leg.

Lethbridge-Stewart must have had some sleep, because he was able to sit awake under the stars as the others slept. Out there the sky was scattered with bright points, blurring in places to patches, giving the dunes and boulders a thin sheen of silver light. He stood and started pacing around the campsite. The slightest tap of a stone against his foot echoed.

He paused. The tapping continued.

He froze, listening. The sound was solid, not fading. As he stood, listening, trying to place it, it stopped. He tried to focus on which direction it had come from.

'Hello?' he called, turning around. There was no answer, no sign of anyone else in the dim light. He held his breath, listening for any sound, hearing nothing.

He started walking again, taking care to keep his feet moving as softly and quietly as possible. The tapping came again, from behind him. He spun, walked directly to where the sound was coming from.

It stopped again. Then he realised that it was still coming, again from behind him. He turned constantly, searching for the source of the sound. It was always behind him. The steps were getting louder now.

Warrior.

The voice came instantly, only a single, deep tone that sat just behind his right ear.

'That's not my name.' He spoke softly. 'My name is

Lethbridge-Stewart.' This was no dream. He had all of his faculties, no confusion, no dread. 'You, I imagine, are Montu.' The other made no direct reply.

I will name you if you fight for me.

A hint of disapproval, even anger was in that voice now.

'And if I don't?' He already knew the answer to that. He had seen it struggling in the Nile.

The threat didn't come. The voice seemed to move around him, as if the being was walking around, surveying him from every direction. He still couldn't see anything except the tents, the jeep and the desert sands.

Are you one of them? it asked.

'One of who?' Lethbridge-Stewart rejoined.

The ones that stay constant, as the timelines shift. Like buildings as the sands blow. The landscape and even the roads that lead to them change, but they remain the same.

'And who are you?' Lethbridge-Stewart had no desire to play this game.

Maybe you are one, maybe not. But you are certainly connected with one. Maybe it has rubbed off on you. Maybe you and he are pulled together.

Lethbridge-Stewart felt like a new specimen being considered at an animal market.

'You seem to think you know a lot about me,' he said. 'What about you, Montu?' He felt a shudder through the still, dark air as he said the name. It was good to know that he was on the right lines.

To you, I am a god.

He felt the air blow, as if a wind was picking up. Particles of sand brushed against him.

'To me?' Lethbridge-Stewart said. 'And what would you be to someone else?' Silence. 'Alien? A space traveller?'

There was a murmur.

I travelled far to get here, it said.

'And what would you be to your own kind?' This was a dangerous step. But Lethbridge-Stewart had to know exactly what he was dealing with. What was this thing? 'A leader? A general?' The wind increased. 'A soldier?' It was whipping at his face now. 'A slave?'

With the wind came a roar, strong enough that his eyes

were forced shut as sand was blasted against his face. He pulled them open, as, for the first time, light flashed, a flicker like a strobe light. And then he saw the outline. Just two feet from his face and towering above him, was a bull's head, huge and black.

Then the light shut off and he was lying down in the sand. He felt the grains down the back of his shirt and looked at the sky. No more stars, but he could see a red flickering light creeping across it from the east. Sunrise.

He pulled himself to his feet, swaying slightly. His hand went to his watch. Five hours since he had started his lookout, but there was no sign of anyone around him. The campsite was exactly as should be.

There was a sound, movement, to his right. Instantly, he crouched down, his hand going to his waist before he realised that the only weapon was still in the jeep. Nearly ten metres away.

He tensed before he realised what the noise was, canvas shifting as a man climbed out of a tent.

'Well, I won't be able to sleep in this light,' said Greaves as he emerged. 'You might as well get yourself another hour.'

Lethbridge-Stewart accepted gratefully and pulled himself back to the tent.

Laying down inside, he felt Fiona's body pushed against his. He lay still, seeing the faint dim light of pre-dawn filter through the thin tent material. There was no other sound, the desert outside still and quiet.

He had finally spoken to Montu. Clearly, it was some sort of alien, although he doubted it would do him the courtesy of telling him where it was from.

The thing had become so angry at the mere suggestion that it was simply a follower, a slave. He was no psychologist, but he could almost swear that the creature had some sort of aversion to being seen as simply one of the crowd. It wanted to be a big fish in a small pond. Better for it to be the god Montu than to simply be one of many soldiers of whichever army it had fought for.

It was a soldier. That much was clear. It was testing for warriors in what appeared to be the most twisted recruitment drive Lethbridge-Stewart had ever encountered. A sly smile crossed his face. He seemed to be doing reasonably well. He wondered how the rest of his command would fare. If anything would make an alien recruitment sergeant give up and go and take up gardening, being faced with Corporal Evans would be top of the list.

Lethbridge-Stewart must have started to actually laugh, because Fiona stirred, her arm stretching over him.

'A shame we're in a tent with Greaves nearby,' she whispered in his ear.

He rolled back to look at her. Even when waking up from a night on the hard sand, blonde hair in a tangled halo, she still reminded him why he had fallen for her.

Then he remembered what he had to do today. What he had to say now, before it was too late. Especially now with an enemy that may well want him dead and anyone else with him. That enemy that had grabbed him, sunk its claws into his own heart.

He had to protect her.

'Fiona,' he said, taking her hand in his as he stared across at her. He pulled himself upright in the tent. 'I think we may have an interruption.'

'What can be more of an interruption than this?' She gestured at the tent they now sat side by side in.

'I need to keep going into the desert. You need to go back to the oasis, the hotel,' he said it. Those words effectively brought their planned adventure to an end. 'It won't always be like this. But this could end up related to work. There may be problems as we get closer to the border.'

'What?' Her eyes were awake now, focused on him. 'What is happening out there?'

'I can't say. My call at the hotel yesterday, it confirmed it. Out there in the desert is something that I need to deal with.' He took a deep breath. It was a lie, he knew. 'I need to go. It goes back to when I was stationed in Libya as CO.'

'You need to tell me what you do.' A statement.

He tried to ignore it and sighed. 'You know I can't. There's some help on its way for you. I'll make sure that Cosgrove comes up, too.'

'To look after me while you run off?' Fiona took a deep breath, throwing the sleeping bag off and turning to her bag to rummage for some clothes. 'Alistair. It's too damn early to have this discussion. At least let me get some coffee first.'

Outside, the sand dazzled in the brightness of the morning sun, casting sharp shadows from dunes and rock.

'Good to see the two of you up and about,' called Greaves. Fiona could see that he was already reclining against a sand dune, as if sunbathing. The small fire was burning again, and he had rigged up a stand for the kettle. 'You're just in time.'

He was right, the steam was rushing from the spout and the thing seemed to be on the verge of whistling. She looked meaningfully at Alistair. He took the hint and started ladling spoons of the military grade instant coffee into three mugs. She took one, holding her hands around it. The sun may have been up but, right now, the desert remained cold.

'I suppose you're cleared to keep going?' she said to Greaves. 'It's just me that has to go back.'

The man at least had the decency to look embarrassed. 'I know how to get to the tomb,' he mumbled.

She turned to Alistair. 'Right. I will go back. You will take me, and I will find my own way back to Asyut. It will take Cosgrove an age and a day to get here. I'll need the rest of your dollars to pay my way.'

Alistair looked lost for a second, before his brisk manner asserted itself. 'Excellent, we'll get started and Professor Greaves can start packing up the camp.'

'I hadn't finished.' Fiona took a deep breath. 'I know that it's got to be like this. That's the way with the Army. They snap, you jump.' He nodded. He probably didn't even know he was doing it. 'I also know that you're in an administrative role. This sort of thing won't happen back home.' She looked at his face. Did it fall then, just for a moment? 'This is our first holiday together. I need to know that you are going to make this up to me. We go on to Luxor. We do not get interrupted again. Please, I know you have to go where you are ordered, but this last week has been the most frustrating time I have ever spent with you.'

She searched his eyes, those dark yet bright and oh-so-serious eyes that would occasionally twinkle with a mischievous glimmer when he managed to forget himself long enough to let his guard down. They were hollow, giving nothing away. It was like the Army had called and now the mask was up.

'Of course. That's exactly what we'll do.'

Alistair's voice was almost hollow as he said the words. *Be the lady* she heard. It was already becoming a hard creed to live by. His world suddenly had no room for her in it.

'Right,' Fiona said. 'You can pack. I'm going to take one last look at this desert we were so desperate to get to.' She turned and set off up a nearby dune, feet sliding down and shoes filling with sand as she forced herself to make it to the top and take in the ruby dawn that had woken them.

From the rise, she could see the dunes spreading before her like waves on a sea. She breathed in, feeling the cold air flooding in, calming her breathing.

'Fiona.'

The voice behind and below her sounded uncertain and out of condition. She knew that it was Greaves before she turned to see him, scrabbling up towards her, occasionally falling forwards as he did so.

'How can I help you, Professor?'

He reached the same level as her, the sand dropping off his jacket in the still air.

'I just…' He sighed, looking embarrassed. 'I wanted to talk to you. It's not as easy travelling across Egypt as it can be at home. You've got a long way to go to get back. The roads aren't easy to navigate, and they can be dangerous. And, well… you're…?' It was as if he couldn't bring himself to say it.

'A woman?' she suggested.

'That's it.'

She sighed. What did he expect her to be?

'So, it's too dangerous to go with you and too dangerous to go back. Any suggestions?'

'I… Look. I don't know what the background is between the two of you, but I think you should consider waiting for your friend when you get back to the oasis. At the hotel.'

Fiona noticed that Greaves was looking down, away from her. The man clearly wasn't lying, but then she realised. He was simply all but incapable of speaking to a woman. He must have spent his whole life speaking to either other male archaeologists or male locals on site and the biggest interaction with a woman would be to an audience at one of his tours or lectures. She felt almost sorry for the man.

'I'll see if I can find somewhere. Thank you for your concern.'

He shifted and went to back off and walk back down the dune. Then he stopped and turned back to face her.

'Actually, there is one more thing.' He reached behind his neck and unhooked the chain that was holding something around his neck. He held it out to her.

She reached out and took the beautifully carved and jewelled scarab beetle.

'This was taken from the same dig that my grandfather brought back many of his treasures. It's a scarab. It brings protection. Please, take it.'

'You'll need more protection than me.' Fiona made to push the thing away.

'I've got it.' Greaves nodded down the hill towards where Alistair was emptying the tent. 'This is my compensation to you for depriving you of him.'

Slowly, she took it off him and, as her hands closed around the little beetle, she felt a sense of comfort, like her mother had just scooped her up in her arms after a fall.

'Thank you,' she said, looking at Greaves, at once uncertain but so enthusiastic for the things he cared about. 'I know it means a lot to you.'

He gave a half-hearted shrug. 'It is the least I can do, for leaving you in this position. Please don't be angry at Alistair.' Greaves rubbed his cheek absently. 'He is simply doing his duty. As best he can.'

It was an hour later that they set off from the campsite in the jeep.

Behind them, Greaves worked on striking the campsite and kicking the sand across the fire to ensure there was no trace that they had been here. Alistair had been careful to take a clear bearing of the city so that he could find the place again and pick up Greaves on his return.

Fiona had no idea why the other man couldn't simply come with them back to the town, but Alistair seemed adamant. More things she wasn't being told, things that she would never know.

The journey back to civilisation was an easier one than Greaves had brought them on to escape. Alistair had clearly far less faith in the jeep's abilities than Greaves had. He took it around each dune and rock formation, the compass propped up on the dashboard acting as his guide both to and from the little hotel at the end of the road.

They stayed silent for the journey. It was as if the sudden shift in Alistair's purpose had changed their entire relationship. She tried to remember what she knew of Libya. There had been trouble not long ago, Gaddafi had seized power from the King. Not long after Alistair had been called away suddenly. It had calmed down since of course.

Or had it? That had to be part of the reason. She shuddered, despite the growing heat. Some of these new regimes that had taken over the older empire colonies could be brutal. Especially to the British.

'You'll be careful, won't you?' she said.

Alistair looked across at her. The terrain had flattened out now and the town was once more in sight. 'I'll do what needs to be done.'

'That's a "no" then?' Once she would have put some amusement in her voice, even if it wasn't justified, however, here and now, his taking risks with his own life was simply not a joke anymore.

'I'll come back,' he said.

'In one piece?'

'In as many pieces as you leave me in.'

At that, she finally gave in and giggled. 'Am I really more terrifying than whatever is waiting for you in that desert?' The thought gave her some comfort. That if she were really worse, he could come to no harm.

He paused.

'Absolutely,' he finally said. It was just slightly too late to convince.

The hotel was the same as it had been when they were last

there, the same dust that filled the car park and coated the few vehicles, the same slowly spinning fan in the reception and the same bored teenager behind the desk.

Alistair immediately picked up the phone, directing Fiona to the bar. She entered. The shutters were down on the bar itself, which was only to be expected. The lounge had clearly once been luxurious, but now it contained just a few scattered tables and threadbare pouffes across a floor once smooth but now cracked and undulating. She dropped into one pouffe, putting her feet up on the nearest chair; she could feel it rocking back and forth on its misshapen legs.

Alistair entered.

'I've called Cosgrove,' he said. 'He will be along as soon as he can. He hopes by today.'

She felt herself nod. 'Why…?' she began speaking then swallowed. 'Why didn't you contact him yesterday? He could have arrived here by now.'

Her fiancé was silent. He opened his mouth to reply to her. She stopped him.

'Truthfully, please, Alistair,' she said.

He dropped into the chair next to her, his head back and staring at the ceiling where flies hopped between a broken fan and the crumbling plaster.

'Last night was when I realised that I couldn't bring you into the desert. That was when I truly understood the risk.' He sighed.

'What risk?' Just asking was putting him in a difficult position, she knew. He put his hands over his face and groaned before turning his face towards her.

'I can't say. Something incredibly sensitive.' He sounded pained.

'Something to do with Greaves' lost city?' She knew by the look on his face that it must have been.

'Please…' he said. 'Please don't put me in this position.'

She folded her arms. 'Why? Is it worse than being in a shoddy hotel in the middle of nowhere, on your own, no transport and relying on the least trustworthy man in Egypt to get you home?'

Alistair's face fell. She knew from his expression that this wasn't what he wanted.

'Duty is everything to you, isn't it?' She made his point for him. He nodded, slightly.

'It was. Before I met you.' As he spoke, she knew that he was remembering that night in the hotel in England when they had finally met after years of prompting from her cousin.

'I'm not just a temporary transgression you know, Alistair. I'm here for good.' She tried to keep her voice level, and kindly. She knew she was failing.

He leaned over, took her hand from the fold of her arm despite initial resistance.

'You're not. You make this more difficult than it has ever been before.' His voice cracked.

She let her hand rest on his. 'Do you think it's difficult enough yet?' As she met his eyes, she couldn't help but smile.

This man was so dedicated to his job and his service that he would always put it before everything. As he should. But his love for her was strong enough that he was now in agony about it. She squeezed his hand and lent closer to kiss him.

For now, that was enough.

CHAPTER ELEVEN
New Day

THE RETURN to the camp was just as frenetic as the previous night.

Without Fiona to look after and with the knowledge that the government might be closing in on him at any moment, Lethbridge-Stewart pushed the poor jeep to its limit as the wheels span on the dunes, throwing sand across the rock outcroppings in lumps. With each crested dune, the bonnet of the jeep pitched down, and Lethbridge-Stewart felt his stomach lurch as if he was about to fall before the vehicle's momentum caught up and threw it down.

Across flatter sections, he slammed his foot onto the metal. He could feel the vehicle's clutch protest as it was flung forward. He kept the same bearing as he flew along the boulder strewn landscape, aiming back to the camp. Now, more than ever, he needed to pick up Greaves and then to get out into the desert.

Lethbridge-Stewart felt infected. The thing that was stalking him, getting inside his head, was like something he had caught. Something that could make him hurt Fiona. He screwed his eyes up briefly and punched the metal of the steering wheel with the bottom of his fist. He cursed his own mind. Somehow, having a fiancée again made Lethbridge-Stewart think of what had happened, like an old wound that twinged when the air was cold. Sally would always be there, sleeping in his mind, reminding him of the risks that he faced.

Would he ever be able to let his guard down? He thought back to the last time he could remember being able to truly open up in a relationship. It could have been… No, that last time in Brighton was gone now.

It was as Lethbridge-Stewart was lost in the memory that a sudden bang brought him to the present. The jeep had crested the peak of another dune. As it rolled down the other side, he heard a thump followed by a rattle. The noise continued while he floored the accelerator and the jeep gradually picked up the pace again. He swore. The last thing he needed was an issue with the jeep.

Lethbridge-Stewart pulled to a halt, letting the dust cloud that he had brought with him clear. He sighed and went to check the rear of the jeep. The chassis was fine, no roll bars were loose, no problems with the canopy, which was fortunate as the sun slowly climbed to its zenith. He checked the back seats as well: some water barrels, a good supply of petrol.

He looked under the seats to check that the rifle was still strapped there. Then his heart skipped. There was a small, barrel shaped object, wrapped in old linen resting there. He knew it immediately. It was the same size and shape as the jar that Greaves had been carrying, the same that had sat between the two of them at the campfire yesterday. It was the jar that contained the Heart of Montu.

Had it somehow followed him?

Biting his lip, Lethbridge-Stewart reached under the seat and brought it out. In his hands, the thing weighed almost nothing.

Taking the thin cloth between finger and thumb, holding his breath, he unwrapped the linen. As he did so, he gritted his teeth and looked around him. If it had followed him, then the shade that had stalked him, that had spoken to him, that had killed Mortimer, could have done as well. Yet, here he was, out in the desert with no one else for miles.

Lethbridge-Stewart peeled off the last layer and looked down at the object.

Then he laughed. It was the hideous fake jar that Fiona had found in the souq in Cairo. The one that Cosgrove had claimed showed a copy of the Contendings of Horus. The thing must have fallen from her luggage and got jammed under the seat, only working its way loose and rolling around when he had started heading back into the desert.

He wrapped the damn thing up and wedged it into the front footwell. He needed to remember to give it back to Fiona the minute he saw her again. Maybe he should try to find some rice to put in it, show her that, despite the demands of this daft old jar's doppelgänger, he really couldn't wait to build a home with her.

Lethbridge-Stewart stood, straightening his back after the morning's bumpy ride. This wasn't going to get any easier, especially with the sun climbing. He could already feel the sweat pooling in the small of his back.

He paused again, his heart beating fast once more. There, in the distance but close enough to worry, was another plume of dust. The sort that could only be made by a vehicle.

A vehicle that appeared to be heading straight for the camp where Greaves waited for him. Lethbridge-Stewart reached below the seat, rummaging for the rifle. He checked the breach and satisfied himself that the thing was loaded. Good. Safety engaged, he placed it in the passenger side.

Ahead, he could see that the plume had stopped and was fading in the desert wind. He was sure that it was on the exact spot in which Greaves waited.

As it faded and settled back to the ground, like a collapsing shroud, Lethbridge-Stewart gunned the engine again and slammed the pedal down.

The camp grew closer and closer, and Lethbridge-Stewart found his hand reaching for the rifle. He was sure that, somehow, the Egyptian authorities had found their way to their camp. That was the only conceivable group that could have found them, despite his finding the radio tracker.

Should he stop here and approach on foot? No. They would likely have seen him coming and when they saw him, he would be trapped on foot. He needed to find Greaves and the jar, if he could. Then they both had to get away as quickly as possible.

One last set of dunes stood in his way. Lethbridge-Stewart circled them, coming into the camp from the south-west, the better to get back out into the desert afterwards. Finally, at the last moment, he revved the engine, sliding sideways into the space in which the tents had been, and braked with a tug on the handbrake.

Lethbridge-Stewart crouched below the windscreen as the dust and sand cleared, the rifle in his hand and safety off.

He saw the vehicle first, a battered old truck, rusted and dented that started as a dark silhouette before resolving. His tent was next, still standing. He could see no sign of Greaves.

Lastly, the various figures stood around became clear; all young, dressed in a western style, but conservatively. He knew from their hair length and facial hair that they weren't military. They held various weapons: old British, German and American rifles. Shotguns, a revolver, newer Russian models. The men were strung out around the campsite as if they had been searching, some in the open, some behind boulders, with no cohesive effort by them to surround the jeep. They were, without doubt, a group of armed amateurs.

Which made them dangerous in Lethbridge-Stewart's eyes. For a start, unlike soldiers, these men were completely unpredictable.

'Where is it?' shouted a voice. It had a familiar edge. He turned to it, keeping the rifle ready.

'Where is what?' Lethbridge-Stewart snapped.

'The heart.'

The dust had cleared enough now that Lethbridge-Stewart could see who was speaking. The man at the centre, crouched behind the bonnet of the truck, holding a revolver. A revolver, even among a group as disparate and ill-formed as this one, usually meant a leader.

But it was the man's face that gave Lethbridge-Stewart his biggest shock. It was a face he had seen before, firstly in the restaurant of *Keberia*, then later, streaked with soot, in the vessel's engine room.

The leader of this group was Dawoud. He imagined the rest of them were fellow students.

'What do you want with it?' Lethbridge-Stewart chose his words carefully.

'You have it then?'

As the reply came, Lethbridge-Stewart scanned the group in front of him. Seven men. Maybe more were hidden where he couldn't see them. He would be doing well to make even a dent in their numbers if this came to a firefight.

'Answer my question, and I'll answer yours,' he called back.

'You know the answer. You searched my room, Mr

Lethbridge-Stewart.' There was still a slight edge of panic to Dawoud's voice. That was, of course, a worry. A panicked man could easily pull the trigger, and then the rest of his goons would no doubt jump to it with him. Then Lethbridge-Stewart's jeep would be riddled with holes from bullets and shells.

'I was trying to help,' Lethbridge-Stewart said. 'I was trying to find out why someone wanted to kill you.'

'I am very grateful, Mr Lethbridge-Stewart, for helping me out of that firebox. Your argument would have more weight, I think, if you were not pointing a gun at me.'

As Dawoud spoke, Lethbridge-Stewart scanned the ground in front of him, risking the occasional glance to the front and side. He could see no further men hidden. Then, out of the corner of his eye, he saw a quick movement in a dune to his right, sand tumbling down from a hollow that had been dug, facing away from the armed men.

'And I am a reasonable man,' Dawoud continued. 'If you give me the heart now, then I will let you go. I have no quarrel with you.'

Lethbridge-Stewart's attention was on that hollow and the familiar face that peered out of the dune. How Greaves knew how to hide like that was a mystery.

A new voice cut in. Female. 'We must have Montu's heart.'

She stepped from behind the truck. A western trouser suit, but with a headscarf. Lethbridge-Stewart guessed he had found Professor Mariam Salem.

'Why?' Lethbridge-Stewart called back.

She sighed, holding her head to the side. 'It's taken three years to teach this lot. And they know the language. I really haven't got time. Just break the habit of your nation and do as you're told.'

Lethbridge-Stewart saw the rest of the men crouch and tense, as if ready to spring into action. He had to accept that he had very few cards here. His eyes flicked around, looking for a way out of this, before alighting on the package, still wrapped, in the passenger footwell.

Outside the jeep, he could hear safeties being unclicked and chambers being filled. Maybe he could outrun the old truck in this jeep. His vehicle was certainly better built for the terrain, but he needed a head start of not being shot at.

'I have it,' he finally said.

There was a stir of excitement among the gathered men.

'Then give it here,' called Salem. 'It is essential that we have it.'

Lethbridge-Stewart transferred the rifle trigger to his left hand and left the barrel balanced on the door of the jeep, pointing at Dawoud behind the truck's bonnet. He reached across the handbrake to the passenger footwell. There he felt the reassuring round object that was the jar from the bazaar. He pulled it back to himself and held it up, briefly, like a magician showing his cards, before pulling it back down to his chest and taking the rifle in both hands again.

'It's here,' he called. 'If you want it, I'll throw it to that sand dune there.' He pointed over at another large dune to his left, far away from the nearest man. 'Then I'll drive away, and we can both be happy. You will understand if I can't trust you entirely. But you have hidden rather a lot from me already.'

'That is because this isn't your fight, Mr Lethbridge-Stewart,' said Salem.

Tell that to Montu, Lethbridge-Stewart thought. 'Here,' he called, quickly bowling the jar in a classic underarm movement that saw it arc out and over to the dunes. The eyes of the men followed it and so didn't see Lethbridge-Stewart turn to the dune to his left and motion to the occupant.

He needn't have bothered, Greaves was already running towards the jeep, a canvas bag in his hand. Lethbridge-Stewart gunned the engine, depositing the rifle back onto the passenger side again.

'Can you shoot?' he snapped as Greaves vaulted into the jeep. Before he could answer, Lethbridge-Stewart had the throttle down sufficiently to spin the wheels and cover the area in dust once more as he executed a perfect doughnut and pointed the jeep out into the desert again. The vehicle leapt forward.

'I can point it and pull the trigger,' said Greaves, taking the rifle and turning in his seat to look behind him. 'What did you throw for them?'

'A piece of tourist tat. I will probably get it in the neck for throwing it away,' said Lethbridge-Stewart. 'Please tell me that you've got the damned heart in your bag?'

'Heart, food, whisky.'

'Excellent. We have all the essentials.'

At that moment, over the roar of their engine, they heard another sound, the rattle behind them of a vehicle that was far less well-serviced. Lethbridge-Stewart risked a glance back and saw, ahead of another dust plume, the truck shaking and rattling its way towards them.

He swore.

'Time to point and shoot, I think. Just a couple of shots. Give them enough to keep them out of the way while we try and get away.'

Greaves pulled himself up in the seat, sighting down the barrel and squeezing shots off towards the pursuer. He was taking far too long to refill the chamber and Lethbridge-Stewart knew that the shots would be going wild, but at least they would be giving those behind something to think about.

It was then that he heard the unmistakable sound of metal on metal. The sound of a bullet striking the jeep's shell.

'Please tell me that was you aiming really badly, Greaves,' he shouted.

Greaves had ducked into his seat, lifting himself up just enough to see the truck behind.

'I wish it were.'

Another bullet chipped off a strut holding up the canopy.

'Right.' Lethbridge-Stewart saw more dunes up ahead; he could only hope that the jeep was faster over them than the truck was.

He hit them hard, keeping his foot down.

Of course, it wasn't enough, their speed slowed and the truck caught up. He weaved as he crossed the dunes, trying to make a harder target, but more bullets ricocheted around them before they crossed the apex of the dune and picked up speed on the other side. As they cleared it, Lethbridge-Stewart looked back again. The gap was larger but, as a high-pitched whistle nearby told him, the truck remained within firing distance.

'Okay, time for some guerrilla tactics,' he said to Greaves. 'Tear a strip off your shirt, soak it in the whisky and stuff it in one of the jerry cans.'

He had already used plenty of petrol to get back to the oasis. He was about to throw away litres of the stuff. They might never be able to drive back. But it had to be better than being caught.

'Then light it and drop it behind us,' Lethbridge-Stewart said.

Ahead of them was a rocky outcrop. If he could circle it, then he could put something between them and the pursuing truck. Greaves squeezed off another shot and then dropped into the passenger side. A loud thump behind Lethbridge-Stewart told him that a shotgun shell had narrowly missed the jeep.

Greaves already had his own sleeve off, before opening his bag and pulling the whisky from the top. Lethbridge-Stewart saw the man take a deep glug of it before tipping out half the bottle onto the cloth.

'A shame to waste it, you know. It's a good bottle.'

'Never mind the damn bottle, man, get that bomb ready to go,' snapped Lethbridge-Stewart.

He hauled hard on the steering wheel as they rounded the rock, putting them out of sight of the truck. He saw Greaves grab at a jerry can. From the way he struggled to move it, the thing must have been full of fuel. Four gallons if Lethbridge-Stewart remembered rightly.

'Have you got a light?' asked Greaves.

Lethbridge-Stewart looked sidelong at him.

'I don't smoke. What did you light the fire with?'

'I think we might have left the matches behind.'

Lethbridge-Stewart swore loudly and thumped the steering wheel hard enough to shake the front wheels.

'Then find something quick, man.'

They were reaching the end of the outcrop now; the truck hadn't appeared in the rear-view mirror yet. Dare he hope that it had turned away?

Any such hopes were soon dashed as the truck sped in front of them from the other side of the rock wall, its broadside facing them, but still fifty metres away. He must have misjudged the twists and turns behind the outcrop, allowing the truck to speed past and cut him up.

A fusillade of shots rained out of the truck and Lethbridge-

Stewart instinctively ducked as he feathered the brake and yanked the wheel round, sliding the jeep in line to climb another dune. The bullets and shells clattered around the stones and boulders on the ground. At least one, he heard, ricocheted up and struck the undercarriage of the jeep.

'They're shooting the tyres,' he shouted at Greaves.

'Good. I don't like being a target.'

'Not really, they're dreadful shots.'

To prove Lethbridge-Stewart right, as the jeep started to ascend the dune, another shot whipped over their heads.

Greaves was pulling items out of the bag. Apart from the jar for the heart itself, it was mostly odds and ends; Greaves' own textbooks, phrase books for Arabic, a trowel and brushes.

'What in God's name did you grab hold of those for?' snapped Lethbridge-Stewart.

'I didn't. I grabbed at my own bag. It tends to have my things in it.'

That was a fair answer, except…

'Then what is my whisky doing in there?'

'Saving our lives if I can find some matches,' muttered Greaves, barely audible over the over throttled jeep engine.

As they reached the top of the dune and started down the side, Lethbridge-Stewart heard the loose items shift and tumble over each other. He hoped no water or food fell out. If they got out of this, those things would be the difference between life and death.

He looked out ahead of them. About a mile or so away, there was a small range of cliffs and hills. Through the middle of them he could see openings, presumably to various valleys that led through the rock.

'We're going to try and escape through there,' Lethbridge-Stewart shouted, pointing. 'I need that bomb ready to go before we reach there. We need to use it to stop them following us.'

'I see. You need the bomb, do you?' Greaves turned back and threw himself in the seat, picking up the rifle again, ready to fire it again at their enemy. 'I'm not sure if you have noticed, Alistair, but I am not one of your soldiers.'

'Fine,' Lethbridge-Stewart snapped. 'Then feel free to get out of the jeep and *walk!*'

'Did you pay attention to anything I just said?' shouted Greaves back, slamming the butt of the rifle down on the dashboard.

Lethbridge-Stewart instinctively ducked as the thing went off with a loud crack.

It was then, thanks to the hard blow, that the glove box finally fell open. Greaves peered inside for a second, then quickly reached in.

'Found a lighter,' he said briefly, as if nothing had happened.

Lethbridge-Stewart raised an eyebrow. 'Get that bomb ready to light. Here we go.'

The wall of rock was getting closer now as the truck finally cleared the dune behind them. A further shot cracked against the scree that they were crossing.

Greaves was back on his feet, letting off another round before ducking back down into the footwell.

'Have you hit any of them yet?' asked Lethbridge-Stewart.

'I'm happy to swap places if you want me to drive. Just pull over.'

When this was over, Lethbridge-Stewart would be very happy to have his command back.

'Right,' he said. 'As soon as I say, light the rag and drop it off the side of the jeep. Try and keep it as central to the ravine as you can. We need to block the whole thing off.'

'I hope this works,' said Greaves. Then a pause. 'Thank you, Alistair.'

'Don't mention it.' *Because if you do*, thought Lethbridge-Stewart, *I may have to bring up the fact that you knew that your jar got me into this mess.*

As they approached the wall, the terrain under the wheels got bumpier. They slowed and Lethbridge-Stewart knew that the truck was nearly on them. It was confirmed when the rocks began to echo with the sound of bullets that splintered and shattered against them.

They were nearly there. He aimed the jeep carefully, looking for the gap that was just big enough for it and hoping it would take them out the other side. He would have prayed, but was starting to feel that gods were not a massive help.

They passed into the rocky ravine. He checked over his

shoulder, the truck was still following. Ahead, the ravine continued. He hoped it would take them back out into the desert.

The truck was certain to go down the same path that they had picked, clearing the entrance.

'Now!' shouted Lethbridge-Stewart.

He saw Greaves fumble with the lighter. It would be just their luck that the thing was a dud.

But then it caught, and the flame lit up the alcohol soaked cloth.

'Drop it, drop it!' Lethbridge-Stewart shouted.

The other man didn't need telling twice. He let the jerry can fall out of his hands. The way was dusty, and they were travelling at speed. It was very possible that the flames would go out before the bomb would go off.

The truck grew closer, getting nearer and nearer to where the bomb had been dropped.

Lethbridge-Stewart needn't have worried; the bomb went off like a treat, a fireball that filled the ravine between them and the truck. He heard, after the explosion, the sound of the truck coming to a halt.

'Good work,' he said to Greaves as he turned his attention to the way ahead. Lethbridge-Stewart patted the side of the jeep as well. 'And thank you for holding together, girl.'

'You should name her,'

Lethbridge-Stewart thought hard. One name sprung to mind, and out here, Fiona would never know.

'Doris,' he said.

CHAPTER TWELVE
Looking Outwards

THERE WAS no hope of a good drink here. It was too far from the Nile and its tourist spots.

Fiona had spent the morning wandering around the deserted streets of the oasis, marvelling that the only vegetation for miles was weeds forced through the pavement.

Cats, their fur matted, missing in parts, lounged against cracked concrete, eyes fixed on her as she passed. The heat grew too much, and she retreated back into the hotel bar, where she was given warm water. She tried to order wine, but a confused look and a glance at the clock told her all she needed to know.

She sat by a wilting plant, staring at the meal in front of her. It seemed to be a mix of rice and lentils. Half an hour earlier, she had tentatively tried some, to find that it was at room temperature. She tried not to think about how long it had been sitting on a plate in the kitchen before being served to her. The ever-present flies took turns in landing on it.

It was probably better to wait for Cosgrove to arrive before she ate.

The clock showed it was only one in the afternoon. There was no telling where Alistair would be by now, or what he was doing. She knew it shouldn't anger her as much as it did.

This was her lot in life. That phrase again swum into her mind. *Be a lady*. It was a hard thing to do. To her mind, it was only right that she be compensated for being left behind, while her man was out there, by spending that time enjoying the better things in life.

Instead, she had peeling, flaking walls, warm water and food that invited vomiting.

It wasn't the lack of home comforts that really bothered her. It was the lack of Alistair.

She stood, taking another sip of water to calm her aching head, and walked towards the bar.

'Where's the nearest train station?' she asked the bored looking youth.

He shrugged. 'I don't know.' His head rocked from side to side. 'Maybe the nearest is Asyut?'

'Asyut?' Fiona fought to keep her mouth from dropping open. 'That's where we arrived from. It took the best part of a day to get here.'

'If you like, there is a bus.'

That was a bit more like it.

'When does the next one leave?'

'Early tomorrow. Sorry, miss.'

She sighed. 'Is there no way of getting there earlier?'

The boy smiled. 'If a nice girl stands by the road. She will definitely get a lift.'

Fiona's stomach churned. A further night of rotten food was preferable then. If Cosgrove didn't show up.

It wasn't until she was sitting back down on the pouffe that she heard booted feet out in the lobby. She hoped that it was Cosgrove finally arriving. Possibly even with some back-up that he was sending on to help Alistair out. She pulled herself back up and went out to the lobby, ready to greet him.

She should have known that it would be the olive uniform and black berets of the Egyptian military that awaited her. Who else would have followed her here? As she stepped out, all eyes turned to her.

Rifles were raised, pointing straight at her, before the officer spoke sharply to his troops in Arabic. He had three stars on his shoulder; a captain.

'I am sorry, ma'am.' He switched to English. The voice was familiar. 'I have told them that they should treat a lady with more respect.'

Fiona realised that she knew the voice, and, as he stepped into the light, the face as well. She had last seen it at the foot of the gangplank of the *Keberia*.

'Azmy,' she said. 'What are you doing…?'

He came closer, took her by the elbow and led her back

into the lounge, snapping in Arabic at the troops.

'Please, over here.' He pulled out a chair for her, then sat opposite, before clicking his fingers at the poor youth. 'Two coffees,' he snapped. His accent was changed, more clipped. Less the helpful local and more a man used to commanding. 'I hope you don't mind,' he said to her. 'I have been awake a long time and I think we need to talk.'

Fiona crossed her arms. She definitely wanted to talk to this man. People lying to her and hiding things was the one constant of this holiday

'Early start?' she asked. 'I'm surprised. You knew where to find us.'

'We aren't looking for you, ma'am.'

'Why?' Fiona asked. 'Why were you hiding on that boat?'

'I can't say.' Azmy looked down at the table, before his eyes snapped back up.

'Well, you're not alone,' Fiona said, just as the coffees were placed down in front of them. She took a brief sip. It was good, full of flavour but not too bitter, better than she expected. 'Alistair can't tell me where he's going either. So, you're out of luck.'

'Miss Campbell.' Azmy lowered his voice. 'Can I call you that?'

'If you tell me your real name.'

He shrugged, as if embarrassed. 'Azmy. It makes sticking to the cover story easier. Captain Azmy Mahmoud.' He sipped his coffee. 'We believe that the man with your fiancé is dangerous. You need to tell us where they are.'

'I'm not sure I believe you.' Fiona took a deep breath and picked up the coffee, staring at the contents to make sure that her hands weren't shaking. 'Professor Greaves never pointed a gun at me.' She could feel the cold metal of the amulet that the man had given her against her chest. She remembered his nervousness as he placed it into her hand. She was certain that Greaves was one of the safest people for Alistair to be around. In any event, 'Alistair can look after himself,' she said.

'He's a brave man and a good shot. But no one can watch their own back all the time. Sooner or later, as poor Mr Dawoud found out, it ends.'

The mention of Dawoud's name jolted her.

'Dawoud? What have you got against him anyway?'

Azmy looked saddened. 'He must have been a good man once. But he has made some bad friends at university. Terrorists. Absolutely ruthless. They will stop at nothing to get what they want.' His hands left his coffee, reaching out to her. 'That is why I had to go undercover on that boat. I needed to keep him under observation. I fear that Greaves is part of the same group.' He shook his head slowly. 'I might still be able to help Alistair if you can tell me where they are heading. But if the terrorists get there first…'

Both his fists snapped shut, the sound was like a gunshot in the silent lounge.

'What do they want?' Fiona asked.

Azmy gestured with his hands, holding them about ten inches apart. 'They have a small jar, about so big. It contains very dangerous material. Stolen from Russians. Have you seen it?'

She shook her head.

'It's very dangerous. Toxic, infectious,' Azmy said.

Fiona's City experience had not prepared her for being fired at, for trips in battered vehicles across the desert or clandestine government operations. It had, however, made her an expert at telling angry and manipulative clients, firmly, that they weren't going to get what they wanted.

'Really?' She tried to put on the breathless dizzy air of the dumb secretary. 'I had no idea. But I'm really sorry, I just can't tell you where he's gone, because…' Her voice hardened. '…he hasn't told me himself.'

This was actually easier than the City, because she always knew the traders and advisers were really around the corner in *The Red Lion.*

Azmy's eyes narrowed. 'We don't know where the terrorists are right now. You've got a room here?' She nodded, almost without meaning too. 'Then I will make sure that you are directed to it without delay. We wouldn't want anything to happen. Don't worry, my men will remain here until we know where Alistair and Greaves have gone. We will keep you safe.'

She hadn't really expected anything less of course.

*

'So, which way now?' Lethbridge-Stewart stood, leaning on the jeep's windshield while looking through his binoculars.

There was now nothing to see except miles of dunes, stretching out to a horizon that reflected off the water mirage that formed in the heat haze.

'It's hard to say,' muttered Greaves. 'The difficulty with your escape from those chaps is that you couldn't keep to your bearing.'

'Come on, man!' snapped Lethbridge-Stewart. 'You're supposed to be navigating us so that we can finally get rid of that thing.' He nodded at the bundled-up jar in the back.

Greaves folded the map up carefully, ensuring that the folds went back in the correct place, before taking his feet down from where they rested on the door.

'I feel, Alistair, that you may be under the impression that I am a subordinate.' He sighed heavily. 'I am not. This is my family's heirloom.' He reached back to the back seat and patted the jar. 'This is my expedition and I have taken the time to locate the correct route.' He tapped the map on the top of the windscreen. 'Despite appearances, you're on civvy street now, whatever you have told your good lady. Feel free to wait for the military to turn up if you like. We can see if they arrive before the Egyptian Government or Professor Salem's gang catch up.'

Lethbridge-Stewart dropped into the seat. 'Now see here…'

Greaves shook his head. 'Not really, Alistair. I can see that you've been in the military a long time. Not much time for people outside of it, I imagine?' He sucked air into his cheeks. 'At least until Miss Campbell arrived.'

'There was someone else,' Lethbridge-Stewart said.

'Please, take some small advice from someone that has spent his life mucking these things up. That young lady isn't marrying into your life. You're both marrying into each others'. And that means that, sometimes, what you say won't always go. Even when those orders come from the top.'

Lethbridge-Stewart stretched his arms forward and breathed out, pursing his lips. 'I'm sure you're right.' He thought for a moment and gave voice to the thought that was gliding below the waters of his mind. 'Maybe this isn't the right path for us.'

'Come on, old chap. Not even I'm that inflexible. Just buck your ideas up. Speaking of which.' Greaves pointed at a precise point on the horizon and lined up his compass. 'If we aim in that direction, it should keep us back on track again and, with any luck, we might make it there at some point tomorrow.'

Lethbridge-Stewart smiled and gunned the engine, giving the pedal just the slightest tap to send the jeep off the dune with a small puff of dust behind it.

'So, we know that Dawoud's professor is behind all this. What sort of research does she do?'

Greaves sighed. 'She looks at matters from a less analytical viewpoint. For most of us, we look at Ancient Egypt's religion for what it tells us about their society. For Salem, she treats the texts of the tombs and temples as the gateway to a solid truth. She tries to draw connections to try and find a sort of core of truth that stands at the heart of what the Pharaohs believed.' He gave a wry smile. 'She thinks the gods really existed.'

The window looked out onto the car park, a blasted corner of cracked concrete half hidden beneath drifts of sand.

It would have been instant death to try and jump. Fiona lifted her eyes up to the horizon. From there the white of the sky met the haze of the desert heat in an almost straight line that extended as far as she could see.

Alistair was out there. The man she loved and who had left her to go out there and do... what? Here she was, stuck in a small room, an armed guard on the door and certain death from the window. That's if the exposed wiring and crumbling ceiling didn't get her first.

She sighed and dropped into the bed, hearing the springs squeak as they dropped her down. She closed her eyes, feeling the dust on her forehead stretch the skin and thought about what her holiday should be like. They should be in Luxor by now, walking around the temples in Thebes, probably listening to Greaves droning on about the New Kingdom, the Old Kingdom and the flaming Piggy-in-the-Middle Kingdom. Alistair would be half listening, but she knew that he often struggled to pay attention to that sort of thing.

She smiled, the stories of the gods bored her too, but the

kings of old fascinated her when there were many parallels to the people of today.

The more Fiona thought of Alistair, the more she was drawn back to the window. She opened her eyes and walked over to it again, opening it and letting the hot dry air in. As she gazed out at the pale soup of the horizon she felt suddenly no longer alone in the room, as if something was out there watching her, listening to her.

The presence grew on her mind as her fingers gripped the sill of the window, knuckles tightening. Her every instinct suddenly told her to go out there. Jump from the window and run out into the desert. She knew that if she did so, that was where she would find Alistair again. She tensed, grabbed the sides of the wooden frame and pushed the pane open, placing one foot on the sill, keeping her head up and her eyes on the fair horizon, picturing perfectly the exact spot to aim for after she jumped and was free.

That was when the here and now broke through in the form of shouts in Arabic. She glanced down, past the end of her open toed sandal to the car park below.

Two soldiers stood there, rifles aimed at her.

'Go back!' was the broken English command of the first. The other glanced up, then immediately ran back inside, shouting as he did so.

Azmy was soon next to the first soldier, putting his hand out to push down the rifle's barrel and barking at the man in Arabic, then to her in English.

'Please, ma'am, stay where you are. We will talk.'

Fiona stayed frozen to the spot, she felt the pull coming from out of the desert, felt the tug at her heart. She let go of the sill with one hand and reached for the scarab around her neck. An item of protection. Why shouldn't it protect her now?

As she held it in her hand, her eyes were drawn to the horizon, to the spot where the two largest dunes framed the place that she and Alistair had spent the previous night.

'Ma'am, stay there. Hold on to the side!' shouted Azmy.

He doesn't need to worry, thought Fiona, *the scarab will protect me and then I would be able to join Alistair, out there, in the desert.*

She heard running feet behind her, coming up the stairs. Whispered conversations in Arabic outside the door. Perhaps she should move now, make the next step on the road back to joining Alistair again. She tensed as she heard the door open behind her. Just one strong jump would get her clear.

That was when she felt arms around her waist, pulling her roughly back inside. Her hands went back to the sill, she tried to kick with her feet before she felt a swift kick to her shins that made her yell in pain. Down below, she could see that Azmy had now left the car park. As her hands were wrenched back from the window, she struggled to free them, reaching out for that spot on the horizon, where, somewhere, lost in the haze, she was being drawn.

It was just seconds later that she heard Azmy's voice snapping at the soldiers, saw the window dropping down and began to feel where she was rather than just seeing it as if in a dream. She was on the floor now, face down, held there by two soldiers.

As Azmy went to the window, one of the other soldiers joined him. They had an urgent conversation in Arabic as the soldier pointed out the window, towards where she had been reaching for.

Azmy knelt in front of her; she could smell the tobacco on his breath.

'Is that where they went?' He paused. 'Fiona, is that where they are?'

She stayed silent.

'I think that's the best we will get from you.' Azmy sighed. 'I don't think you know what you are dealing with out there. I hope, for his sake, that your future husband is better informed.'

He snapped at the other troops around him. They jumped and ran downstairs. Fiona was left alone with him.

'You can come in now,' he called to the doorway.

Fiona gasped as she recognised the man that entered. Complete with pith helmet and his moustache now waxed and prominent, Cosgrove looked apologetic.

'I think you've given me as much as I can hope for,' said Azmy. 'We're going to send a chopper over to try and find Brigadier Lethbridge-Stewart and the archaeologist. So, I'm releasing you to General Cosgrove here. He's been waiting downstairs until you were free to leave. Now that you've given us somewhere to go…' He shrugged. 'I don't want to keep you here longer than necessary. In my line of work, you don't draw attention to yourself. I suggest you do the same.'

As Azmy left, Cosgrove crossed the empty room to close the window before returning and dropping to one knee next to Fiona.

'My dear, are you all right?'

She felt her arms and legs, some bruises where fingers had gripped her and feet had knocked her legs away, but beyond that, she was fine. Her head felt clearer, like the sky emptied after a storm.

'Yes.' She gulped. 'They were just trying to get me away from the window.'

Cosgrove looked closer, into her eyes. 'What were you trying to do?'

'I don't know.' Fiona looked back over to the window. It seemed so ordinary now; there was no sudden tug at her chest or desire to go through it. 'It just felt like I needed to be out there, trying to follow Alistair and Greaves.'

Cosgrove looked over her, using the back of his hand to feel her forehead. He tutted. 'Touch of sun I would guess.'

She wasn't convinced by his tone.

'And what are you doing here?' Fiona struggled to her feet. 'Alistair only called you this morning. More to the point, what were you doing downstairs when I was locked up here?' She folded her arms, cocking her head to one side.

Cosgrove shifted his weight from side to side. 'A man in my position hears many things. When I found out they were heading here for you, I knew I had to get here. Even if it were only to show my face and make sure they knew someone was watching them.'

'Is that all you did then?'

Cosgrove spread his hands and shrugged. 'When you're known to work in intelligence, like me, but are nonetheless tolerated, again, like me, then you often find that the most you can do in these situations is ask nicely.'

'Thank you for asking nicely if they would stop keeping me imprisoned.' Fiona dusted her clothes down. 'Can I assume that you are going to ask them nicely to not chase after Alistair into the desert?'

'I can only hope that he has got enough time to finish what

he has to do.' Cosgrove offered her his elbow. She took two unsteady steps towards the door before finally making it. 'The nearest bases are in Minya or Aswan. That chopper will take a while yet.'

'You seem to know more about what he is up to than me,' Fiona said. 'You could have told them where they are.'

Cosgrove nodded. 'I could. But they know better than to try to take it from me. Come on,' he said. 'Your adventure is over. Hopefully, Alistair will join you back at my house sooner rather than later.'

She dropped her hand from him. 'You need to make sure he's safe,' she said.

Cosgrove took his helmet off and ran his hand through his wispy grey hair. Again, he looked like a tired old man underneath it. Perhaps he was. He must surely be too old for this sort of thing by now.

'What can I do?' he said. 'I can't chase after them. I can't take up arms, or fight off the Egyptian Army. The British, I'm afraid, cannot do anything in this country. We discovered as much in '56.'

'Then what will happen when they catch him?' Fiona leaned against the door frame as she spoke. She felt drained, as if something had sucked the air from her body.

'When he surrenders, they'll stick him in a helicopter. They'll tell me, I'll make some diplomatic sounding arguments and then they'll let you go on your way.' Cosgrove smiled. It didn't quite reach his eyes.

'Alistair doesn't surrender,' she said.

'Yes. I hope that he learns quickly.'

'What's he doing out there anyway? You know, don't you? You set him up to this.' Fiona leaned away from the doorframe and jabbed Cosgrove in the chest.

The man nodded. 'I can't hide much from you, can I?' He puffed out alternate cheeks, as if rolling something around in his mouth before swallowing it. 'I may have ensured that he was in the right place at the right time. I need to, you see. Interfere too much with another country's military and they hurl you out. But if a tourist just happens to stumble in at the right time...' He smiled, like a child that thought he had outwitted a parent.

'Cosgrove! People have shot at us. A man died on that boat. I need to know what is going on.'

Cosgrove ran a hand through his hair again, tugging at a few strands, almost in frustration, before placing his helmet back on his head. 'I wish I could tell you. All I can say is that in military terms, sometimes things need to be done. And when that happens, it doesn't matter if you're a private, a brigadier, or a general. What you would like no longer matters.'

'Then stuff the military.' Fiona forced herself to move as she left the room, keeping one hand on the wall to steady herself and ready to shrug off any further attempt by Cosgrove to assist her.

By the time they got to the bottom of the stairs, the Egyptian Army truck with Azmy and the troops had already left.

'Wait. Your bags,' said Cosgrove.

'Still upstairs,' Fiona muttered. 'Just leave them.'

'Don't be daft, I'll nip back up and grab them, my dear.'

With that, Cosgrove was off, leaving her standing in the spartan lobby. Even the boy had now disappeared, presumably after the troops had found their way in. Fiona doubted if any staff would show their faces again today. She dropped onto a settee in the lounge. She felt so tired. Perhaps this was sunstroke?

There was a jug of water left on one of the tables, presumably for the troops. She helped herself to a nearby glass, not caring if anyone else had drunk from it, and downed the water quickly.

Who are you?

The voice was behind her ear. A female voice. She jumped up and turned, but there was still no one there.

'Where are you?' Fiona said.

I am with you. The voice sounded quietly amused. Fiona's hand went to the scarab around her neck again. The voice giggled slightly. *So, who are you?*

'It doesn't matter.'

But it does. It matters so much. It stayed behind her. She could feel the breath against her neck, a warmth that shifted her hair ever so slightly. *Because that amulet is ours. It binds.*

'It was given to me. It's a gift. To keep me safe.'

She felt a quick gust of wind on her shoulder. As if someone had gone to place a hand there and then snatched it back.

So it seems. But he needs soldiers now. He needs their essence. Their skill and their drive.

'I want nothing to do with soldiers.' Fiona spat the words.

Something between a hiss and a growl came from behind her. Something primal, like an animal straining at a chain.

Why? You must! She felt a tug at her chest as the thing spoke, like fingers of ice scraping like claws. *You have the amulet.*

Fiona's hands went to it instantly, her eyes tracking down to see that there was nothing there.

'The best I am is a soldier's wife.'

There was a rattle behind her, like chicken bones being crunched together.

A wife? You think your sex betrays you? It never betrayed me. That terrible rattle only grew louder. She realised it was laughter. *My race wouldn't recognise such cowardice. I'm surprised to hear it from yours.* The voice calmed. *We have slept, but have heard much. I know the girl in white that could fire a weapon with such accuracy. I know the manipulative ones in their masks that thought they could control history with spells and shadows. What's your excuse? Why do you hide behind another?*

Had Fiona ever thought she would be anything different? She'd had her good times and her career, but it all felt like a sidestep, like she was waiting for the right man to come along. For the right marriage to come along.

The breath was in her face now. She couldn't see what caused it but got a fleeting glimpse in her mind's eye of something lithe and swift, a sudden stench of sweat rising from a leathery hide. She suddenly knew that it could see into her thoughts.

Now, what made you think like that? The voice was quieter now, almost amused. *You are strange creatures. You follow such stringent rules but you're never told what they are. You simply do what others do and place yourself in the most woeful situations.* The breath moved across her face as if the beast were shaking its head. Then Fiona heard the voice hiss into her ear. *Throw away the amulet, cattle. You don't deserve to carry it. Give it to a warrior, not a slave.*

Fiona's hand went to the amulet again. Her other hand grabbed at the empty glass on the table. She whirled around, looking for the source of the voice, this mocking, needling sound.

With a hiss, the great cat lunged at her.

Fiona shouted out in a sound that was almost a roar as she threw the glass.

It shattered across the wall, shards tinkling to the ground. There was silence. No cat and no voice. They had simply faded like a mirage.

'Don't worry about that, my dear,' Cosgrove's voice cut through the hush from the lobby.

He stepped into the lounge, looking at the shards on the floor. 'Glasses get dropped and these things are easily cleaned up.'

She slowly turned to face him where he stood with her luggage.

'Come on,' Cosgrove told her, 'let's join my driver and get back to Cairo. We'll stop for the night at Asyut.'

CHAPTER THIRTEEN
Between Two Worlds

THE EARLY evening sun bathed the tanks in a red illusion. Even after thirty years, there was still no rust on them. Time stood still in the desert.

Lethbridge-Stewart compared the state of the armour, sitting there half buried in the sands, to the jeep that was now cooling and making soft plinking noises. They could be from the same battle.

'There's a hundred sites like this,' mused Greaves gazing around. 'Scattered across the whole of the Sahara.' He slapped the swinging end of a torn caterpillar track. 'Something for future archaeologists to get their teeth into. For now, the world's had enough of these.'

Lethbridge-Stewart nodded towards the jeep. 'This is a good place to hide Doris for the night. One more rusting hulk won't look any different.' He walked over and pulled out the tent. 'If you can get this up, preferably hidden behind all this armour, I'll have a scavenge and see what I can find that's been left behind.'

'Yes, sir,'

'Carry on.'

Lethbridge-Stewart hadn't noticed the sarcastic tone from Greaves and his own automatic reaction until he heard the soft cough as he walked away. He groaned inwardly and turned back.

'I'm terribly sorry,' he said. 'I meant to say, thank you very much indeed.'

Lethbridge-Stewart kept walking past the Challengers that had died there. The war had passed through the desert thirty years ago, but the state of the hulks it left behind, preserved in the heat, made it look like yesterday. No civilians had been anywhere nearby, this had been pure war. Nothing here but what they brought with them to fight. Rommel and Monty. The stuff that boy's adventures were made of. No doubt after the battle was over, the men that had died had been recovered and repatriated. These tanks however, once stripped of whatever could be carried, had been left where they fell.

He searched each one, looking for something that could be used: guns, ammunition, even a trench digging tool would be helpful. There was nothing. The holes in the armour of the vehicles told their own story of what had happened. All were at the top of the tanks. Luftwaffe bombs, falling from a clear blue desert sky to destroy this small group that had struck out across the desert.

It was a strange place to find the debris of a battle. Most battles in the Desert War were fought far to the north. What had happened there, thirty years ago?

There was one last tank, with limited damage to the front. Lethbridge-Stewart put a foot on the rungs of the ladder leading up to the hatch, before pulling himself up and to the top of the hulk. No hatch door, simply a hole in the body of the tank, leading down into the seats where the driver once sat.

With the sun's light hitting it just right, the interior was well lit, but looked as empty as the rest, with leather seats that had long cracked and shattered in the sun and exposed steel corners. He didn't envy the men that had driven these tin cans through the hottest months of the year.

There, just visible past the edge of a seat, was a familiar dark piece of material. He dropped into the cockpit, pulling at it. As he thought, a black envelope, waterproof and stamped with the familiar words *Top Secret.*

Lethbridge-Stewart climbed back out and held the envelope in his hand. Thirty-year-old top secret orders. He paused, turning them over. Surely his security clearance was sufficient to read whatever was in here. He pulled out a set of keys. In the absence of a bayonet, they would have to do. A minute or two of frantic sawing later and he had the orders in his hand.

He read them. Then stopped to look up at the sky,

breathing a single curse word. Then he read them again.

Lethbridge-Stewart had enough clearance to read these, but it was a close-run thing. They were headed *Home-Army Fourth Operational Corps*, his own command's wartime forerunner. The name at the end was also very familiar. Professor Edward Travers, Anne's father. It was pp'd, not signed, of course. Lethbridge-Stewart could imagine the middle-aged Travers bawling the dictation from the far end of his lab at some poor conscripted young lady sent to take the letter. Lethbridge-Stewart allowed himself a small smile. He missed the old man.

But the content was something else. It sounded like a fairly routine matter, at least for a corps like Travers'. Proceed across the desert to a specific point. Locate the city of Zerzura. Secure the sarcophagi of the bodies entombed there.

It was enough that the Fourth had known not only the city, but its location. The final paragraph was where, characteristically, Travers had added some warnings to the troops as an afterthought.

He cautioned about powerful mental powers, including projection, control and even links to animals. He drew parallels to something he had encountered back in England.

His final sentence was a classic. 'If you come under attack by such methods, keep a clear record of the effects so that I can make a comparison.' As if any young soldier out here, far from home and being tortured by mental energies, would think to help Professor Travers with his research.

Lethbridge-Stewart folded the letter and replaced it. He would check the directions against those of Greaves before they set off the next day, but he saw no reason to let the man into the contents of the letter.

Documents went missing all the time. Particularly wartime documents from a time when nearly every square inch of Britain and every citizen was a military asset. Yet the Fourth had known about Zerzura. They had known about the risks of what was there. They may even have known about a link to an incident back home.

Lethbridge-Stewart couldn't help but feel that other, now elderly, members of the military also knew something that had never crossed his own desk.

And he was going to ensure that they knew his displeasure.

When Lethbridge-Stewart got back to the jeep, Greaves had the tent up; it was pitched below and following the line of the barrel of a Challenger's turret gun. A good choice for concealment.

'Did you find anything?' asked Greaves.

'Not a thing.'

'I'm not surprised. If the British hadn't taken everything useful, I'm sure others would have got it.'

A mug was waiting for Lethbridge-Stewart. He took a sniff of the contents. It was the whisky.

'That's the last of it,' said Greaves. 'I used too much on your makeshift bomb.'

Lethbridge-Stewart settled on the ground next to him. 'It will do. How's our water lasting?'

Greaves grimaced. 'In this heat? A day, maybe more. We left too much behind.'

Lethbridge-Stewart nodded. 'Let's hope that we find the place soon then.'

Greaves stared at him in disbelief. 'What about getting back again? I wasn't planning on dying out here.'

Lethbridge-Stewart took a deep drink of whisky, letting the familiar taste slide down his throat. 'We won't. Not of thirst anyway.' He licked his lips. 'Apart from the Egyptian Army, who will probably find us eventually, I've left a message with one of my men back in Edinburgh. There will be a push from the top brass to come and get us.' He raised an eyebrow in the direction of Greaves' bag. 'Our challenge is getting rid of our bovine passenger before they get to us.' He added in a lower tone. 'And, of course, hoping that will put a stop to him.'

'Military men from every direction. Wonderful. I'm glad I missed the fun and games that came with this lot.' Greaves slapped the side of a tank as he stood. 'Right, food. What will you have? Flatbread with sugar, flatbread with water or plain flatbread?'

'I'll save the water for now. Plain please.' Lethbridge-Stewart caught the thrown package and started eating before Greaves returned with a canteen of water.

Greaves took a swig, swirled it around his mouth and spat

it out, before tearing off his own mouthful of bread.

'Why have you never served?' Lethbridge-Stewart said. The question had been irritating him. That man should have seen active service in the last war at his age. There was no way that Egyptologist could possibly have been a reserved occupation.

The other man sighed. 'Initially, I was a conscientious objector.' Greaves winced as he said it.

'I see,' said Lethbridge-Stewart. 'Only initially?'

'Then it was off underground. I much prefer digging up relics to digging up coal, but at least I was doing something.'

Lethbridge-Stewart was silent for a moment. 'A difficult job, I hear, being a Bevin boy.'

Greaves shrugged. 'I was a Bevin man. Had a few years over most of my colleagues. Other men did more dangerous jobs.'

'And still others had cushier.' Lethbridge-Stewart thought of his father's tutting at Uncle Matthew's term as a civil servant in the War Office.

They sat in silence for a moment or two. The light was dying now. Building a fire would only advertise their presence.

'What do you know about the city?'

Greaves looked up at the sky, silent and dark pink above. 'Very little. The map in Pakhet's temple showed a triangular shape. Very meaningful. It must be underground. Maybe hidden within a rock formation.' He turned away. The subject was over.

'Come on,' said Lethbridge-Stewart. 'You must know where we're heading. It was your grandfather's expedition that found the place. You must have some knowledge of where we're going. What about his own books? His records? Was there nothing left?'

Greaves sighed. Then took a long sip from his mug. 'We did find a diary. A meticulous account of all of his expeditions.'

'Well then, perfect.'

Greaves turned and looked Lethbridge-Stewart straight in the eye. 'My brother and I burned it.'

Lethbridge-Stewart coughed on the flatbread in his mouth. The archaeologist was making a habit of this.

'I beg your pardon.' Lethbridge-Stewart spat the bread

out. 'What on the earth possessed you?'

Greaves chewed on his bread, staring out past the ruined tanks and out to the desert. 'Zerzura wasn't his only expedition. He wasn't an archaeologist either. Like a lot of men of his time, he thought of himself as being a lot of things, an explorer, an administrator. Someone bringing civilisation to these dark places.'

'He was a true polymath.'

Greaves' mouth twisted as he thought of his grandfather, like a man who had bitten into a lemon. 'I can barely remember much about him. My abiding image is of an angry man that looked for the worst in everyone.' He looked back at Lethbridge-Stewart. 'Don't feel that you need to smooth over what he was to me. We read his own words. We know what he was.'

Lethbridge-Stewart finished the bread and took another drink of whisky from the mug. 'And who was he?'

'A monster. But not an exceptional one.' Greaves took a deep breath and sat in silence for a moment or two. 'He led a number of expeditions. He and the British would usually come home in one piece with sunburn. Any Africans he recruited? Not always so lucky.'

Lethbridge-Stewart kept his own counsel. His own family seat came from a gift after Waterloo, but he doubted that any military family had clean hands when it came to the scramble for Africa.

'The worst,' continued Greaves, 'was what he did to those under his command. Beatings. Grown men beaten as discipline. Simply because they were African and made a mistake. He listed the reasons in his diary, innocuous, minor things…'

'Any man that loses his temper with his command loses their trust,' said Lethbridge-Stewart. 'And to do that over something trivial…'

'The people he met lost more than their trust in him. He was making a land grab as he passed through the continent. What do you think he did when the people he was taking it from tried to fight back? What do you think happened to those unarmed people? Those *savages?*' Greaves pointed at Lethbridge-Stewart's rifle. 'That's what happened. There was one entry in which he wrote about a group of boys. When the expedition started firing, they turned and ran. So, they kept firing. In his entry he described it as like being on a grouse shoot.'

Lethbridge-Stewart had no words. He had been a soldier, but he knew, he always knew, that when he pulled the trigger on his rifle he was doing it as a soldier. As a man that represented Britain. To treat other human beings as animals, as vermin, was something he could barely comprehend.

'And that's what goes through my head every time I see men marching or that flag.' Greaves drained his drink now, licking his lips like a man that had reached the end of a meal. 'What it meant to some of those people that he took pot shots at. That's why my brother and I both turned against King and Country. That's why I ended up underground in the war. And why I think this…' He tapped the jar. '…needs to go home.'

Lethbridge-Stewart felt a lot of things. He wanted to shout about who they had fought in the war, that the Victorian age was a long time ago. Things were different then. But deep down, he knew that knowing that your own grandfather had done such things was something that Greaves had every right to struggle with. He had every right to have it colour his whole perception of his own country.

More than that, Lethbridge-Stewart knew the real reason that this matter had annoyed him so much.

'Still,' he said. 'It would have been damned useful to have his diary…'

Greaves glared at him.

CHAPTER FOURTEEN
Onward

'I MUST say, you're taking this all in your stride,' Greaves said. 'Ancient gods, armed bandits, mysterious cities…'

'This is all a rather familiar part of my life, these days.' Lethbridge-Stewart shrugged as he reclined in the passenger seat. It was Greaves' turn to drive for the morning and that meant that the going was rather more sedate for the moment. He kept the rifle close at hand.

'An exciting life. Don't you think it would help me if I knew something more about it? You know all the background you need about what brought me here.' Greaves glanced at the compass and map, propped up on the dashboard.

Lethbridge-Stewart had already surreptitiously checked this against Edward Travers' own directions before they had set off.

Lethbridge-Stewart considered; Greaves was a civilian. He probably wouldn't know the Official Secrets Act if it slapped him in the face. But he did have a point.

'The stranger threats that Britain faces have become my job. It sort of fell on my shoulders by accident. You remember the London Event?'

Greaves chewed his lip for a moment, deep in thought. 'I remember. The evacuation. Nerve gas escape, wasn't it? Don't tell me that you were responsible for that?'

'That was the cover story. In truth, there was an attempt by something very old and very powerful to seize control of the capital. It used automatons to control the streets and mind control powers to infiltrate my team. I was the CO in the end. It was a dashed close-run thing I can tell you. Since then, the strangeness has just kept coming.'

Greaves was silent for a moment. 'I can see why that was suppressed. If it wasn't for our friend Montu back there, I doubt I would have believed it.' He tapped the wheel absentmindedly. 'And you think this…' He searched for the word. '…this being is connected with Montu?'

Lethbridge-Stewart shook his head very quickly. 'No. This isn't the Intelligence's style. That's much more connected with another ancient civilisation. But there are similarities.'

'So, a busman's holiday then?' said Greaves.

Lethbridge-Stewart was silent a moment. 'Not for the first time. Something similar happened when I travelled to New York once.' When Greaves didn't respond, Lethbridge-Stewart added. 'My fiancée at the time was involved in the same work that I was.'

That at least got a reaction. 'You've been engaged before?' Greaves continued to drive in silence for a moment, Lethbridge-Stewart could see his mind working. 'So, was that any easier for you?'

'In the end, no.' Lethbridge-Stewart sighed heavily. 'We separated. Then she died, back in September. Badly. In a way that was connected to my work. I had hoped that having a relationship with someone outside of the Forces would be easier. I could keep her at arm's length from the work. I could keep her safe.' He choked slightly at that last word.

'Just have a little woman at home to bring up the children, out of the way of all the demons that you face?'

Lethbridge-Stewart knew from his suddenly quickly beating heart that comment had struck a nerve, even if he wanted to pretend it hadn't.

'That was unfair,' he decided to say. 'I was happy enough to marry a woman who served in the Forces. Fiona doesn't serve and good for her. I just don't want to deal with that again.' He gazed at the unchanging horizon. 'To have a command over someone that I care for.'

'And how does Fiona feel about this?' said Greaves. 'She's ready to give up a career, move to the other end of the country to marry you and, in return, you're going to keep her shut out of the only life you have ever known.'

'What would you know about it? You've never served, and you've never married.'

Greaves shrugged. Absolutely nothing. Or at least, very little. Just what I've picked up in scraps and pieces here and there. Much the same as I approach archaeology really. And I've not done too bad at that.' He paused. Lethbridge-Stewart let him sit there. 'You can't shut her out of everything, you know. No one can be safe forever. Unless they are also imprisoned forever.'

Lethbridge-Stewart nodded, unseen by Greaves.

As he was about to reply, he heard a low thrumming sound in the dunes behind them. He turned to look at the gathering dust cloud. Just above it, and getting closer as he watched, was a helicopter. Desert camouflage. He brought the binoculars up to his face and he recognised the type. Soviet built. It was a small craft, but one that was occasionally armed. He looked down at the Lee Enfield in his hands. It would not be enough.

'We've got company,' he said.

'Government or loonies?'

'Government. How far to the city?'

'I've no idea,' said Greaves. 'I've got a bearing but no distance. It could be a mile, it could be another fifty. Thousand-year-old maps aren't the most accurate, you know.'

'Damn.' Lethbridge-Stewart looked around. 'They'll have seen us by now. We're throwing up enough dust to choke a camel.'

'Do you not think Doris will get us out of this one?' Greaves was joking, but the crack in his voice betrayed his thoughts.

Lethbridge-Stewart pointed ahead. 'The dunes flatten in that direction.'

Greaves glanced quickly over at him, then at the desert ahead.

It was then that the steadily growing roar of the chopper behind them changed in pitch. Lethbridge-Stewart glanced back to see it bearing down on the jeep, so close that he could make out the two figures piloting it. He snapped a hand out to the steering wheel and jerked it down. The jeep rolled as it turned, sliding sideways and sending Lethbridge-Stewart pitching over towards the driver's side before the vehicle righted itself.

The chopper was now wheeling off towards the south. Lethbridge-Stewart pulled the rifle to his eye and sighted down it, straight at the chopper. It was, quite literally, worth a shot. He pulled the trigger, the rifle recoiled as the bullet flew wide.

'Keep going,' he snapped at Greaves. 'Towards where I pointed.'

'Why?' Greaves asked.

'Because that's where the city might be. Flattened land.'

'That's what you're basing this on?' Greaves shouted back. 'The dunes would have moved in the last thousands of years.'

'If you can see any other clues in the landscape, please point them out.'

Lethbridge-Stewart pulled back the bolt on the rifle and followed the chopper's arc back as it returned towards the jeep.

It was low in the sky again as it aimed directly at them. He sighted along the rifle, waiting until the chopper was close enough so that he could again see the pilot and co-pilot clearly. He squeezed another shot off. He was sure that it struck the canopy of the Mil. The craft immediately started to climb again.

Lethbridge-Stewart tensed as it did so, but could see that the craft wasn't armed. Suddenly, he was very grateful for the Egyptian Government's failure to buy decent kit for its troops.

'Keep going,' he said. 'With a bit of luck we can find this city.'

He turned back to the chopper, it appeared to be keeping its distance, holding back, as if watching for the jeep to do something.

'We've got a bit of time,' he said to Greaves. 'Not sure how long.' He kept the rifle trained on the chopper.

The jeep thundered on, Greaves guiding it around the dunes as they dropped in height, before suddenly hauling the wheel to the side and releasing the gas pedal.

'What are you…?' Lethbridge-Stewart slowly trailed off as he saw what lay just off Greaves' side of the vehicle.

A scree cliff dropped away from where the jeep's wheels now trundled slowly, leading to the flat bottom of a valley below. A sheer rock wall rose on the other side. Lethbridge-

Stewart looked both ways up and down the valley.

'What's this?' he said.

'I think, it could be what we are looking for,' muttered Greaves.

He put his foot down again as the sound of the Soviet helicopter ramped up behind them. The ravine next to them continued until, without warning, it seemed to meet another valley coming in at what, to Lethbridge-Stewart, looked to be a perfect sixty-degree angle. The two ravines met at that pinch point and stopped, giving way to nothing but more sand. Greaves hauled the wheel around and started accelerating along the second valley.

The chopper flew over, again. Lethbridge-Stewart tracked it as it hovered behind them, closer. He kept the rifle up against his shoulder.

'Where are you going now?' he snapped at Greaves.

'Following a hunch,' he replied. 'Geometry is very important in Ancient Egypt. And, if I'm right, this ravine is not the natural system it looks like.'

Ahead, Lethbridge-Stewart had an inkling of what the man meant. Yet again, the ravine they followed met another at an angle.

'They form a perfect triangle,' he said.

The helicopter came at them from the desert. He had let it out of his sight, and it now swooped down low. Lethbridge-Stewart turned and fired a shot at the thing, knowing it could only go wild. He stood to get a better aim as it passed just metres overhead.

That is probably what saved him, as the helicopter dipped; Greaves must have jerked the steering wheel at that moment, panicked. The jeep suddenly tilted under his feet and Lethbridge-Stewart lost his footing, falling from the jeep. The rifle flew out of his hands as he impacted in the dust and rocks of the desert floor, rolling.

He lay there for seconds that seemed like minutes, the wind knocked straight out of him. He heard the chopper climbing up and away. For the first time since he'd noticed it, the sound of its engine faded and the total silence of the desert returned. Not even the sound of the jeep's engine.

Lethbridge-Stewart thought the worst and pushed himself

to his hands and knees, feeling for that tell-tale sharp pain of broken bones. Nothing. Just the dull ache of bruises that threatened to become far worse, and the acrid taste of a bloody lip. Lucky him. He pulled himself to his feet and staggered to the edge of the ravine.

Just as he thought, the jeep lay at the bottom, bodywork dented, fuel pouring out of cut lines.

Greaves lay about a hundred yards back, where he had fallen. The angle of the man's neck told Lethbridge-Stewart that he'd died instantly.

'Would you like anything for the journey, sir?'

Cosgrove's driver was impossibly happy for the time of day when they stepped out into the morning sun in Asyut. Fiona spoke up before Cosgrove had a chance to reply.

'Cigarettes,' she said.

Cosgrove turned to look at her. 'My dear, I didn't know that you…'

'I didn't.' She took her bag, lying near the car's boot and threw it inside. 'Well, I used to, occasionally. I haven't since Alistair and I…. Well, since we met.'

The driver left them to find a shop. Fiona watched him go, through the early morning traffic of Asyut. They'd arrived late last night, to the same hotel that Cosgrove had used a couple of nights ago. She had immediately left for her room, slamming the door and making it clear that she didn't want to see anyone. Fortunately, she had been left to catch up on sleep.

She missed the feel of Alistair's arm around her and the warmth, even in this heat, of his body next to hers.

Cosgrove leaned against the car, looking out at the surrounding red stone buildings and then past them to the wilderness beyond.

'Is everything okay, my dear?'

Fiona kicked a pebble, watched as it skittered across the ground. 'Yes.' The pebble bounced up at the last moment and hit the door of the hotel. 'No. I feel like I've fallen through the crack between two worlds. I've left my old life for Alistair. But I'm not in his life.'

Cosgrove took his pith helmet off and turned it over in his

hands. 'It can be difficult, this world. And you are right, of course.' He drummed his fingers on the hat brim. 'We ask you to share our lives and take on duty in the same way that we do.'

'And what do we get from it?'

Cosgrove breathed out slowly. 'I wish I knew, my dear. I don't even know what I get out of it. It's more of a calling.'

Fiona stood in silence for a moment or two, before she heard footsteps that crunched across the carpark. It was Cosgrove's driver.

'Excellent, we can get going.' She took the cigarettes and pulled one out. 'Light?'

The driver produced a lighter and flicked it on for her. She took a deep drag and let the smoke out slowly. A small piece of rebellion, a tiny piece of control over this object and what sat in her lungs.

Cosgrove looked at her; she couldn't quite make out his expression. It sat somewhere between sorrow and pity.

'Let's go,' he said.

The shadows cast by the cliffs stretched across the rocky floor, shrinking as the sun rose. Lethbridge-Stewart crouched next to the body, feeling the pulse, just to be sure. He sighed and closed Greaves' eyes.

'There's not much of a forbidden city here, Greaves,' muttered Lethbridge-Stewart as he fanned himself with his hat.

He set off for the wreckage of the jeep. Fortunately, crashing vehicles only burst into flame in films. This one had simply rolled until it came to a halt in a heap of metal and rubber. Somehow, it had landed on its wheels. He patted it once.

'Sorry, Doris.'

Somehow, the rifle still lay in the footwell. He pulled it out. The sights looked crooked, but the barrel was still straight. He sighted along the barrel and paused. The chopper had flown off. Presumably, the Egyptian military thought they were both dead. He could risk the noise, but the bigger risk would be the bullet exploding in his face. He turned his head away and held the gun at arms-length before he squeezed the trigger.

The gun fired. He heard the bullet strike the rock wall with a crack.

'Made in Britain,' he muttered. 'Of course.' He searched the rest of the jeep.

The jar was still wedged in the back and wrapped in cloth. Carefully he unwrapped it, to check that it remained intact. It was and he covered it again. He also found a small cloth rucksack, full of trail rations. He emptied them out and put the jar inside.

Lethbridge-Stewart started to walk towards one side of the valley, then paused. There was something else that needed to be done. He grabbed at the tent in the back and unfolded it as he walked back to Greaves, and stretched the fabric over the body, weighing it down with rocks. He stood back, feeling that words were called for.

'You brought this here,' he said, hefting the jar in one hand. 'It's affected people. Tested men. Turned a man into a killer, caused another to jump to his death.' He paused. 'And men will kill for it. The government, others… It wasn't you. You've lost a lot. And maybe bringing this thing…' He looked at it in his hand. '…back here will stop all of that.'

A man alone in the desert stood over the body of the only man for a hundred miles. He paused.

'I hope you're right. Something needs to come out of this.'

A salute would have been wrong, so he gave the poor man a small bow.

Lethbridge-Stewart turned and walked away down the ravine, the rifle slung over his shoulder and the jar in his rucksack. As he passed the jeep, he pulled out a miraculously unbroken bottle of water from the back. He upturned the bottle, letting some of it trickle down his face where dust and dried sweat had mingled in the stubble of a few day's travel.

He walked on, his eyes on the walls on both sides, searching for a clue, anything. This ravine was completely unnatural, a perfect triangle that enclosed a mesa. It was deserted, the outer rock walls were natural, even sloped. That was, after all, how he scrambled down after the jeep.

The inner walls overhung the valley bottom, the rock uneven, like a concertina, such that the folds were dark openings at irregular intervals. He worked his way along the walls. Each apparent opening turned out to be only a few feet deep at a time, with no obvious way in.

He sighed and slumped to the ground, taking another drink. His heart was still beating fast, and the sweat was springing up on his forehead as the shade retreated behind the sun. He had to find his way in, and quickly. That helicopter would have reported this position to the Egyptian Army. They would be along quickly. He had no doubt that Dawoud, Salem and their truck were also on their way. The entrance had to be somewhere.

This must *be the city.*

Lethbridge-Stewart opened the rucksack and looked again at the jar that contained the heart, still wrapped up. As he did so, he remembered what Greaves had told him about entering the tomb. He felt the jar itself tingling in his hand.

Lethbridge-Stewart pulled the cotton wrapping off the jar and held it in his hands, closing his eyes. There was the slightest tingle in his fingertips. He jumped up, picked a direction back to the jeep and started walking in it.

After a few hundred yards he stopped. Was it his imagination, or had that sense of warmth gone from his hands? He couldn't feel anything, but it was hard to feel anything outside of the sun's heat. He would chance it. He turned and walked back the other way, still holding the jug in both hands.

He felt like a cross between an altar boy and a water diviner.

His hunch was right; the warmth grew in his hands. He was now clearly walking in the right direction and approaching one of the corners of the triangle. Once there, he looked around, seeing nothing except the point of the mesa, rising above him like the hull of a ship and scattered boulders. He headed down the other side of the triangle and, within another hundred yards, stopped and swore.

The damn jar was cooling again. That cornice he had passed must have been the place to enter the city, or the tomb and whatever it was. He turned and headed back to it and paused, staring at the cliff edge rising up in front of him. There was nothing except the gullies that ran down it.

Then he saw it, as if it were a hidden picture, an optical

illusion. Rising out of the side of the mesa's point, he could see what were clearly two huge bull's horns, carved into the rock itself. Below them were eyes and an outcrop that could only be a nose.

Lethbridge-Stewart looked down at the jar and the carving on top. The features matched exactly. This was it.

The question remained, how to get in? He started by walking towards the apex. The rock remained solid. No hidden doors. He thumped it with the base of his fist for good measure then sat on an empty rock, casting his eyes around, looking for…what? A doorbell?

What would Greaves have looked for? He wished that he had listened more to what the man had said. Archaeology was not Lethbridge-Stewart's strongest point. None of the humanities ever had been, come to that.

Then he remembered what Greaves had been talking about in the jeep. Something about the importance of geometry in the architecture.

He looked at the rock he sat on. His brain started to fill in the gaps. The distance from where he was to the bull's head carving was the same as the distance from both the carving and where he sat to…

Another rock. Flat, just like this one. As if both of them were altars. Perhaps he had been an altar boy after all. So, what needed to be triangulated?

The bull's head certainly. A jar, possibly. What else did he have that could possibly unlock the entrance? Something connected to the power inside. He feared that he knew the answer.

He walked over and placed the jar on one of the altar stones, then he retreated and stood again on 'his' stone.

He crossed his fingers and slowly pulled the rifle down from his shoulder. He held it ready, hearing nothing in the still air except for his own heartbeat. Perhaps he was wrong.

Then he heard it.

A crunch and a scrape and, below the bull's head, a tiny crack in the cliff appeared, growing larger and larger as doors made of the rock face itself swung open until they were wide enough to drive a horse and cart through. He jumped off the rock and picked up the jar that sat on the other, throwing it into the rucksack.

The doorway remained open, so Lethbridge-Stewart advanced towards it, the rifle at the ready.

Inside, he found himself in an archway. It looked like the type of arch he had seen in ruins across Egypt; straight up and down and topped by a slab. Yet, unlike every other ruin, the material looked brand new and polished.

Beyond the arch, he could see only blackness. He took a breath and stepped straight into it.

Immediately, light began to grow around him, dark pink to start with, then growing through red into orange. The vast space beyond ballooned in front of him.

He breathed in as he saw it. He stood in the entrance archway of a city and before him were streets upon streets, filling the triangular mesa in a grid pattern and packed with buildings that were cut from stone. The place had the appearance of something purely functional, long low buildings and occasional larger storehouses.

He realised what this looked like to him. The lost City of Zerzura was nothing of the sort. There were none of the decorations, the colours of Ancient Egyptian ruins. It was a barracks. He looked up at the ceiling, searching for the light source. There was none. The light simply grew brighter and brighter until the ceiling was lost in the glare.

Definitely alien, he told himself. He was almost glad that Greaves wasn't here to see the base truth behind the civilisation that he had spent his life exploring.

Steps led down from the archway to the street level, so he took one more chance to look around, to get his bearings and work out where he needed to go next.

In each of the two opposite corners of the city there was a pyramid. One larger than the other. He remembered something else that Greaves had told him. There was rumoured to be a king and queen asleep in the city. He was willing to bet that in one of those buildings was Montu, waiting.

The damn alien was going to get his heart back. Then he was going to leave Lethbridge-Stewart and his family alone.

Fiona sat in the back of Cosgrove's car, watching the blue and brown of the Nile slip past the window. It was like watching a super 8 film of a holiday. Something she had felt and smelt so strongly now just glimpsed through glass.

It had been a matter of days since they had passed this stretch on the *Keberia*, but it felt like a lifetime.

She reached up and held the scarab between finger and thumb, rolling it around and watching it catch the sunlight. The thing must have been worth a fortune. Greaves really must have felt terrible when he left her like this.

Somehow, she still felt tired. Not as much as she had yesterday, when she experienced the bizarre hallucination in the Hotel Royale, but the scenery still blurred as she watched it, sharpening as she blinked. Ahead, she could see that the heat had sent Cosgrove to sleep in the front seat.

She cradled the amulet as her eyes closed again, feeling as though someone was talking to her as she drifted.

When are you coming back?

She twisted in the seat, trying to shake the feeling of being spoken to.

He needs you. You need to fight.

'I'm not fighting,' she muttered. She had no idea why. She stuffed the scarab back inside her shirt.

We need a warrior.

She closed her eyes. She didn't need to fight sleep either. Just as sleep grabbed hold of her, the car halted. She was alert again, her eyes snapping open.

The driver had pulled on to the side of the road. She jerked up, looked around. There were no buildings nearby, no other traffic.

Except, parked behind her, a large black car. It looked like a Rolls. From out of it jumped two men, both in black suits, incongruous in the sun, and with bulges in their jacket pockets. She didn't need to ask what they were carrying. She turned to face Cosgrove. He gave a grim smile.

'For me, I think, my dear.'

He opened his door and stepped out, striding out to meet the two men halfway between the cars. Fiona could see them gesturing back the way they had come, Cosgrove shaking his head, pointing to the car, shrugging, throwing his head back. She couldn't help but smile. The man had picked up so many mannerisms from his time here that when he switched to

Arabic, he spoke in body language as well. Finally, he turned back to the car, resigned.

The larger of the suits returned to his own car, the other followed Cosgrove. He tapped at the window for the driver to wind it down before leaning in to speak to her.

'I'm sorry, my dear.' Cosgrove looked back at the suit. 'It appears that I won't be able to accompany you the rest of the way home. Urgent business.'

This was becoming a familiar story.

'What urgent business?' she growled.

'Top secret I'm afraid.' He sighed. 'I really can't turn this one down. It could cause major problems for relationships. Ahmed will get you home and Venessa will be ready with a good spread. I'll get back to you as soon as I can.'

'Is Alistair going to join us?'

The slight pause before he answered told her all she needed to know.

'I hope he can,' was all Cosgrove could assure her.

As he walked back to the black Rolls and Ahmed started the engine again, Fiona stared out at the Nile. Those white sails represented something so simple and free.

Instead, she was in this car and very alone.

CHAPTER FIFTEEN
The Magic City

EACH BUILDING looked the same. Sixteen beds, each one a stone slab, covered with the tattered remnant of cotton sheets, just visible in the dim light from outside. Lethbridge-Stewart picked at the wall. It was made of clay, not the polished material of the archway that led into the city.

The troops made the buildings. The voice was where it always was, just behind his shoulder.

'What do you want with me?' Lethbridge-Stewart gripped the rifle, knowing that it would do no good here and now. The thing was simply following him, again.

You could lead an army like the one that once lived here. Even from here, still trapped in that jar, you have seen what we can do. The troops we can summon.

'What troops?'

The man that attacked you at the tombs. The animals that followed the boat. Lethbridge-Stewart thought he could hear an amusement to the voice. He sighed.

'That man couldn't shoot straight to save his life.' He started to walk out of the building. 'And, as for the crocs… I'm not particularly impressed that you got a carnivorous aquatic animal to follow a boat and eat a man that you threw off it.' He swallowed. 'No matter how impressed a few marine biologists were that it was there at all.'

He stepped out into the red light of the city and looked around. Footsteps followed behind him.

Think about it. The chance to fight wars across more places than just this planet. The chance to travel the universe. Montu's voice was earnest now. *My brothers used automatons in battle. Slow moving, cumbersome things. Instead, we perfected a true army. A thousand species that fought together, their commanders augmented as gods themselves…*

'And who would I be fighting for?'

The voice was silent for a moment.

Why do you need to fight for one person? it said. *I am offering you the universe.*

Lethbridge-Stewart paused outside another building. 'My country is important,' he said, looking through the doorway, 'And, for that matter, my planet. The fighting that I do is simply something that needs to be done.' Through the doorway, he could see shapes on these slabs. He entered, seeing row on row of man-sized bundles of cloth, one on each stone bed. He took his rifle and pushed aside a covering.

A skull rolled across the slab and dropped to the floor with a loud crash. He jumped back as it shattered. As the echoes faded, there was no other sound. Below the cloth was nothing but bones, grey and dusty from centuries in the city. Clearly, mummification was not something reserved for simple soldiers like these men.

They were trapped here, hissed the voice in his head. *They starved to death over many days while they suffered with us in our imprisonment. They were denied their chance for battle and for life.*

Lethbridge-Stewart bent down, placing the rifle on the cold stone floor, and he picked up the broken pieces of the skull and placed them reverently back on the slab. He covered them with the cloth and stood back.

'A dreadful way to treat a defeated foe. Not something I want any part in.'

He inclined his head at the rest of the room and made to withdraw.

We weren't defeated, Montu said. *Our side won. The two of us were imprisoned here because we didn't want to stop fighting. We left the army after the battle was won and continued the war. This is how they repaid us.*

Lethbridge-Stewart stood, gathering his breath.

'It's a novel way to desert. Most do it to stop fighting. I have nothing more to say to you.' He kept walking. The footsteps didn't follow.

Lethbridge-Stewart continued down the main street, watching

the identical buildings slip by on each side as he went. One of the two pyramids in the far corners had to be Montu's tomb. The other? Well, he had time to look at both, he supposed. Unless one of the other parties arrived first.

The larger one made sense. He picked the left-hand path. As he walked down it, he got a sense of something, a sound at the edge of his hearing. He stopped and realised what it was.

It was the roar of an engine, echoing through the entrance to the city. He turned around, searching for somewhere he could use as a vantage point.

He thought quickly, it could be a bit of a jump, but it was worth a risk. With the rifle over one shoulder, he placed one foot up on the sill of one of the holes that served as windows to the dormitory buildings, then pulled himself up, throwing his hands onto the roof as he reached his full height. There was a small wall around the top of the building. Not enough to stop a man falling, but enough to hide behind.

The sound of the engine cut out. Lethbridge-Stewart tensed and waited.

Through the gateway he could see the figures coming. A motley collection of sizes and clothing. Even from this distance, he knew that it was Salem, Dawoud and his friends. They walked down the street, heading towards where he lay hidden, still holding their weapons. Professor Salem led the way. Dawoud was carrying something else, however. It was difficult, but as he approached, Lethbridge-Stewart saw that held in both hands was another jar. The carving was different. It appeared to be sleeker, a feline shape, rather than a bull.

Lethbridge-Stewart dropped down to the floor behind the rampart, then heard the booted feet ambling, not marching past.

Two jars, two pyramids. What did they want from this god? The tablet that Dawoud held had said that Montu would seek revenge until the heart was returned. What would this other jar do for whatever was in the other tomb?

The footsteps faded after they clattered past until Lethbridge-Stewart thought he may be safe enough to raise his head. From there, he could see the direction they had taken. The group was still moving through the city, heading for the smaller of the two red bricked pyramids.

Lethbridge-Stewart slid over the edge of the rampart and dropped back to the street, the stone paving doing little to break his fall. He breathed hard, recovering his breath before continuing his path.

As he walked the streets, he tried to remember what Greaves had told him. 'Return the jar to the tomb,' was what the tablet had said.

Lethbridge-Stewart paused, his mind whirring.

Return the jar to the tomb to stop revenge on the ones who had stolen it and their family. That was the supposed curse. Except, that wasn't what had played out. Greaves' brother had died after he refused to fight in the tests. Frederick Mortimer had run from some apparition and fallen to his death with the crocodiles. He had been plagued by dreams as well. Mortimer had no connection with the jar. The camel man had jumped off a cliff after Lethbridge-Stewart had cornered him. Lethbridge-Stewart was not unconvinced the man hadn't been a test himself. A simple pawn that had outlived his usefulness.

It was as if the jar had wanted to be taken from its tomb, out into the world, and then returned, having found a suitable warrior.

The term it put him in mind of was *recruiting sergeant.*

Enough was enough. He was not going to be a pawn to a jumped up god. Especially one that had such a twisted idea of what military service entailed.

Lethbridge-Stewart sighted the pyramid and set off after it. There was nothing he could do about Dawoud and Salem. He didn't even know what they were up to and whether they were gunning for or against the creatures locked in the city.

As he approached the thing, his boldness faded. Closer to the pyramid, he saw more buildings full of skeletons. Some were even lying in the street. They hadn't been able to die in bed. Or worse. Had they starved to death, had they been cut down by their comrades? He started walking again, feeling the emptiness of the city weigh on him.

He almost wished that those interminable footsteps would start again behind him, just so that he had some company. With the weight of the jar on his back and the rifle in his now cut and calloused hands, he simply wanted something to shout at. To blame.

That's what gods were for.

Lethbridge-Stewart reached the wall of the tomb. It inclined away from him. He remembered hearing, just a few days ago, that when newly built, the Giza pyramids had been clad with additional stone, which formed a smooth cover to the steps that were so familiar to the tourists.

This pyramid still had that cladding. It had been sealed away from the wind and the rain and looters. Or, at least, all looters except for Mr Greaves senior, and Lethbridge-Stewart was now pretty sure that was a set-up.

He ran his hands across the stone, hoping that it would open up in front of him. Nothing. He resigned himself to walking around the edge of the building, rifle in front of him, ready for anything that may happen. Somehow, he doubted it would have much effect.

The other pyramid jumped to mind, and he stopped, listening. There were no sounds from the far corner of the city. Whatever Dawoud and company were up to, they were doing it quietly.

He continued around the walls, his eyes grazing over the stone slabs, flicking over to the surrounding buildings. More utilitarian mud dormitories. More skeletal remains of Montu's army.

The row of buildings continued around the corner of the pyramid. That was when he realised that the entrance had been hard to miss. Twelve feet high and arched. Clearly, he had been intended to find it easily.

Between its supporting pillars, he saw the stone doors, closed. Somehow, he knew which way this was going. He shrugged and stepped towards them, not breaking his stride.

His thoughts were confirmed as he heard the sound of stone scraping on stone, the dust dropping from the top of the doors as they inched open. He continued down the corridor that opened beyond them as the walls started to glow, lighting his way along the path that continued upwards. It narrowed as it went, the ceiling rising such that he felt like he walked at the bottom of a deep cut in the fabric of the pyramid.

The walls were as bare as the rest of the structures of the city. This was no place for the Ancient Egyptians to live, it was no decorative tomb. This was a military citadel. The pyramid was a prison.

The passage came to an end at another stone door, one that remained closed as he approached. He nudged the door with the butt of his rifle. It didn't give an inch.

He pushed it with his boot.

'Oh, come on!' Lethbridge-Stewart shouted at the empty tomb. 'If you want me to bring this damned thing back to you, at least make it easy!'

There was, of course, no response. He aimed a kick at the stone slab, it shifted an inch. He was almost relieved. Somehow, he had been expecting it to be another test of arcane knowledge and geometry. A test based on sheer brute strength and persistence was almost a relief.

He continued to kick at the door until it opened sufficiently for him to slip through. Rifle in hand, he pushed his way through to the darkness beyond.

The walls began to glow, a low red light to start with, rising through pink to orange. Lethbridge-Stewart looked around, at alcoves set at intervals in each wall. He could see the curved upper sections, but the lower halves were dark, like tunnels. Lethbridge-Stewart readied the rifle, the butt up against his shoulder, swinging it around the chamber.

The light was still too dark to see what could be in those alcoves. His mind filled with the thought of mummies, skin decaying and eyes hollowed, lurching out.

They failed to appear.

He stepped through the chamber, listening for anything and hearing only his own footsteps and breathing. How long had it been since someone had last walked in here? Had Greaves' grandfather made it this far? The thought occurred that Lethbridge-Stewart might be the first human to have set foot in there since Mortu had been imprisoned thousands of years ago.

So, what was waiting for him here? He wished he had a torch, just something to allow him to see into the darker recesses. The dim orange light was completely useless. One of these alcoves had to be a disguised tunnel entrance. What did the rest hold?

Lethbridge-Stewart stepped towards one, ready to fire, straining to see inside. There was some sort of shape there, an amorphous black mass. What he wouldn't give for a decent British bayonet. Taking a deep breath, he took the rifle and stabbed into the alcove, jumping back afterwards.

He wasn't sure what he was expecting, but the sound of metal components collapsing onto each other was not it.

He kicked the remaining lump, back heeled the metal into the light and looked down at it. He was no expert, but it looked like pieces of some sort of framework. He picked one up. It was light but immensely strong. There were thicker pieces inside, looking like some sort of hydraulics.

'My jailers.' The voice didn't come from behind him as it so often did; it came from the opposite side of the chamber. 'They've been dismantled for some time.' Montu sounded almost sad at the reality.

Lethbridge-Stewart kicked the littered pieces of robot that were scattered across the floor. He shrugged, shouldered his rifle and set off towards the source of the voice. Clearly someone had been here before. And, unless they had been very lucky, it had probably been several someones, several times before they managed to dismantle a robot army.

On the other side of the chamber, Lethbridge-Stewart paused, picked an alcove at random, reasonably close to the centre. It was also occupied by the mixture of metal and fabric. He worked his way along, kicking and meeting piles of scrap metal until he found one that seemed empty. He crouched down, feeling his way forward with the rifle. The alcove was the entrance to a low tunnel.

He sighed and dropped to his hands and knees, crawling through it as the tunnel inclined upwards. Dust and debris ground into his hands. Unlike previous tunnels and chambers, this one remained pitch black.

It may have only been a few minutes that he crawled through the narrow space, bruising his shoulder as he went and feeling his knuckles scraping along under the weight of the rifle, before a sudden sense of air and a breeze above his head told him that he had managed to exit the tunnel.

Lethbridge-Stewart stood. Standing in the blackness, he couldn't see a thing.

'Well,' he said. 'I'm here, and I've brought the heart.' He unslung the rucksack, reaching inside it for the jar.

The same pinkish orange light that had suffused the previous chambers started again.

As it lit the chamber, he saw that the room was bare except for two items. Immediately before him was a plinth, narrow, just large enough to take the jar, but empty. Its use was obvious.

Behind the plinth was something else. A sarcophagus or, at least, it looked like one. Plain and upright. Colours still decorated it, not faded like a museum piece, but bright as if they were painted yesterday. The image on it was the body of a man, dressed in black robes, but the head was that of a bull, the features, the horns, matched that of the carving on the jar that Lethbridge-Stewart now held in one hand.

He placed the jar on the floor, ignoring the plinth in front of him. The rifle dropped easily into his hand, from where he raised it to a firing stance.

'Right, Montu.' His voice echoed in the small chamber. 'It's time to have a talk.'

There was silence for a moment or so. Then he heard footsteps echoing through the small passageway behind him. They continued, even through the small crawl space, without a change in rhythm, before he heard that familiar low voice, now echoing around the chamber.

'Simply place the jar on the plinth.'

'You're in there aren't you?' Lethbridge-Stewart nodded at the sarcophagus. 'You've been imprisoned. So, what is the jar? Your key?' He pulled the rifle butt into his shoulder, simply to make the point. The bruises in his torso and arms ached as he stood there.

'It is immaterial!' The voice snapped now. 'Place it on the plinth.' Was that anger? Desperation?

'No. I am not in your army. I've been forced into this place by many people, not least, I believe, you.' Lethbridge-Stewart moved the rifle a few degrees to the right and squeezed the trigger. The crack of shot and its ricochet was loud enough to hurt his eardrum. Montu gasped and hissed in his ear as he pulled the bolt back to reload another bullet and re-sighted the rifle on the jar. 'Now,' Lethbridge-Stewart said in the silence that followed, 'what is that jar?'

He could feel the beast behind him shifting its weight.

'It is a device. It holds my essence apart from my body. Keeping me imprisoned by holding my powers separate. Within it, I am compressed, made so small. So ineffectual.' Montu sighed. Lethbridge-Stewart risked a glance over his shoulder, seeing only a flutter of deeper darkness fading. 'It does give me a small amount of freedom. Some power over the world around the jar. Some control of the weak or the unconscious. It took a long time before I discovered that.' There was a chuckle. 'It wasn't until your race's greed brought them here that I was removed, taken into your world. I have gathered power from the strong.'

'Just the strong. That's why you tested people on your little jaunt. Haunted the ones that you found wanting. Drove them to suicide. Delightful.' Lethbridge-Stewart's fingers tightened on the rifle. He could end this now, but he wanted answers. 'You knocked me out in the temple. Floored me.'

'That was Pakhet. My lieutenant. She is very powerful in that place. It was constructed to her specifications many years ago.'

'The cat god? Buried in the other pyramid?'

Montu's voice rattled with dry laughter.

'She was not a god, but she was a good soldier. She believed as I did. She commanded a legion of beasts. Easier to control and more powerful, but oh so stupid when left to their own devices. I preferred sentient life as my army. They sealed us both in here together.'

Lethbridge-Stewart thought. The jar with Pakhet's heart must have been on the boat as well. Pulling those damn crocodiles with it. Following him to the temple. He couldn't help but feel a twinge of sympathy for Mortimer. The man must have been terrified by something that caused him to leap into that river. He had no idea what was waiting for him.

'This jar, you're using it to test people. And to remove the failures. When you establish a connection, you need it to be with the right people, don't you? Otherwise, it all goes wrong. What do you need them for?'

Silence.

'Are they helping you break free?'

Lethbridge-Stewart heard the footsteps behind him, felt something tense, the breathing from the creature behind him grow faster. Montu hissed.

'Don't you dare. Talk!' snapped Lethbridge-Stewart, finger on the trigger. The breathing grew steadier. More controlled.

'It is a conduit for our power,' said Montu. 'It links me with all those souls that are marked. When it returns to this place, I can draw on those souls.'

So. Only the right souls in touch with the jar would be sufficient to help him break free. That's why the others had to die.

'You draw on them?'

'You've felt the slightest touch. The dreams. The tests. You would be a part of the greatest army. My army. It will be reborn.'

Lethbridge-Stewart shook his head. 'I don't want to be a soldier in your army.'

'You wouldn't be a soldier. I can offer you power beyond what those pathetic peons out there had. I can feel your potential. You could be the greatest warrior. I can share my power with you.'

Lethbridge-Stewart sighed. 'This again. The duty motivates me, not the fight itself.' He thought back to the numerous robot parts that had littered the previous chamber and his suspicions. 'This isn't the first time it's left and returned, is it? How many times? How many times has a fake prophecy brought the "right stuff" back to your cell? And how many more times is it going to come back again before you can escape?'

Montu took a deep breath behind him. 'I can hear the sound of one of your flying machines, coming closer. It brings many troops. I look forward to meeting them.'

Lethbridge-Stewart raised his rifle again at the jar. 'Not without this.'

This time Montu's laughter became something full blooded. It echoed around the chamber, pounding at Lethbridge-Stewart's head. He tried to force his mind against it, but it was no use. Eyes screwed shut, he knew he no longer had the jar in his sights.

Then the sound stopped and in front of him was Fiona.

She was stood in the alleyway in Cairo, just outside Cosgrove's front door. The dust and muted roar of traffic washed across him, fumes where there had previously only been the dry air of the tomb. He recognised Ahmed, Cosgrove's driver. He was nearby, chatting to the Bawab. Cosgrove, himself, of course, was nowhere to be seen.

In Fiona's hand was a small amulet, a scarab, that she turned over in her hand.

'I show you this, because you will have to return the jar,' Montu hissed. 'And then, when you have, you will join me. That amulet she holds is also a conduit. One that Pakhet and I share. Our link. We communicate through it. Primarily to each other, but also to the one that holds it. And we have power through it as well.'

Fiona screamed, a shrill sound that Lethbridge-Stewart had not heard before, and dropped to the floor, her body writhing on the paving stones as she held her head. He lunged toward her, his arms reaching for her.

Then he opened his eyes to the floor of the tomb, the dust coating the side of his face. The rifle lay abandoned just beyond his fingertips. He scrabbled across the floor, pulling it to him and getting back to his feet.

'You keep saying that your duty is more important than the fight,' said Montu. 'Then let us see. Your duty is to destroy the jar. But if you do that, I can still kill her through the amulet. If you want her to live, place the jar on the plinth. Then prepare to join my army.'

Lethbridge-Stewart looked at the rifle in his hand, then down at the jar. He knew what the right thing to do was. He had a duty, to Britain, to the world, to make sure that this monster stayed in his prison.

But he also had another duty, one to the woman he loved, even if he never saw her again. He thought of the plans for the wedding, images of a big house in the country, children. They felt so distant from this place. This tiny room in a tomb, in the middle of a desert, like an island for a castaway. There was no return home.

He lowered the rifle, clicking the safety on before swinging it over his shoulder, then he bent to pick up the jar. The room was in silence now. He couldn't feel Montu behind him. He held the thing in both hands, feeling the sudden desire to throw it to the ground, as he should have done when he sat around the fire with Greaves.

He lifted the jar and placed it on the plinth. The light in the room grew brighter, the orange changing to yellow.

CHAPTER SIXTEEN
Street Named Hell

THE LIGHT outside the pyramid was burning brighter too now.

Lethbridge-Stewart staggered out of the archway, still feeling the bruises from the jeep crash and his impact with the tomb's floor. He glanced behind him. The pyramid itself seemed to be glowing, the building now waking from centuries of slumber.

Paths led away from him, each one a line intersected by others, regular, like lines on a parade ground or racks in a filing system.

Something had changed even more than the light that blazed from above, covering the whole ceiling and chasing away the shadows. He leaned against a doorframe as his mind groped through what it had seen only an hour ago. What had changed?

Footsteps hammering on the paved surface brought him back to reality. Someone was heading directly for him. He pulled himself into the doorway, trying to focus on the direction the running feet were coming from. The steps echoed between the buildings, he pulled the rifle into him, his fingers finding the trigger again.

He risked a quick glance out of the doorway and recognised the figure now heading from the direction of Pakhet's pyramid. Dawoud ran like a rat, his head down and feet scampering in short steps. He didn't appear armed.

'What happened?' Lethbridge-Stewart said, stepping out of the doorway.

The man stopped, his eyes flashing. Arms jerking up, he ignored the rifle, lunged at Lethbridge-Stewart, throwing him backwards into the building.

'You tell me,' Dawoud hissed. '*We* followed the instructions on the tablet exactly in the other tomb. What have you *done?*'

Lethbridge-Stewart brought the butt of the rifle up into Dawoud's stomach, winding the man enough to cause him to stagger backwards against one of the empty stone slabs.

'So did I,' he said. Then paused. 'After some persuasion. Isn't this what you wanted? You and your little cult.'

Dawoud leaned against the slab, gasping for breath. 'What I wanted? I wanted those beasts buried in here for good.' He swallowed, recovered his breath. 'We are not a cult. The professor has discovered so much lost knowledge about this place. Working with her, we knew what they are, where they came from. We know why their kind buried them here and what they will do if the two of them get free.' He spat on the floor, clearing his throat. 'That's why I bribed the cleaners at the Russian embassy for Pakhet's jar and returned it. That's why we needed Montu's. To imprison them both back here for good. What were you doing?'

He stole Pakhet's heart from the embassy? Well, that explained the Russian couple on the boat and their hostility to Dawoud. Had anyone on *Keberia* just been on a simple holiday?

'The same,' replied Lethbridge-Stewart 'But I tried to negotiate when I realised what was really happening.' He sat down on another slab. Dawoud seemed to be listening, or perhaps was just trying to get his wind back. 'I think that the tablet may have been a poor translation of the situation. Or a very good one dictated by Montu himself.' He took a deep breath. 'I have it on rather good authority that the jars are actually essential to releasing the pair of them. Sadly, by hook or by crook, that's exactly what they both have. '

'So, you know the history of this place better than us Egyptians do? Than Professor Salem who dedicated her life to this research? Why am I not surprised by that attitude?' Dawoud pulled himself up against the slab.

'You've come a long way from the meek little man that wanted Greaves to tell him all about his country's history. Believe me when I say this, the tablets, the prophecies… They are all designed to bring the jars home. To let the gods draw from the people that have passed their perverted little tests to become good soldiers.'

'I don't believe you.' Dawoud spat on the floor. 'You are telling me that a cause I have devoted myself to has been in service of these…' He threw his arm out to the doorway, as if searching for words. '…these monsters. They are not gods.'

'I can only apologise. For my own part as well.' Lethbridge-Stewart thought back to the image of Fiona dropping to the ground. 'But that is how it is. In any event, we need to stop Montu from gathering an army.'

Dawoud looked at him. Over his fussy, round little glasses, Lethbridge-Stewart could see something in his eyes. The expression was a haunted one, a man that had just lost everything.

'He already has an army, that's what destroyed my friends. And the professor.'

Lethbridge-Stewart stood up. 'He can't have that many. He has only just got the jar back. He's killed more recruits than he's taken. Even I'm not feeling any loyalty towards him yet. And I'm supposed to be his prize recruit.'

Dawoud shook his head sadly and looked around the empty building.

Empty.

That was when Lethbridge-Stewart noticed what was now missing from the streets and buildings that surrounded the pyramid. Corpses, skeletons, bones of long dead soldiers. All were now gone.

Lethbridge-Stewart's head jerked around. 'He can't, can he? He can't control bodies, corpses?'

Dawoud walked to the door, looked out at the street, glancing both ways. He turned back.

'This was their city. They created this city to build an army. Here, they can control everything that was theirs. Those skeletons were once people. People recruited into his army, like you. Like me.'

'They serve even after death,' said Lethbridge-Stewart.

Dawoud nodded again, looked back out of the doorway.

'But what about outside the city?' Lethbridge-Stewart was grasping. He knew. There must be something else that he could do now. This could not be the end of it. He couldn't simply drift away from his world, his future with Fiona, his duty and become a cog in this pathetic god's machine.

Dawoud shrugged. 'Who knows. I doubt that the dead could leave here. The writings said that the dead guarded the city. They made no mention of the dead fighting the battles.'

'Right,' said Lethbridge-Stewart. 'In that case, we need to get out of here. There's only two of them. Surely alone they can't control a full army.'

Dawoud sighed, like a teacher dealing with a particularly stupid pupil. 'That's what you and I will be for, don't you see?' He leaned on the doorframe, his back to the street outside. 'Their powers outmatch the rest of their kind when it comes to starting an army. That's why they were such a key part of the war that was fought here before the time of the Pharaohs.' Dawoud's face was grim. 'They can give their chosen generals powers that approach their own. They make a man into a demi-god. A tactic similar to that which your country used in India and south of the Sahara I believe. Not that it lessens the servitude of the men at the bottom of the pile.'

'This is not the best time for a history lesson.'

'Far too late you mean? Imagine, a whole army, a whole race in Montu's image and with his power to manipulate the mind. That's his plan for us.'

Lethbridge-Stewart checked the rifle. Only about four shots left in the magazine.

'And you have been part of it. You and your people. Always bringing these stupid jars back. Every time they got looted, you would follow the prophecy. Follow the tablet. And every damn time, you brought them back.' Lethbridge-Stewart slammed his fist into the flaking clay wall. 'And every time, you brought them back, their power grew.'

'That was the instruction. You stop the haunting by returning the jar. But your people are always greedy and always want more. They take and take and take again.'

Lethbridge-Stewart fixed Dawoud with a glare. He could feel anger inside him at this man, who had let himself be duped into doing the gods' dirty work.

'You could just leave them in England, or Russia, where they were. Our government could have looked after them and kept everyone safe. Instead of leaving us sitting here waiting for our call up papers.' He paused. 'Call up papyrus, then.' Lethbridge-Stewart knew he was being unfair. He knew that he was lashing out at the only person he could without any good reason.

Dawoud pulled himself to his feet. 'You arrogant—'

Lethbridge-Stewart didn't get to hear the rest of it. A sudden sharp pain in his temple heralded darkness that blurred into the edges of his vision.

The light faded back into Lethbridge-Stewart's eyes as he came to. A boot was worrying his ribs like a terrier with a bone. His eyes focused on the blurred outline of the man stood over him.

'You had better be okay,' came Dawoud's voice. 'You're the only other one in here that's not a walking corpse.'

Lethbridge-Stewart scrambled to his feet, picking up the rifle. Had that been the start of Montu taking over?

'Let's go,' he said.

The streets were still deserted when they left the building. Lethbridge-Stewart was reminded of his team's ill-fated trip to the streets during the London Event. A dead city and somewhere out there was an army or automata controlled by an alien power.

Two pyramids, each in the corner of the triangular mesa made the decision on direction easy. Aim for the empty corner and the gate out of the city. He chose an appropriate street and started jogging down it.

'What happened to the rest of your chaps?' he said to Dawoud who panted behind him.

The man's story was familiar. The pyramids had the same layout, right down to the plinth in the 'burial' chamber.

'I prefer the term "cell",' said Lethbridge-Stewart.

The group of Egyptians had considered it a job well done, and then retreated out of the pyramid to the entrance.

'That's where they found us,' said Dawoud. 'We didn't know it at first. We were just heading back to the entrance when Waaiz shouted behind us.' He took a deep breath. 'When I turned to see him, he was already being dragged away by them.'

'Walking corpses?'

Dawoud nodded, glancing behind him to check that nothing was following.

'Silent. They just came from every direction. All over. Some were bones. Some covered in rags. Maybe mummies.' His words were coming out in gasps. Lethbridge-Stewart knew that he was pushing the other man hard, but they had to get out of the city.

'Come on,' he said.

'Just one minute.' Dawoud stopped, leaning against the nearest door frame. Lethbridge-Stewart could see that his arm was shaking.

'Come on, man,' he snapped.

Dawoud didn't move. 'This is a lot for me.' His eyes looked out to the far corner of the city. 'I was a student. That's all I was. I had some experience at drama. As an actor. When we knew the jars were coming back to Egypt.' He swallowed. 'We all got together to decide what to do with the professor. That's when they put me on that boat.'

Lethbridge-Stewart stood in the street, looking quickly from side to side. Both ends were deserted. There was a sick feeling in his stomach. The knowledge that something was out there. They had covered some ground since the pyramid, but not enough. The dead were out there somewhere. Waiting for them.

'I'd really rather they hadn't,' he muttered.

'Me too,' said Dawoud. 'Since then, I've been shut in a boiler, shot at by a crazy man, forced to lead my friends across the desert, and then I had to watch them get slaughtered along with my professor.' He punched the wall next to him, sending clay dust down onto the floor. Dawoud slid his back down the wall to join it, sitting in a heap next to the doorway. 'This is not my life!' he shouted. 'I did it because it was right. And because I believed her. And it was all for nothing. And she's dead. She looked straight at me as they grabbed her. I'm never going to forget that.'

It wasn't shortness of breath that had got to him. He was in a full-on funk. Lethbridge-Stewart sighed. He couldn't blame him. Over the last few days, he had seen too many civilians, including Fiona, encounter things that were not their business. His duty was to deal with these things. It should never have fallen to the others.

If this were one of his troops, he would have snapped the man to attention, told him to pull himself together and act like a soldier. But he wasn't. This was a man whose best intentions had been to stop the two gods imprisoned in this city. That's what had led him here.

Lethbridge-Stewart placed a hand on the man's shoulder. 'They've spared you,' he said. 'You've had those dreams, haven't you? Those pernicious little tests.'

Dawoud nodded.

'Then they've got you marked for something. They think you've got some worth. Let's show them they're more right than they know, eh?' Lethbridge-Stewart clapped the man's shoulder. 'Come on, man. Let's get out of here and take the fight to them.'

He reached for Dawoud's hand to help him upright. Then he saw the look in the man's eyes and froze.

'My right-hand side,' said Dawoud. 'It's there.'

Lethbridge-Stewart was standing on the man's left. He pulled the rifle out and silently padded around to the other side, where there was a doorway into the building.

It was a hand, clutching at Dawoud's tunic, skeletal, the flesh mostly gone, the fingers flexing as they scrabbled upwards. Only a wrist was attached, the stump dragging along behind the hand itself. Dawoud sat, rigid, as it worked its way up his body. Lethbridge-Stewart checked the safety on the rifle. He hoped that its recent mistreatment on their expedition hadn't damaged the mechanism.

Taking the barrel in both hands, he took an experimental swing. He had never been much of a man for sports. He jabbed down at the hand with the rifle butt, knocking it away from Dawoud and trapping it against the wall of the building with the barrel.

'Go now!' he shouted.

Dawoud was up, scrabbling away from the doorway. Lethbridge-Stewart released his hold on the hand, and it immediately dropped into its fingertips, racing towards him like a spider. He stamped on it, hearing the bones crunch under his heel as he did so, raising his foot again and again as the thing lay there.

It may not have been dead even after that. He decided not to wait to check and took off after Dawoud.

From the corners of his eyes, Lethbridge-Stewart saw movement coming down every side street, from behind him, from the tops of buildings. Silent movement, just glimpsed in many cases as bleached white bone and cream rags against the bright yellow light shining from above.

Skeletons, bodies, wraiths still clad in tattered sheets, tens of them, hundreds maybe, all converging on where he now stood in the street.

He ran for Dawoud, grabbing him by the collar.

'Come on!' he shouted.

Dawoud just stood, shock still, and pointed a trembling finger forwards at the street in front of him. The direction that led to the gate.

The road in front of them was filling with the dead, staggering, limping, some scrambling on all fours and all blocking the way forward. Lethbridge-Stewart looked about him. Side streets were the same; each one that could have led away from this road was full of them. They blocked doorways, stood on rooftops. He hadn't heard them approach. These bodies that had lain for centuries, now moving, advancing, like an army.

His army. If he became Montu's general.

'Wait here,' he said to Dawoud. 'I've got an idea. Get ready to run.' He stepped forward. 'Right then, you chaps!' he snapped. 'All of you, halt!' The skeletons stopped moving. Their grinning pale skulls staring eyelessly at him as if laughing at him. 'None of you are to move,' he said, nudging Dawoud and nodding in the direction of the gate. 'You know that we are not to be harmed. And you will follow that order.'

Dawoud wasn't moving, his hand was shaking.

'Come on,' hissed Lethbridge-Stewart. 'This is our only chance.' He pointed at the shock still skeletons. If he said it out loud, they would know what was going on, they could be caught, killed or dragged back to Montu and Pakhet. Surely the man knew that.

Dawoud started to take tentative steps down the street, following Lethbridge-Stewart towards the entrance. Lethbridge-Stewart grabbed him by the collar.

'Walk carefully. Act like an officer. We can make it past them.' He could feel the sweat on the man's neck, see him shaking. 'Snap out of it.'

The first skeletons were within touching distance now, the faces turned to face them, the constant grins still there. He could see that flesh still clung to some among rags and tatters of clothing, draped from brittle shoulders like thick cobwebs.

He tried not to think that some of these corpses may have been more recent than others.

Dawoud stopped dead, when Lethbridge-Stewart turned back, the man was visibly shaking.

'Come on!' he snapped at the Egyptian. 'We can't stop here.'

Around him came rustling, faint, on the edges of hearing, like a soft breeze through new leaves. He turned slowly. The heads of the skeletons were cocked to one side now. Quizzical, sizing him up.

He grabbed for Dawoud. The man simply jerked away from him. Instinct.

Instinct seemed to drive the skeletons as well. At that moment, they lunged for him.

Lethbridge-Stewart wasted no time, he immediately bolted away. He could see the empty street behind this group.

In a flash of white, one stepped in front of him, he felt the arms encircle him like a pair of steel rods. He twisted, throwing his shoulder in first and felt the body that held him stagger and give way, without letting go.

They both fell onto the hard stone surface of the road, where he heard and felt the ribs crack on impact. Brittle twigs that splintered, releasing him from the grip of the arms. He pulled himself up onto hands and knees and leapfrogged over the empty eye sockets of the skull that now glared at him.

Lethbridge-Stewart was back on his feet and running down the road before he started to hear the sound of running feet behind him, clicking as they pounded over the road surface.

He kept his head down, risking the occasional look back.

The chaotic and uncoordinated mass behind him appeared to be making some headway. He snapped his eyes forward again. There was the archway that opened out to the desert outside. He hoped that maybe, if he could just get to it…

The pain hit his head again, and he stumbled as it did so. His eyes forced shut. Legs wobbling, he weaved across the road, bouncing off the side of a building. They would still be coming behind him. Those rictus mouths, looking so gleeful atop those jerking bodies, were still following and they would be on him soon.

Eyes open. Focus on the arch. Run for the arch. Most of all, don't think about how some of those men had been trapped here before. Don't think about why, if he was far from the first person here in millennia, the door was closed when he arrived.

Don't consider how he might be entombed with these gods.

He could barely feel his own legs. The arch was closer now, waiting for him. He had no idea what he might find on the other side, if he would simply get there and be dragged back inside, indentured to service with Montu and Pakhet.

There was a buzzing at the back of his head, something that grew and grew.

The buildings on either side blurred, the gate ahead seemed to wave in the light. He blinked, forced himself to keep going, to just take another hundred or so strides.

Then he saw at the bottom of the archway, shapes. Dark shapes that strode through it, heading straight for him. A sense, a whisper at the back of his head said one word.

Enemy.

He knew the voice.

'Get out of my head!' he roared.

But still the hollowing clicking of running skeletons came from behind, still the buildings on either side funnelled him down the road, still the figures stood in the archway, waiting. Waiting for him.

Join your troops. They can clear a path.

Was the voice right? It made sense. He had fought like this in the tests. This should be easy. He could marshal the troops. He could coordinate them. Make sure that the invading force was dealt with. Protect the city.

Lethbridge-Stewart blinked, shook his head.

This wasn't his city. He had protected his city. London, a city of a thousand ideas and a million fashions. As many gods as people. Not a barracks that held only two.

Neither of whom impressed him.

Vision had faded to just showing outlines. Now, he knew that whatever was in his head was taking over. It was going to control him. It was going to stride right into this city and through that archway and it was going to destroy the pyramids where the gods slept before they could fully awaken.

Was that right?

Lethbridge-Stewart stopped dead, just before the archway, as those dark shapes rushed for him. The rifle was in his hand. He could easily take a few out. If only he could see. He pulled it up to his eye, sighted along it, seeing only the figures that milled in front of him. He could hear shouts, in a foreign language, see many scattering as he squeezed the trigger. None fell. They dived out of the way, as he let off one, two, three, four shots.

The rifle clicked as he tried to put another round in. Empty. He reversed it, using it as a club and ran for the nearest figure.

He was hit from the side, fleshy muscled arms wrapping around him and throwing him against the wall of the nearest building. A hand grabbed his own collar, dragging him towards the archway.

'Alistair, stop it, what are you doing?'

The voice. He recognised it, from a boat thousands of miles away and a million years ago.

'Azmy?' he croaked.

Lethbridge-Stewart's vision started to clear; he recognised that once cheerful Egyptian server. The man was dressed in an olive military uniform.

'What…?'

It seemed so long ago that he had last seen the man. He had wanted to join up, didn't he?

'Congratulations,' Lethbridge-Stewart said. 'I knew you could do it.'

He was dragged further, up the steps to the archway. Shots thundered around him, he could hear the rifles cracking, the sound of the occasional bone splintering as the skeletons followed. His head cleared to the familiar sound of battle. Azmy pulled him behind the lee of one of the buildings, out of the line of fire.

'Blunt force,' Lethbridge-Stewart said. 'You need blunt force, break the bones.'

Azmy snapped an order, and a soldier dropped his rifle, pulling out a grenade. Lethbridge-Stewart smiled. A good tactic. The small object arced through the air, out of sight of where they stood, before the dull crump of an explosion shook the ground, dust blowing back over the troops. As it did so, Lethbridge-Stewart felt a weight lift from his shoulders.

'Wait,' he said. 'It's clear now. You were spying on me. You followed us here.' He paused, before grabbing the lapels of Azmy's uniform. 'You killed Greaves, chasing us with that damn helicopter.'

'Service of the country,' said Azmy simply. 'The same as you. Where are the jars?'

'Never you mind!' Lethbridge-Stewart kept a hold of the man's shirt, knowing that as soon as he let go, he would be fighting the urge to punch him in the face.

The buzzing at the back of his head faded, he could feel the pins and needles in his arms now, like a line of insects marching down each one, heading for his hands and flowing through them.

Flowing into Azmy. The other man winced in pain, screwing his eyes against the sensation. Lethbridge-Stewart's own legs began to shake, he felt himself falling forward, at the same time as he felt Azmy's weight against himself. The sounds of the battle faded.

They both collapsed in the rock and dust of the city.

CHAPTER SEVENTEEN
Body and Soul

IT WAS dark. Silent.

He could feel others around him. Hundreds maybe. Some felt close, as if standing in the same room. Azmy was one. Dawoud too. Other soldiers were nearby, he recognised something in them that told him, like a sense beyond sight, beyond hearing.

That same part of him knew that others were further away. Souls that the jars had selected and kept alive. Some were guests of the Greaves' house through the years. Some were Egyptians. Others came from far away. Somewhere cold, regimented. Pakhet had recruited the Russians in some numbers. The space, whatever it was, was filled with anyone that could lead a part of the army that these aliens wanted to create.

He tried to speak, but like the worst dreams, no sound would come out. His mouth wouldn't open, his arms remained frozen next to his sides.

They must have all been stood in a circle, because at the centre of their gathering, light suddenly burned.

They were there. The two gods, or aliens, whatever they were. Both clad fully in black robes with the bodies of what looked like large humans.

Their heads were another matter. Montu stood with the head of a bull, two huge golden horns that stabbed into the darkness and eyes that burned green as he looked around.

Pakhet looked like the depictions of her in the temple back on the banks of the Nile: lithe and topped by a feline head of silken fur and upright ears.

'Our minds are free.' The voice was familiar, but no longer

a whisper behind a shoulder, it filled the space. 'But our bodies remain imprisoned. Thank you. All of you. We can draw on you. You will help us. We can break free.' He paused. Even here in this unreal space, Lethbridge-Stewart could see that the corners of the bull's mouth had turned up. It was smiling. 'We are so grateful.'

Pakhet's voice was one that he had never heard before, soft and sibilant. 'Then, the crusade can begin, and we can reach out to the universe. All of us, together. We will escape here. And you will all accompany us. You who are blessed and chosen.' There was no sense of artifice in her words. She meant everything she said. 'You will be raised up with us. To become more than the crawling apes of this world. To become one with us. A family, enhanced and powerful.' Her arms raised. 'Be one with us.'

Pain, like shards of metal, pounded into Lethbridge-Stewart's skull from every angle, pain that made whatever passed for his body here twist and writhe. He tried to scream and failed.

Around him the others did the same. He knew this, in the depths of his agony, as if connected to them all in some way. Something was being pulled from them all, yanked out like a fish being filleted. All the time, the light around the gods burned brighter and brighter.

Fiona opened her eyes to the guest room in the Cosgrove household. Her head heavy and throbbing, as if she'd just had a night full of gin.

She was sure that she'd felt fine in the car, right up until she was outside the door, then she had collapsed. A sudden sense of being elsewhere as her legs had slid from underneath her.

Then she was in the bedroom with vague memories of Venessa Cosgrove and Ahmed helping her up the stairs, into bed.

Pushing herself up on her elbows only made her head swim more. She cast about, her hand grasping, finally finding a glass, the water now warm in the heat of the day. It was enough, she gulped at it, spitting some back as her throat, too dry, retched.

Out of bed, she staggered to the window. That same

window that she had stood in before they had joined the *Keberia*. When she had been so happy because the holiday had started and she and Alistair were together. She had thought he would protect her.

She was back here, alone. Left out and left behind. Her future was mapped out and it would be this one.

Out there, in the smog and the dust of Cairo, lives continued, cars threaded and horns honked. It was a maelstrom of life that sucked her in, made her feel as she had in the Hotel Royale back in the oasis, being pulled out.

And on the rooftops below her window, cats. All stopped shock still and staring at her. Waiting for her.

She turned back to the room, the dark furniture blurring after the bright sun outside. A single step back inside and she felt her legs shake. Perhaps she should lie down again. Another step back towards the bed, the blurs coalesced, flowing into each other, the darkness filling her vision as her knees hit the carpet.

She opened her eyes to darkness, surrounded by others; soldiers, warriors and, at the centre of the ring, a light burned. She felt in that instant the tug at her chest, where the amulet sat.

There was that voice again, the strong, sibilant voice that had spoken to her in the Hotel Royale. The one that had taunted her, tried to persuade her to be a warrior.

And it spoke to her again, asking her, pleading with her, to be content. To join them. To be one with all the warriors and champions present.

She pulled away.

To Lethbridge-Stewart, it was a symphony. A collection of the themes, each one a note from the mind of a person. The strands combined, swirled together, gathering above the gods as they breathed in the fruit of the threads that mixed above.

There was a single thread, a single note even, that pulled away, fleeing, spiralling through all of the others, jerking away as they got closer, then dodging out to the edge of the space. Lethbridge-Stewart felt something, some kinship with it. In his mind, he reached out for it, to whatever this thing was that was no part of this gathering of the minds.

'No…' groaned Montu. 'The convergence, the flow is disrupted at the nexus…'

Lethbridge-Stewart pulled himself towards it, feeling the pull back, the pain in his temples growing as Montu and Pakhet grabbed him with their own minds, his mind becoming ever more theirs, ever more a part of their army.

Then he was linked. They all were. Montu was all of them and they were all Montu.

That's when Lethbridge-Stewart knew everything. All of the souls that were present, they were an army and a power source. As Montu drew their power, they became like him. As they became like him, they fed his own strength. That strength that would allow Montu and Pakhet to break free.

They had been selected. Like a breeder might select the best specimens because any mistake, any discordance now would be fatal. Like a trip switch plunging a house into darkness. And Montu would have to start again.

That discord was here. Montu was nevertheless trying to pull through, to use all of the power of the chosen ones to break through that discord and escape, before being thrown into darkness.

Fiona could feel something familiar as she thrashed around.

Something that was at once hers, but at once a betrayal, a whole that she wanted no part of.

She jumped away from every sensation, her mind flipping around as it did so and then, suddenly, there was Alistair. She couldn't see his face, but she knew it was him. Whatever this sensation was, he was at one with this place, growing into it like water rushing into an empty channel, filling it.

And in that moment, the evasions, the secret midnight trips, the army and the country that came first, that always came first, jumped to her mind.

Fiona tore away, throwing him back as she pulled further and further away, an instinct, a simple desire that kicked in as her future stretched in front of her.

Montu screamed, Pakhet's voice joined him as the symphony of minds abruptly ended.

Lethbridge-Stewart felt the snap of a connection being

severed. It echoed through the assembled throng, reverberating across the men and women that lay, writhing, across the space.

'I will go to her,' hissed Pakhet. 'The nexus is breaking. The amulet…'

'It has broken,' said Montu. 'This chance is gone. Thousands of wasted years.'

The pain subsided as everything went black again.

Soft light danced across his eyelids as he felt hands under his arms pulling him upright.

'What the devil's going on?' Lethbridge-Stewart muttered.

Azmy stood alongside him, supporting his weight. They were back inside the city again, surrounded by soldiers that were just stirring and skeletons that lay shattered across the rock and dust.

'No idea. My guess, a short circuit. Someone really did not want to be there.'

The ground shook. Lethbridge-Stewart glanced back to the pyramids. The light that was now dimming in the rest of the city almost seemed to be rushing towards the giant structures, like water escaping a sink. Blinking his eyes did nothing to make the image easier to see.

His eyes screwed up in the glare as each pyramid simultaneously flashed and then went dark, like a bulb burning out.

'Come on!' snapped Azmy, yanking at Lethbridge-Stewart's shoulder. 'Whatever's happened, it's trapped them again. We don't want to be stuck in here with them.'

He was right. Lethbridge-Stewart could see the doors on the other side of the archway starting to narrow. Around him were men, some groggy, others looking around in confusion.

He grabbed at the neck of the uniform of the man nearest him, throwing him forward, towards the gate.

'Go!' He pointed. 'Go now!' If the words were lost, he hoped the intent was clear.

He looked around, running to the other soldiers, pointing them, pushing them, shouting loudly and clearly, yet hoping for the best, as only a British man abroad can do. Azmy did the same, speaking quickly in Arabic, barking orders, grabbing his most confused troops and almost throwing them towards the narrowing doors. Finally, Lethbridge-Stewart knew that he had to go now. He put his head down and ran for the crack, bright sunlight glaring through it. Azmy was next to him, the last of his troops already disappearing through.

Azmy reached the gate first. There were two metres left to go before it sealed shut. As Lethbridge-Stewart put an extra spurt on to reach it, he felt his leg, already weak from the fall, collapse to one side.

The doors continued to close, sealing off the outside world, leaving him here, trapped with the mad gods. One and a half metres, nearly just one. He struggled to his feet, feeling his legs wobbling.

That's when he felt a hand on his bicep, dragging him along, another pushing his back, propelling him through the gap as he closed to one metre, half a metre and then the final crunch behind him as he lay in the gravel and rock of the desert once more.

'I couldn't leave you in there, could I, Brigadier?' Azmy smiled, through the sweat and the dirt on his face. 'Not after what happened in there. Somehow, I just know you had something to do with getting those two back in their tombs, where they belong.'

'If I had anything to do with it, I'm damned if I know what,' said Lethbridge-Stewart. 'You seem pretty happy about the way it's turned out.'

Azmy shrugged. 'Orders are orders. Our government wanted the gods and their power, but I cannot say I was thrilled at the idea. Sometimes, it is best to leave these things alone.' He gave a secret grin, one that took Lethbridge-Stewart back to *Keberia*. 'One god is enough for Egypt now I think.'

They looked around at the men strung out, confused, shaking their heads. Some, in the quiet that followed the battle and their trip to that other place, were praying, hunched to the ground.

Over the sounds of relief and barely suppressed panic came another sound, a familiar thrumming noise of a large transport helicopter.

'Here come reinforcements, Brigadier.'

'For you, Captain. Not for me.'

'You acted honourably. I will make my report. Explain the confusion that caused us to chase you, the issues that caused the gods to go back to bed.' As the dust started to blow at the top of the ravine, Azmy dropped his voice. 'Please, not a word about my own views of this mission.'

'You have my word,' said Lethbridge-Stewart, watching the dust boil and settle down the slope from the clifftop above.

The newcomers weren't all soldiers. Behind the olive clad troops that confidently jogged down the scree slope to the bottom of the ravine, others followed, in overalls, suits and civilian clothes. Lethbridge-Stewart recognised one that brought up the rear, slower, maybe even older than the rest, his fatigues and pith helmet once more in place. Lethbridge-Stewart waited for him to reach the bottom.

'Cosgrove,' he said.

'Alistair!' Cosgrove jogged up, red-faced, short of breath. He panted, leaning on his knees. 'I'm so glad you made it through.'

Around them, orders were barked and experts were updated. Lethbridge-Stewart could see that Azmy was speaking quickly to two senior officers. A pointing finger in his direction and a dismissive gesture appeared to tell him that the other man was sticking with the story that the chase across the desert had been a mistake.

'What are you doing here?' Lethbridge-Stewart measured his words carefully.

'I'm really here as part of the civilian cleanup crew.' Cosgrove waved at those that surrounded him. 'A bunch of scientists, archaeologists, history experts. The sort of thing a place like this needs.'

'And what are you supposed to be cleaning up?'

Cosgrove stood, his eyes fixed on the former gate that was surrounded by the soldiers and various other officials. 'Well, you as a matter of fact. I seem to have got you into this.'

'Yes, you did.'

Across the ravine, one archaeologist aimed a kick at the rock wall that marked the former gateway. He howled in pain and hopped around.

'Right.' Cosgrove gestured at the helicopter up on the cliff. 'I think you and Fiona are due in Luxor about now. We should go and get her.' He set off across the sand.

Lethbridge-Stewart clenched a fist. General or not, he had had enough. 'Just one moment.'

He could see Cosgrove's shoulders drop, like the mask falling away. 'Lethbridge-Stewart,' he said as he turned. Last name basis, as if he were only now trying to pull rank.

'You set this up. You knew who was on that steamer. You knew *what* was on that steamer. You knew the dangers that we were in.' Lethbridge-Stewart's arms waved towards the sealed city, hidden in the mesa. 'You know what was in that place. That the government were after it. You pushed me through all of this. Hijacked our trip to throw me into this mix.'

'I needed a man I could trust close to the action.' Cosgrove's face barely moved a muscle.

'Fiona? Did she need to be close to the action? You could have just got your agents to do it, instead of throwing us in there.' Lethbridge-Stewart leaned forward, he could feel his blood pounding as he realised the enormity of what he was saying. 'My fiancée could have been killed. You didn't even have the decency to warn me.'

'Warn you?' Cosgrove took his helmet off, ran his hand through his hair. Without it, he looked like an old man, out of place and out of depth. 'Alistair, you're as straight as an arrow. If I had told you what was going on, the whole of the Arab League would have been told about it in five minutes. I couldn't have it known that Britain was interfering. We got in enough trouble for that twenty years ago.'

'I didn't hear of any aliens in Suez.' Lethbridge-Stewart almost spat the words.

'It makes no difference. Without some sort of united international response to this kind of thing...'

'... you need to put civilians at risk. Wonderful work, Cosgrove.' It was somewhat immature, but Lethbridge-Stewart took some pleasure in referring to the man as he would a subordinate, as a civilian would refer to a member of the services. Cosgrove needed a discreet reminder that at this very moment, Alistair Gordon Lethbridge-Stewart was not on duty and certainly not subject to any orders.

'Look. It's all turned out for the best, hasn't it? Whatever those things are, you seem to have them safely sealed away.' Cosgrove leaned forward. 'I'll debrief you later,' he muttered.

'No, you won't,' said Lethbridge-Stewart.

'If you like.'

'Here's your debrief, General. Walk up that ravine. Pay your respects to Mr Greaves. Then come back here and pay the same to all of the men dead and trapped in the city. And a woman too. A professor. Not a great one, but she didn't deserve to be killed in there.'

Cosgrove didn't let a muscle move on his face. 'I may do that. I usually find it easier not to. Let's get you to the next helicopter out of here before the Egyptian authorities decide what they're going to do instead.' Cosgrove turned away. 'Feel free to stay here and find out if you want.'

Lethbridge-Stewart looked around. About him, bodies were busy, taking measurements, jotting down reports. Their disinterest in him would soon fade. He had no choice.

It was late when they landed at the Air Force base near Cairo. It had been a long wait before the helicopter lifted off. A medical flight had gone first, taking the walking wounded and their less lucky comrades back. Cosgrove and Lethbridge-Stewart had been forced to wait for the scientists and other experts to finish their measurements and photographs, throw up their hands in despair and give up the city as once more being lost. The army had then agreed to fly them all home.

He'd pointed out Greaves' grave and told them about Dawoud and his fellows, likely dead and entombed.

He hadn't spoken more than a dozen words to Cosgrove for the entire journey. He had nothing to say to the man. Cosgrove felt that everything had gone swimmingly.

As they emerged from the oven-like interior of the helicopter to the cooling tarmac of the airstrip, Cosgrove clasped him on the shoulder.

'Look, old chap. I am truly sorry. But the nature of command, the nature of our lives, there have to be some sacrifices. You know that.'

'I do,' said Lethbridge-Stewart. 'But did Fiona have to find out now? Did she have to find out like this? On our holiday?'

Cosgrove sighed. 'She would have found out sooner or later,' he said. 'That's simply the way it is. But trust me. And trust my own wife. Fiona will adjust. She will realise what your role is. And her own, of course. The two complement each other so well. It's difficult to pick it up at first. It always is for them. But they've got such remarkable fortitude.'

Lethbridge-Stewart kept quiet. He felt it was easier to understand the Arabic speaking airmen that rushed about them.

'Excellent,' said Cosgrove. 'There's my car. They must have let Ahmed in to pick us up.'

It was even later when Lethbridge-Stewart finally knocked on the door to the Cosgroves' guest room. He heard Fiona's voice from within, calling out, before he pushed it open, darting across the room and enveloping her in a hug as she stood from the bed.

'You're here,' she gasped. 'I was so worried…'

He kissed her, rapid pecks becoming more deep and meaningful as he did so.

'I made it through,' he said finally. 'And we won't be staying here again.' He gave a grim smile. 'Although Venessa has said that she has dinner cooking. She's tried her hand at a Moroccan tagine.'

Fiona laughed, and pulled him down to the bed to sit next to her. 'We may give it a miss,' she said. 'Tell me about where you've been.'

He thought of the final moments in the city, the nightmarish world, the pain and the feeling that he was being turned into something he could never be. He shook his head.

'I said tell me, Alistair.'

'I can't,' he said. 'There's too much that we need to keep under wraps. I can't. Not even to you.'

Outside the traffic roared and a distant siren sounded. A world that was as close to normality as it could hope for. He thought of his decision in the tomb. To abandon his duty, to give up his own future, for Fiona. He wished he could tell her. It would all be so much simpler.

'Why can't you just tell me?' She sighed.

Lethbridge-Stewart held her tightly as she buried her head in the crook of his neck, feeling her breathing through choked sobs. As he did so, he felt her relax, her head still turned away. She gave nothing back to him.

Some deserts were too far to cross.